JACOB LOMAX, PRIVATE EYE

"Another Jake Lomax mystery is reason to rejoice... Crisp dialogue, good plotting, suitably sleazy bad guys, and the requisite romantic subplot. This can be confidently recommended to any fan of American private-eye fiction." *Booklist*

"Allegretto's prose is vivid as well as wry and laconic. He's an expert at the quick size-up, a hard trick to pull off... I'm hoping Allegretto has further plans for Jake Lomax."
Chicago Sun-Times

"Lomax and his adventures are very welcome additions to the literary landscape... A real pleasure." *Denver Rocky Mountain News*

"Writing in the Chandler mode... Allegretto has found his own voice within the chorus, and all moves trippingly across the pages." *Boston Sunday Globe*

"Gritty, mordantly witty adventure... A many-layered mystery that ought to win Allegretto another prize." *Publishers Weekly*

Other Jacob Lomax Mysteries by
Michael Allegretto
From Avon Books

BLOOD STONE

THE DEAD OF WINTER

MICHAEL ALLEGRETTO

AVON BOOKS ◆ NEW YORK

This is a work of fiction. Names, characters, places, and incidents either are the product of the author's imagination or are used fictitiously. Any resemblance to actual events or persons, living or dead, is entirely coincidental.

AVON BOOKS
A division of
The Hearst Corporation
105 Madison Avenue
New York, New York 10016

Copyright © 1989 by Michael Allegretto
Published by arrangement with Charles Scribner's Sons, Macmillan Publishing Company
Library of Congress Catalog Card Number: 89-6178
ISBN: 0-380-71120-6

First Avon Books Printing: March 1991

AVON TRADEMARK REG. U.S. PAT. OFF. AND IN OTHER COUNTRIES, MARCA REGISTRADA, HECHO EN U.S.A.

Printed in the U.S.A.

RA   10   9   8   7   6   5   4   3   2   1

For Pam

THE
DEAD
OF
WINTER

CHAPTER

1

IT WAS BELOW FREEZING, but Joseph Bellano wanted to walk.

"Can't we talk in my office, where it's warm?" I suggested.

"Your office might be bugged."

Bellano was shorter, heavier, and twenty years older than I; I'd say five ten or so, two hundred pounds plus, and mid-fifties. He was also more immune to the cold. I had on corduroy pants, a shirt, a wool sweater, heavy socks, boots, a ski parka, gloves, a scarf, and a knit cap pulled down over my ears, and I was still shivering. I was also certain my office wasn't bugged.

"How about we sit in my car and turn on the heat?"

"That, too."

"Come on, no one bugs cars, not even in the movies."

Bellano shook his round head. His ears and bulbous nose were turning red from the cold. He should have had on a hat—his hair was thinning on top. The rest of it was long, the way barbers like to wear it. There was a lot of gray mixed in with the black.

"You're right," he said. "I'm getting paranoid. But you gotta understand, the feds are on me like fleas on an old rug, and I don't know how far they'll go. I know for a fact they've tapped the phone in my shop. So let's just walk and talk, okay?"

"Sure." I pulled the scarf up around my chin.

We headed north on Broadway. The afternoon traffic mushed by the other way. There was still a lot of old snow left over from a few days ago. Most of it was piled along the curb and against the brick buildings. It was so gray from sand and pollution that it hardly looked like snow. At least the sidewalks were shoveled clean. Temporarily. Tiny icy flakes fell from the dead sky. They were sticking to the concrete and soon would make footing treacherous.

"It's my daughter," Bellano said grimly. "She disappeared three days ago. I've called around, friends and all, no one's seen her. Her mother's going crazy."

Obviously, he was, too.

"I can imagine," I said. "Have you talked to the police?"

He nodded yes. "Not that they're that eager to help *me* right now."

Bellano thrust his hands deep in the pockets of his black overcoat. His heavy shoulders were bent, and his collar was turned up. It made him look like a middle-aged mafioso. But he was no criminal. Unless you called someone who runs a sports book out of his barbershop a criminal. Which, by the way, I don't.

"I called the cops Saturday morning," he said, "after she didn't come home Friday night. They told me she's not a 'missing person' until she's been gone for seventy-two hours. I went down there today and signed some papers. So now it's official. She's missing. Then I called around to get the name of a decent private snoop, er, no offense."

"Hey, I'm used to it."

I'd been in the business for four years, and I'd been called a lot worse. Also punched, spat on, and shot. So I guess "snoop" wasn't so bad.

We waited for the light at Twelfth Avenue. The big window of Howard Lorton Galleries on the corner was hung with a twelve-foot Christmas wreath. Tomorrow was December first.

The light changed, and we crossed the street. My freezing toes were thankful for the movement.

"Where did you last see your daughter?"

"In my barbershop Friday morning. A few hours after I'd been busted."

I'd read about Bellano's arrest.

A dozen of the bigger bookies in town had been rounded up by a special crime unit made up of federal agents and members of the Denver police. A truckload of evidence had been confiscated. Most of the bookies were otherwise honest businessmen who also happened to act as clearinghouses for those eager to wager on sporting events. But every ten or twelve years some civic group decided to purge the city of gamblers. Make it safe for their kids. Meanwhile, the state ran the lottery and lotto and dog races, and the sports pages of the morning papers carried the point spread for every ball game in the country, pro *and* college.

This year, though, the feds were trying to tie the bookies to organized crime.

"Do you think there's a connection between your daughter's running and your arrest?"

"Absolutely. You gotta understand, Stephanie is a sweet kid, barely eighteen. Polite, respectful. Her mother raised her to be a good Catholic. She never knew I was making book until the cops showed up at the house Friday. She went to pieces."

"You're telling me that your eighteen-year-old daughter didn't know you were a bookie?"

"No."

"How could you keep something like that from her?"

"Because I didn't want her to think her father was a crook."

"No, I didn't mean it that way. I meant 'how?' "

"Oh. Well, for one thing my wife and I never told her. I always took care of the bets and the money at my shop, where she rarely goes. My books I keep on a computer at home, but it's locked up in the den. Off limits. Anyhow, Steph thought all I did in there was play the stock market, which I do, some. Did."

"You kept your books on a computer?"

"Why not? It's the electronic age."

"Oh, yeah, I forgot."

We passed leafless trees poking up through the frozen sidewalk. They belonged to the new Security Life Building. It stood on the former site of Azar's Big Boy, where a guy used to be able to go in and get a cup of coffee and get warm. I wiped my nose with the back of my glove.

"Tell me about Friday," I said.

"The cops came into my shop first thing in the morning and pulled me downtown. They also went through my house with a search warrant and confiscated all my records. Almost all. The jerks missed one copy right under their noses. Anyway, Stephanie was home with her mother. The poor kid didn't know what was going on. When the cops left, Angela explained it all to her. She didn't take it well."

"What did she do?"

"She drove straight to my shop."

We crossed Thirteenth. A truck had stopped in the crosswalk. Its nose dripped dirty icicles. We had to step around it, out near the lanes of traffic on Broadway. We got frozen slush splattered on our pants. Bellano didn't seem to mind.

"When she came in, I was cutting hair and—"

"Wait a minute. This was a few hours after your arrest and you were already working?"

Bellano nodded. "I'd been charged, printed, pictured, and bailed out. I was back cutting hair before noon. Also taking bets."

"You're kidding."

"Hell, no. No way am I gonna close down, not with the Broncos playing tonight. Monday night. National TV. That brings the part-time gamblers right outta the woodwork."

Which reminded me that I'd laid a nickel with *my* bookie

earlier in the week. After all, the line was Denver by three, and I figured they'd stomp Seattle. Plus, I had money to burn from my last case, so five hundred didn't seem like much of a risk. Actually five fifty, counting the vigorish.

"Anyway," Bellano said as we made it to the curb, "me and Sal are in there cutting hair, a few customers waiting, all of them trying to cheer me up, and in charges Stephanie like the wrath of God."

Bellano smiled.

"I'd never seen her like that," he said. "At first it was kinda funny. To me, anyhow. The other guys in there, though, were staring with their mouths hanging open, like who the hell *is* this broad?

"Stephanie's yelling about how I betrayed her all these years and how she hopes me and my pals all go to prison and how she doesn't want to ever see me again. And then it's not funny anymore."

He frowned. "I tried to calm her down, but it was no good. She threw the keys to her car at me and said she didn't want anything that was paid for with dirty money. Then she ran out of the shop. I went after her, but she was already down the block. She turned the corner. That was the last time I saw her."

"You said you called around. Friends and relatives."

"Me and Angela called everybody. Nothing." He shook his head for emphasis.

"Does Stephanie have a boyfriend?"

"Not that I know about."

"What about her girlfriends? Could she be hiding with one of them?"

"She's only got a couple of girlfriends, and they live with their parents. I've called them."

When we reached the corner, Bellano turned right. Ahead lay the capitol. Its gold dome was as dull as a penny.

"There's probably something else you should know," Bellano said. Then he sniffled—the first sign that the cold was affecting him. He wiped his nose with a folded white handkerchief. "There's more to this gambling bust than they put in the papers. The cops and the feds aren't too concerned with us small fries. They're mostly after one guy. Fat Paulie DaNucci."

"I see."

"The prosecutors are pushing me and some others to turn state's evidence against DaNucci," Bellano said. "They'd like us to admit we were working for him. This would strengthen their case quite a bit. Of course, this is bullshit. We're all independent. Sure, there's guys who lay off bets with Da-Nucci if they're getting too much action on one side or the other. I've done it myself. But it's only because DaNucci's big enough to handle it. On the other hand, I'm a little different than the rest."

I knew that Fat Paulie DaNucci wasn't simply a bookie. He was connected. Mafia. Everyone knew that. Of course, knowing it was easier than proving it.

We turned right at Lincoln and walked south, back the way we'd come.

"I've been making book a lot longer than most," Bellano explained. "I started before there was a bookie in every tavern and office building in the city. You know, before it was 'respectable.' And back then I was, well, acquainted with Fat Paulie. Let's just say that I know one or two things about him that could embarrass him. In a legal sense. Of course, he knows this, too. It might be making him nervous."

"Do you think he might have kidnapped your daughter?"

"It crossed my mind. He says no, though."

"You talked to DaNucci?"

"I called him, sure. At his restaurant. He says he knows nothing from nothing. He got mad that I'd think he'd do something like that."

"Did he hint that Stephanie would return after the trial?"

"No, no, nothing like that. Like I said, he got mad. He hung up on me. I think if he had her he would have let me know by now. At least indirectly." Bellano shook his head. "Maybe she just ran away, I don't know. But no one's seen her, and she left without her car and with hardly any money. Not much more than the clothes on her back."

He took a deep breath and let it out through his nose, blowing vapor like a bull. Then he reached inside his overcoat and handed me a thick envelope.

"Some pictures of her," he said. "Also a list of everyone we could think of who might have seen her. But like I said, we already talked to them. Also five grand."

"Five—"

"If it's not enough, say so."

"It's more than enough. In fact, why don't you just hang on to it and I'll bill you later."

Joseph Bellano smiled briefly and pushed his fists into his coat pockets.

"There's an old Italian saying."

"What?"

"Don't be a jerk, take the money."

"Oh, well, if an old Italian said it," I said, but Bellano wasn't smiling anymore. I could see the pain in his face. His baby was missing.

"Maybe she had some friends from school that we don't know about," he said. "That's the only other thing I can think of."

"Where did—does she go to school?"

"Loretto Heights. She's a sophomore," he said with some pride. "She's a year younger than probably everyone in her class, see, she skipped a grade in elementary school. She was such a smart little kid. Me and Angela, we were always real proud of her, but maybe it wasn't such a good idea, you know, putting her ahead like that, since she'd always be the youngest in her class. . . ."

Bellano realized he'd begun to ramble.

We crossed Thirteenth.

It seemed colder now. The sky had darkened noticeably since we'd started walking. Half the cars coming toward us on Lincoln had their headlights on. Neither of us spoke for two more blocks. We neared Eleventh, where Besant's used to be. Like a lot of other restaurants in Denver, it had changed names so many times I'd lost track.

I glanced at the sign on the door. CLOSED.

"I hear you're good at this?" Bellano had made it a question.

"About average."

He was quiet for a few more paces. Then he wiped his nose again with his handkerchief.

"Find her," he said. "Please."

"I'll do my best."

CHAPTER

2

AFTER JOSEPH BELLANO left me at my office, I deposited most of my new cash in the bank. The rest I took home and locked in the safe with my guns.

Then I popped the cap off a Labatt's Blue and emptied the rest of Bellano's envelope on the kitchen table.

He'd given me two photographs.

One was a studio shot from the waist up of a smooth-skinned young lady in a powder-blue cashmere sweater and a string of pearls. Her black hair was long and sleek, her lashes long. Attractive, not quite pretty. She smiled faintly at something to the left of the lens. She looked content and virgin-pure.

The other picture was a family snapshot of Joseph, Stephanie, and another woman who I assumed was Stephanie's mother, Angela. They were in the backyard, probably this past summer. I could see the corner of a garage and some tomato plants caged in wire. The Bellanos wore shorts and short sleeves and sandals. The sun made them all squint through their smiles. The shadow of the photographer fell on their legs. Ominously, it seemed.

Along with the photos, Bellano had included what looked like his Christmas-card list—six sheets of lined paper with the names, addresses, and phone numbers of forty or fifty people.

Bellano had said he'd talked to them all. None had seen Stephanie. For now I'd take their word for it. Bellano had seemed less certain about the college. I'd start there.

Tomorrow.

Tonight I had a Broncos game.

Except it turned out to be a Seahawks game. In fact, it was well into the third quarter and my second six-pack before the hometown boys finally scored. Way too little, much too late. So I lost five hundred, so what?

I mean, five *fifty*.

Damn bookies.

Tuesday's sky was as cold and gray as dead ashes.

I'd begun to wonder if the old Olds could take another winter. But this morning she turned over on her first try, bless her heart. I let her run with the heater on and spent the next fifteen minutes carefully scraping frost from her windows.

Then I drove to Loretto Heights. More properly, Regis College, Loretto Heights Campus.

The original building sits like a red-stone castle on a hill in southwest Denver. Tall pines, bleak elms, and a vast expanse of snowy lawn insulate it from the mundane traffic on Federal Boulevard.

The college was founded before the turn of the century by the Sisters of Loretto, who turned over its operation to "civilians" in the 1960s. Not long thereafter, the institution began to slide into financial difficulty. Last year it was rescued by Regis. Temporarily, anyway. I'd heard *they* were planning to sell it to a Japanese interest. For a large profit, of course. Regis was run by Jesuits.

I left the Olds in Visitors Parking, then climbed the red-sandstone steps to the main entrance. The Virgin Mary, frozen in white marble over the arch, welcomed me with open arms.

The campus administrator was Father Shipman. He was a thin red-faced man in his sixties. His office was as austere as his clothing. His Roman collar looked too tight. Maybe that explained the red face. I told him who I was and what I was doing. He said he'd spoken to Joseph Bellano yesterday on the phone.

"He wanted to know if Stephanie had missed her Monday classes," Father Shipman said.

"I assume that she did."

"I really didn't know. I told him either I'd check with her instructors or he could talk to them himself. He preferred the latter, so I gave him the names and numbers. That was the last I spoke with him."

"Did you talk to Stephanie's teachers?"

"Not about her absence, no. I assumed that if there was a problem they'd let me know."

"Would you mind if I talked to them?"

He wouldn't. He wrote down their names and told me where to find their offices. Then he cleared his throat.

"Mr. Lomax, don't interfere with the classes."

He'd made it sound like a threat, Roman collar or no.

Stephanie was taking one class each in nursing, art history, business administration, and creative writing. She didn't know what she wanted to be. Father Shipman had made a note that Stephanie's creative writing instructor, Rachel Wynn, doubled as her academic adviser. I tried her first. Her office door was locked, and no one answered my knock.

However, down the hall I did find Stephanie's nursing instructor, Mrs. ten Ecke. I introduced myself, and she waved me into a chair.

"What's on your mind, Mr. Lomax?" she asked me from behind her desk.

She was solid and fortyish, with thick brown eyebrows and a dark cardigan sweater. Her bosom was huge. It pushed out her white blouse like the prow of a hospital ship.

"One of your students, Stephanie Bellano, has apparently run away from home."

Mrs. ten Ecke nodded, then shook her head. "I spoke to her father yesterday."

"Do you have any idea where she might have gone?"

Again, she shook her head. "I'm sorry."

"Who are her friends here?"

"I can only speak about my classes. That's the only time I ever see her."

"And?"

"I don't think she has any friends. At least none that I noticed. She stays to herself."

"I see. What kind of a girl is she?"

"Quiet."

"Is she a good student?"

"Again, I can only speak about my classes. She . . . how can I put it? This year she's struggling."

"So she's *not* a good student."

"That's not what I meant. Last year she was near the top of her class. This year, though, she seems to be having trouble concentrating. I've asked her about it, and she promised she'd try harder. Also . . ."

"Yes?"

"She seems overly sensitive. Even squeamish. Some of the pictures in the textbook actually made her ill."

"Was she like that last year?"

"Not that I remember."

After I left Mrs. ten Ecke, I spoke to Stephanie's instructors in business administration and art history. They both told me pretty much what I'd just heard. Stephanie was a bright student. However, she seemed to lack interest in school work. She was a lone, quiet girl with no apparent friends. Neither teacher had any idea where she might be.

When I went back to Rachel Wynn's office, I found the door unlocked and the lights on but nobody home. She'd

been there and left. I knew she'd be back, because her coat
and scarf were hanging on a hook behind the door.

I went in to wait.

The office was small and crowded with a desk, two chairs,
a file cabinet, and a bookshelf. One wall featured a few diplomas
and a large, colorful butterfly in a frame. There was a spider
plant in a pot on the windowsill. Also some pinecones tied
together with a red ribbon. Beyond the plant and the cones I
could see the mountains, near and white and forbidding.

I sat behind the desk.

On top was an imitation-leather-edged blotter, a full pencil
cup, a stapler, a tiny wooden box with paper clips, and a small
porcelain Santa. His features were delicately formed and
hand painted. There was also a stack of folders.

I opened the top one. It was crammed with short stories by
students. They'd all been graded with a red pen, most earning
merely a *C* or a *D*. I found only one *A*. Miss Wynn was tough.
The *A* was entitled, "The Vase." I started reading it. What the
hell, I had to do *something* to pass the time.

"*Who* are *you?*"

She was a good-looking woman with reddish-brown hair.
It went nicely with her dark green sweater and tweed skirt.
She stood in the doorway with one hand on the knob and the
other holding a beat-up brown briefcase, as big as a valise. It
pulled down her left shoulder. I put her age a few years below
mine. I put her mood somewhere between highly annoyed
and moderately pissed off.

I closed the folder and stood up.

"Sorry, I was just browsing."

"Who *are* you? And why are you going through my
papers?"

"Hey, I said I was sorry." I came around the desk and dug
out a card. "My name is Jacob Lomax. I'm a private investigator hired by the Bellano family to find their daughter. I take
it you're Miss Wynn?"

"Investigator?" She looked at the card but made no move to take it. "Does Father Shipman know you're nosing around in here?"

"He knows I'm here, yes. And I wasn't nosing. I was—"

She hoisted up her briefcase, and for a moment I thought she was going to hit me with it. But she just thunked it down on her desk. Then she brushed past me, went around to her chair, and phoned Shipman to check me out. I waited and tried not to look smug.

"I see," she said finally into the phone. "Thank you, Father." She hung up.

"See?"

She didn't smile. "I was away from my office most of yesterday," she said, as if in apology. "I never got a chance to return Mr. Bellano's call."

"So you didn't know Stephanie was missing?"

"No. She wasn't in class yesterday, but I didn't think anything of it. A number of students are out sick—"

"She's been gone since Friday. May I?" I put my hand on the only other chair in the room. She nodded briefly. I sat.

"Why would Stephanie run away from home?" she asked.

"She learned something about her father that greatly upset her."

"What?"

"That he was a bookie."

"Oh?" Rachel Wynn seemed mildly surprised. "Is that all?"

She was right. It didn't seem like much to be upset about.

"As far as I know," I said. "Do you think there may have been another reason?"

"How would I know?"

"You're her counselor, aren't you?"

"Mr. Lomax, I'm her—"

"Please. Call me Jacob."

Her eyes narrowed a millimeter. They were hazel.

"Mr. Lomax, I'm Stephanie's academic counselor. She didn't confide in me for anything more than class scheduling."

"Did you have private talks with her?"

"A few, yes."

"Did she ever say anything to you about running off? Or talk about a place she'd rather be?"

"No, I'm afraid not." She checked her watch. "Damn, I'm going to be late for my next class." She stuffed the folder with the short stories in her briefcase. She stood up, and so did I.

"Stephanie left with hardly any money and no car," I said, "so she probably didn't go far. I'm hoping she's staying with a friend. But everyone says she has no friends."

"I don't think that's true."

Rachel Wynn motioned me out the door, then closed it behind us. The hallway was busy with young men and women hurrying in search of knowledge.

"I'll ask the students in her class this afternoon," she said.

"Fine. Maybe before that we could have lunch."

Her eyes narrowed *two* millimeters this time. Then she smiled. Or maybe it was a grimace.

"Thanks, no, but I bring my lunch," she said. "Call me here before five and I'll let you know if I've learned anything."

She walked away. I watched her until she'd disappeared into the shifting crowd. Nice walk. How come *I* never had any teachers like that?

I was back home, and I'd eaten lunch before I remembered that today was the first of the month. I wrote out a check for the rent. Then I walked down two flights of stairs and knocked on Mrs. Finch's door.

Mrs. Finch not only managed the huge old building; she owned it. In fact, she'd grown up in it when it had been a mansion—her family's home. Now it was eight apartments, two on each floor and two in the basement. Of course, Mrs. Finch still thought of it as her home and all us tenants as unwanted, but necessary, guests. She kept a close eye on us all.

She opened the door and glared up at me. Her wizened old

face was colored with two smudges of rouge. She was wrapped in a paisley shawl.

"Good afternoon, Mrs. Finch. I brought your—"

She snatched the check out of my hand.

"You're late again, Mr. Lomax."

"Late? Isn't this the first?"

"This is the *afternoon* of the first. I've already been to the bank today."

"Oh. Sorry."

"Sorry, indeed," she said. "Do you have a job yet?"

"A job?"

"Yes, yes, a job. As in 'work.' "

"I work as a private detective, remember?"

"I meant a *real* job."

"Ah, no."

"Just as I thought," she said, and slammed the door.

At least she hadn't raised my rent.

I tried Rachel Wynn's extension at three o'clock. No answer. I called back at three-thirty, then four, then every ten minutes until five. Still no answer.

"Tomorrow I'll *go* there," I said out loud.

I opened a beer and turned on the TV.

I'd come in at the end of a local news story. I wasn't certain I'd heard it right, so I began flipping channels until I found an anchorwoman trying to look grim. She told it to me from the beginning. A car bomb had exploded in a residential neighborhood in North Denver. One man had been killed.

Joseph Bellano.

CHAPTER

3

THE ANCHORWOMAN gave me few details.

"Joseph Bellano was killed this morning by a powerful explosive device," she read. "It had apparently been placed in his car. The blast knocked down a portion of the garage wall, destroyed another car in the garage, and started a fire fueled by gasoline."

Film: Denver fire fighters in dirty yellow slicks and boots pouring water on the remains of an unattached garage. The snow near the garage had been melted, then refrozen into blackened ice.

"Bellano had recently been arrested for bookmaking as part of the city's fight against illegal gambling. It is believed his testimony at the upcoming trial was crucial to the government's case. Police are speculating that Bellano's death may have been related to organized crime."

I switched off the set.

It looked as if Bellano had been right about Fat Paulie DaNucci. DaNucci had been worried about Bellano's testimony, and he'd done something about it. However, that was police business, not mine.

My business was Stephanie Bellano.

The odds were good that she'd hear about her father's death no matter where she was. The story had more than enough

elements to make the national news: car bomb, Mafia, fire on
film. I was fairly certain that when she did hear she'd come
running home to Mama, tears in her eyes.

Case closed.

Which meant I'd have to give back the five grand.

There'd been times in my life, poorer times, when I
would've been tempted to keep the money. Sorely tempted.
Five grand was ten months' rent. It was a thousand six-packs
of good beer. It was a nice long vacation in a nice warm place.
But it might also be the property of a woman recently
widowed. I hoped I'd never be *that* tempted.

The next morning, I drove to the Bellano residence.

I planned on staying just long enough to offer my condolences and return the money. Assuming, of course, that
Stephanie had returned. If she hadn't, I'd keep the money
with Mrs. Bellano's blessing and stay on the case.

Bellano's home was near Forty-fourth and Hooker. It was in
an old, sedate section of northwest Denver—once exclusively
Italian, still noticeably so. The brown-brick building had a deep
front porch, a terraced front yard, and a lot of cops hanging
around. Parked in front were two unmarked city vehicles and
a squad car. A uniformed cop stood on the front porch. He wore
earmuffs under his hat and shifted his feet to stay warm.

I figured the last thing the grieving widow needed now was
another stranger in her house. I left.

Later that morning I phoned the Bellano house. Busy. It
was still busy at noon and busy all afternoon. Either Angela
Bellano was getting a lot of support, or else she'd had enough
and had taken the phone off the hook.

I dug out the list of friends and relatives that Bellano had
given me and called the first name. Then I talked to ten more
people on the list just to be sure.

There seemed to be no doubt: Stephanie Bellano had not
come home.

I phoned Rachel Wynn at Loretto Heights. Maybe she had

come up with a friend for Stephanie. But she was gone for the day. The receptionist gave me her home phone.

No answer.

I was hungry and tired of eating alone. I nearly started downstairs to ask Vaz and Sophia out to dinner. Then I remembered they still weren't back from Phoenix.

Vassily and Sophia Botvinnov had lived in this building longer than anyone but Mrs. Finch. A few decades ago they'd fled Russia via Iceland, at a time when Vaz was ranked high in the world of chess. Soon after I'd moved into the apartment above theirs, I'd begun to notice Vaz in the backyard nudging chessmen around a board. I hadn't played in years, not since college, not seriously, anyway. But I'd been pretty good back then. Relatively speaking. I went outside and challenged Vaz to a game. He feigned ineptness. I promised to go easy on him. He said okay. Then he removed his queen's rook and turned his back to the board. "I play better this way," he said. "Please move my pawn to king four." He beat me in a few dozen moves, and we'd both had a good laugh. He'd asked me in to meet Sophia, and she'd insisted I stay for dinner. I guess after that they'd adopted me.

Now they were visiting some of Sophia's friends who'd recently moved into a retirement community. At this moment they were probably sitting by the pool, sipping cold drinks. Behind them was a platter of steaks waiting for the charcoal briquettes to turn from black to gray.

My stomach growled.

I fixed dinner: cheese, crackers, a tin of smoked oysters, a jar of pickled mushrooms, and a bottle of Jack Daniel's. Lomax cuisine.

The funeral was Thursday morning at Holy Family Catholic Church. It was standing room only. There were enough floral displays at the front of the church to make a bee sneeze.

Joseph Bellano had owned the same barbershop for thirty years. During that time he'd trimmed the locks of a lot of friends, neighbors, and relatives. Also a few politicians and policemen, hoods and priests. They all showed up to say good-bye. I estimated the number of mourners at four hundred.

I saw a few familiar faces jammed into the pews. A former mayor, some past and present councilmen, the chief of police. Also two or three local TV "personalities" and a couple of gangsters—suspected gangsters: lots of arrests; no convictions. I saw Fat Paulie DaNucci. He looked so sad you'd think it was his own brother who'd been blown to bits.

The priest kept the eulogy short and sweet. Kind and gentle man. Devoted to family and church. Loved by all. Terrible loss. Gone to a better place. Amen.

I joined the mourners who stood and moved single file down the aisle, then passed before the flower-draped casket.

Angela Bellano sat in the front pew. She wore black and looked numb. She was flanked by the remains of her family, not including Stephanie. Beside Angela, though, sat a young woman and two little kids. The woman was in her twenties. She resembled Stephanie enough to be her older sister.

Strange. Joseph Bellano hadn't mentioned another daughter.

I went up the aisle and out of the church into the bright, cold morning. Most people were getting into their cars for the procession to Mt. Olivet Cemetery.

Not me.

I can't handle that anymore—when they lower someone, an ex-someone, into the ground and cover him with dirt. It's too scary, too final. It reminds me of where we're all headed. You go watch it; I can't. The next long black parade I'm in will be the one I lead.

I drove south on Federal toward Loretto Heights.

Since it was close to noon, I stopped first at a King Soopers and bought a deli sandwich and two apples. When I got to the college, I asked for directions to the cafeteria. It was crowded. I saw Rachel Wynn eating alone in a corner booth. Her brown paper bag was pressed flat to hold a Granny Smith apple and a half-eaten sandwich. The rest of her table was spread with school papers.

"I brought you an apple," I said, "but it looks like someone beat me to it."

She looked up, surprised. Then she smiled briefly and pushed her papers aside.

"Please," she said.

I sat.

"I heard about Stephanie's father." Her voice was sad. "My God, who would do something like that?"

I shook my head and unwrapped my sandwich. "Did you find out anything from Stephanie's classmates?"

"Yes, but . . ." She sat back, startled. "Hasn't she returned home?"

"No."

"Oh, no. I assumed when I didn't hear from you that she'd come back."

"I'm afraid not."

"Do you still think it's possible she's staying with a friend?"

"I don't know."

"Well, I did talk to some of my students. Only one of them considered Stephanie to be a friend. Madeline Dorfmier."

"What did she have to say?"

"I asked if she knew where Stephanie was. She said no."

"Would you mind if I talked to her?"

"Well . . . no."

"What?"

"If you want to question her here on campus, perhaps I should be present."

"That's fine. Tell me, do you think Stephanie has changed since last year? Her attitude or anything?"

"I didn't know her last year."

At ten minutes to one we sat with Madeline Dorfmier in an empty classroom. Rachel had spotted her in the cafeteria and asked her to accompany us to the nearest available quiet room.

Madeline was a plain-looking girl with a flat forehead and a bony chin. She wore a black turtleneck under a large man's shirt, which hung out of her black corduroy pants. A few untamed strands of hair strayed across her cheeks and worked their way toward the corners of her mouth. A few more danced over her thick glasses. They made me itch. I had to stop myself from brushing them out of her face. I asked her if she knew where Stephanie Bellano was.

"No." She fidgeted uncomfortably. She didn't like speaking to strangers.

"When was the last time you talked to her?"

"Last week, I guess. In class."

"Did Stephanie ever talk about running away?"

Madeline shook her head, and another hair dropped in her face. "Not to me," she said. "Maybe to Stacey."

She'd said "Stacey" the way a maiden aunt says "herpes."

"Stacey?" Rachel asked. "Stacey O'Connor?"

Madeline nodded, dropping a few more dark strands onto her kisser.

"I didn't know Stephanie associated with her."

"What's wrong with Stacey O'Connor?" I asked.

Madeline snorted, fluttering hair away from her mouth.

"She's a bit wild," Rachel explained to me.

I looked at Madeline. She looked offended, betrayed.

"Stephanie started hanging out with her before last summer," she told me. "We were best friends all through high school. We both decided to come here so we could be in college together, and then she . . . got a new best friend. I hardly saw her during summer break. I thought maybe we could start out new this year, but she's been so different, it's like I hardly knew her. I don't know if we'll ever *really* be friends again."

Madeline's myopic eyes searched our faces for sympathy, or at least an explanation.

"I'm sorry," I said lamely.

"For what?"

"Never mind."

Rachel was free for the next hour, so she took me to the front office. We checked Stacey O'Connor's schedule. She had no classes this afternoon. Rachel looked up her home phone, called her, and told her we were coming.

The apartment was less than half a mile from the college. Still, we took my car. The sidewalks along Federal, where there were any, were getting slushed by traffic.

Stacey O'Connor was an attractive girl with blond wavy hair, a turned-up nose, and too much makeup. She wore ski pants and a fuzzy sweater, both of which she filled quite nicely. For a college kid, I reminded myself.

"I haven't seen Stephanie for over a week," she told us.

We sat in angular rented furniture that had been designed to look modern when it was new, twenty years ago. It had been ugly then, and it was ugly now. There was a coffee table strewn with school papers, textbooks, and back issues of *Sassy* and *Self* magazines. At one corner was a big pottery ashtray. It was chock-full of butts and smelled of stale smoke. I could see into the kitchen. Cupboard doors hung open before empty shelves. Dirty dishes were stacked in the sink.

Rachel Wynn glanced about her disapprovingly. Stacey O'Connor looked uncomfortable. She wanted a cigarette.

"When exactly did you last see her?" I asked.

"Oh, God, let's see." Stacey looked at the ceiling. "I haven't seen her in class since I dropped Business. It must've been Wednesday night," she said, looking down at us. "Because we always—" She stopped suddenly and looked from Rachel to me. "Yes, it was Wednesday," she said in a monotone.

Something was up.

"A week ago yesterday?" I asked.

Stacey nodded, then shuffled through the mess on the

table. She unearthed a pack of Marlboro Lights 100's and a disposable lighter. She lit up, blew smoke quickly over her shoulder, then said, "Do you mind if I smoke?"

"Where did you see her?"

She looked at me, then Rachel, then the floor. "The Lion's Lair."

"What?" Rachel said angrily. "You girls aren't supposed to *be* in there."

Stacey hung her head.

"What's the Lion's Lair?"

"A bar," Rachel told me, and glared at Stacey.

"Oh. I thought for a minute it was a depot for white slavers."

Stacey choked on her smoke. Rachel turned her glare on me.

"The college has some clearly defined rules: no drugs or alcohol on campus and no underage drinking on or *off* campus. Stacey and Stephanie are both under twenty-one."

Stacey rolled her eyes.

I looked squarely at Rachel Wynn. "I don't think Stacey will get in trouble with the school for anything she tells us now, do you?"

When she didn't answer, I said, "Because if there's the slightest chance of that, then Stacey and I can—"

"Yes, yes, all right." She turned to Stacey. "But tomorrow I want to talk to you in my office."

"No."

Rachel looked at me. "What?"

"No reprimands, no threats, none of that bullshit."

"*What?*"

"You heard me. I'm looking for a missing girl, remember? And if Stacey can help me find her, then I don't want her holding anything back because she's afraid of you. So I want you to promise her right now that—"

"Don't tell me how to deal with my students."

"If you don't promise, then I'll have to ask you to wait out in the car."

Stacey was staring at us with her mouth open. Rachel Wynn tightened her jaws, stood stiffly, and walked out carrying her coat. She slammed the door without saying good-bye.

"You're going to lose your ash," I said.

"What?"

Stacey was still staring at the door. She looked down at her forgotten cigarette. An inch of powdery ash dropped onto her textbook. She brushed it with the back of her hand, leaving a gray-white smear on the book.

"Winny's got this *thing* about booze," she said.

"Tell me about the Lion's Lair," I said. "How often did you and Stephanie go there?"

"A couple times a week. And it wasn't just us. Lots of girls go there. Well, not lots, but some. It's kind of a nice place. Good music, and everybody's there to have a good time. Wednesday night is Ladies' Night. Drinks are half price for us. It's, you know, a good place to meet guys."

"I'm sure it is. But Stephanie doesn't look like she'd pass for twenty-one. Not from the pictures I've seen. Do they let a lot of underage girls in there?"

"I guess." Stacey waved her hand.

"Did Stephanie ever talk to you about running away?"

"Steph? No way. She lives at home, you know? I think she's still afraid of her parents." Stacey made a face and shook her head. "In some ways Steph is still a kid. I've always tried to get her to loosen up."

"Was it working?"

Stacey brightened. "You know it. When I first met her, which was spring semester last year, she was still a *virgin*, if you can believe that."

"And she's not now?"

"No way. She won't come right out and say it, but she and Ken were getting it on before summer break."

" 'Getting it on,' as in having sex."

Stacey nodded and gave me a knowing look. "A guy I know who's a good friend of Ken's told me. And Ken wouldn't lie about something like that. He wouldn't have to." She sighed. "He's a hunk."

"What's Ken's full name?" I asked.

"Kenneth something."

"No kidding. Does Stephanie have any other friends?"

"No. Well, maybe one. I heard her mention a girl named Chrissie. I don't know her last name. I never met her."

"Is she a student? Or someone from the Lion's Lair?"

"Neither. Stephanie said she met her during the summer."

"Where?"

"I don't know."

"This Ken, do you know where he lives?"

"No, but he's almost always at the Lair. He might be part owner or something. I know he works there as a bouncer. He supposedly knows karate." She sighed again.

"What does Ken look like?"

"Tom Cruise."

"Who?"

"The movie star, silly."

I thanked her and left.

Rachel Wynn was not waiting for me in my car. Okay, so I don't look like Tom Cruise.

CHAPTER

4

I DROVE to the Bellano residence.

By now it was midafternoon. I figured most of the mourners would have gone home, especially since Joseph was firmly underground. I was wrong.

Cars lined the curbs on both sides of the street all the way down the block. I drove to the end and turned the corner. Then out of curiosity I drove down the alley. The Olds practically steered itself through the deep ruts in the snow. Most of the backyards were screened from the alley by privacy fences or tall snowy hedges. Still, the Bellano house was easy to spot.

It was the one with the demolished garage.

I pulled into the short driveway but stayed in the car.

What was left of the garage stood forty feet from the rear of the house and ten feet from the alley. Half of one wall had been blown down, its scattered bricks poking through the snow in the yard. The double garage doors were gone, burned to ashes. So was most of the roof. The entire dead structure was wrapped like an obscene Christmas present in yellow ribbon: Crime Scene—Do Not Cross.

I could see the remains of two cars inside.

The one on the left was blackened by fire, its tires flat and its windows shattered, either by the force of the explosion or the heat of the gasoline-fed fire. The side of the car had been pushed inward, as if kicked by a gigantic foot.

The car on the right, obviously the one that had contained the bomb, no longer looked like a car. It was a burned and twisted metal heap.

I figured it would've been easy for someone to break into the garage unnoticed. The doors, when there'd been doors, were screened from the house by the garage itself and from neighboring houses by fences and hedges. Once inside, the bomber could've worked in privacy. He—or she, for that matter—must have done it Monday night, after I'd talked to Bellano.

Bellano had come home that night, probably ate dinner with his wife, maybe watched a little football or the movie of the week, then gone to bed. In the morning, he'd had breakfast, kissed his wife good-bye, and gone out to his car. Then he'd turned the key. Eternity.

I drove out of the alley and parked the Olds in the street.

The front door of the Bellano residence was open despite the cold. The storm door was shut but unlocked, so I just walked in.

A couple of dark-haired men in suits stood in the entryway. They were holding drinks and talking in low tones. They nodded solemnly at me. I nodded back and went into the living room. It was crowded with people standing or sitting or perched on the arms of chairs. Their ages ranged from little kids weaving in and out of the crowd all the way up to one elderly lady who was so wrinkled and shrunken she might have come over with Columbus.

There was a brightly lit Christmas tree by the front window. Fresh-smelling pine garlands framed the doorways. Except for the clothing of the guests, I didn't see anything black. Everyone talked quietly. No one was crying.

The dining-room table was covered with a fine white cloth and spread with a buffet of prosciutto and salami, cheeses and bread, olives and peppers. I resisted the urge to grab a plate and start loading up.

I asked where Angela was and was told the kitchen.

There were about a dozen women in there, some sitting at the table, the rest on their feet, chopping, stirring, tasting. More food. Enough, it appeared, to feed the neighborhood. It was hot, and I still had on my coat.

"Mrs. Bellano?"

Several women turned toward me. One of them said, "Yes?"

She was a stately looking woman with a face at once strong and gentle, the kind that easily breaks into a smile. Her hair was thick and black, streaked with gray, and pulled back in a loose bun. She wore a dark dress, not the same one I'd seen at the funeral. She held a big wooden spoon in her left hand. The diamonds in her wedding ring sparkled in the bright light. So did the fine line of perspiration on her forehead.

"My name is Jacob Lomax. I was a friend of your husband, and I wanted to give you my condolences."

She nodded and smiled gently.

"Thank you, Mr. Lomax. Take off your coat and sit. Have something to eat."

"Thank you, no. Could we . . . could I talk to you in private?"

The murmuring in the kitchen stopped. All the women looked at me, their eyes alert.

"Why, what's wrong?" Angela Bellano said, her eyebrows pushing wrinkles into her forehead.

"It would be better if we talked in private, Mrs. Bellano."

I glanced at the faces around me. Not a smile in the bunch. Angela looked worried but determined.

"What is it?" she said. "Tell me."

I shifted my feet. "On the day before your husband was killed, he hired me to find Stephanie."

"Stephanie? You've found her?"

"No, I'm afraid not. Has she contacted you?"

Angela's face lost its strength. "Why are you here? What do you want from me?"

Before I could answer, a man entered the room, talking. He was in his late forties—a good-sized dude with pock-marked cheeks and a lumpy nose.

"Angela, we need more wine. We're almost— Hey, what's going on? Who's this?"

One of the women said, "Tony, this guy's talking about Stephanie."

Tony looked me up and down. "Who the hell are you?"

"I was hired by Joseph to find Stephanie and—"

"Hired?" Tony said. "What's he talking about, Angela?"

She shook her head. "Joseph never said anything to me about hiring anyone." She looked at me. Her eyes, already red, were beginning to tear. "Please, if you know where she is . . ."

"I don't, Mrs. Bellano, but I'm still trying to find her."

"Who *is* this guy, Angela? You know him, or what?"

She shook her head and turned to the nearest woman.

"Oh, God, my baby."

The woman put her arms around her and patted her on the back. Angela began to cry.

"Hey," Tony said, jabbing his finger in my shoulder. "What are you, a cop or another goddamn reporter?"

"I'm a private detective, and—"

He made a face and gave me a shove, short but hard.

"Get the hell outta here."

I glanced at Angela. She was still crying. The woman holding her stared at me the way Mussolini stared at train engineers.

I walked out.

Tony followed me all the way, stepping on my heels.

"What's the matter, Tony," someone said as we passed through the living room.

"This *stronzo* got Angela all upset."

I managed to get to the front door before the crowd could

rip me apart. Tony gave me a shove to help me out onto the front porch. There were three or four men standing behind him in case he needed any help, which he didn't.

"The next time you come back here," he told me, "you leave in an ambulance."

At least he hadn't said "hearse."

I got in my car and drove to the rectory of Holy Family Catholic Church.

What I needed was more information about Stephanie Bellano. And it didn't look as if I were going to get it from the immediate family. At least not today. So maybe the family priest could help. After all, that's what he's there for.

On the way, I thought about the possible reasons why Stephanie hadn't returned home after the death of her father:

One, she hadn't heard about his death. Which meant she was somewhere with no television or newspaper. I considered that unlikely.

Two, she'd heard about it, but she didn't care about coming home. Which meant she was a lot more hard-hearted than your average eighteen-year-old Catholic college coed. Again, unlikely.

Three, she couldn't come home.

This was the one that bothered me. It could mean that she was incapacitated or she was being held against her will. There'd been no ransom demand, at least none that I knew about. This seemed to rule out kidnapping. Unless she'd been grabbed by some pervert. In which case, there could be another, final reason why she hadn't come home: She was dead.

I parked at the curb, went up the walk, and tapped on the door. An elderly lady in a print dress showed me into the parlor.

A few minutes later I was joined by Father Carbone, the priest who'd buried Bellano. He was older than I, but he had a boy's face. His hair was dark and curly, and his glasses had tortoiseshell frames. I explained about Joseph hiring me.

Then I asked him how long he'd known the Bellano family.

"Joseph was an old friend," Father Carbone said. "I married him and Angela."

We were sitting at a forty-five-degree angle to each other on hard stuffed chairs in the parlor in the rectory. Between us was a small walnut table. It held a lamp with a green shade and a silver-framed picture of Jesus. He was kneeling by a rock and staring skyward. The clouds had parted to let a shaft of light bathe his face. He looked troubled.

"I also baptized both their children."

"Stephanie and her sister?" I was thinking of the young woman at the funeral.

"Yes. Diane." He removed his glasses and began buffing them with his handkerchief. "That poor woman."

"Who? Diane?"

"No, I meant Angela. First she has the trouble with Diane. Then Stephanie ran off. And then Joseph is taken from her." He shook his head and replaced his spectacles. "God is sorely testing that woman."

When I was a kid, I used to hear that kind of thing all the time. I'd even believed it. Of course, I'd also believed in the Easter Bunny.

"What kind of trouble did Angela Bellano have with Diane?"

"It was constant trouble," he said. "Diane was the opposite of her younger sister. Where Stephanie was restrained, Diane was impetuous, even wild. Where Stephanie was polite and obedient, Diane was rebellious. When Diane was in high school, she even had a brief run-in with the law—shoplifting. Diane and Joseph were always in conflict with each other."

Which explained why Bellano hadn't mentioned her to me.

"Diane left home right after she graduated high school," Father Carbone said.

"She ran away?"

"No. And if you're thinking that there is a pattern between her and Stephanie, don't. Diane made a production out of leaving. She announced it midway through her senior year."

He shook his head and made a grim face. "I talked to her briefly after the funeral today. She told me she'll always regret not making amends with her father before he died."

"Does Diane live in Denver?"

"No. San Diego. She and her children have been staying with Angela for the past few days, but I believe they're flying home tonight."

"Could Stephanie be staying at her sister's house?"

"Dear God, no," he said. "Diane wouldn't keep that a secret from her mother. Especially not now."

I tended to agree. Still . . .

"Do you have Diane's address?"

"I believe I do. If you'll excuse me."

He stood and left the room.

For a few minutes I was alone. My eyes were drawn to the opposite wall and its large wooden crucified Jesus. It reminded me of a time as a kid when my parents—particularly my mother, God rest her soul—had placed me in a parochial school. The older kids told us snotnoses that if the nuns got mad at us, that's what would happen—crucifixion. Barely two weeks later I'd gotten my homeroom nun so angry that she took me to the monsignor. He'd left me in a room similar to this one. I'd sat trembling, waiting for him to return with the nails.

Father Carbone returned with a slip of paper. I stood to take it. He didn't sit down, so neither did I.

"Diane Eastbridge," I read.

"Her married name. Although I'm afraid she's divorced."

I put the paper away. "Father, some of Stephanie's teachers told me she seems different from last year. Did you notice anything like that?"

"Different? I don't know what you mean."

His eyes moved away from mine for an instant. Some priests make poor liars.

"Different in any way," I said. "Apparently her attitude seemed to change between spring and fall. During summer vacation."

His face had become sad. He sat down. So did I.

"There is something, isn't there?" I asked. "Something you know about Stephanie."

He nodded. "Stephanie came to me about six months ago, the end of May or the first of June. She was deeply troubled. It was something she was afraid to discuss with her parents."

I waited.

"You have to understand, Mr. Lomax, she came to me in confession. I am bound by an oath of silence."

"Can you give me a hint?"

He gave me a·pained look.

"Sorry," I said. "I meant no disrespect. But if it could lead me to where Stephanie is . . ."

"It can't," he said firmly. "Besides, the trouble has . . . passed."

"How do you know?"

"Stephanie told me. This was early in September."

"And this 'trouble' changed her?"

"It changed her profoundly. That and . . ." He looked uneasy. "I'm sorry, Mr. Lomax. I can't say any more."

"Father Carbone, if you could only—"

He stood abruptly.

"Mr. Lomax, please. I'm as concerned about Stephanie's well-being as you are. Perhaps more so—I've known her all her life. But I cannot, I will not, break the seal of the confessional. In any case, what she told me during her confession could have no bearing on her present whereabouts. Trust me. If I had any idea where she was, I'd bring her home to her mother myself."

There was nothing more to say. He showed me to the door.

When I stepped out on the porch, he asked, "Are you assisting the police in finding Joseph's murderer?"

I turned to face him. "No, I'm not."

He nodded, his jaws clenched.

"When he's finally caught," he said with suppressed fury, "I pray to God his justice will be swift and terrible."

He softly closed the door.

CHAPTER

5

I FIGURED I now had three leads, none of them great.

There was the sister, Diane, in San Diego. Although I considered it unlikely that Stephanie was staying with her, I had to be sure. I'd have to go there. Besides, maybe Diane could shed some light on the "trouble" that her sister had had during the summer.

There was the hunk, Ken, at the Lion's Lair. It was possible that he knew things about Stephanie that her family did not. I'd find out tonight.

There was the business partner, Sal the barber.

Salvatore Mangieri had been on the list of names Bellano had given me. He'd caught my attention because he was one of the last people to have seen Stephanie before she'd disappeared. I wondered how he was getting along these days, cutting hair and making book all by himself. Probably well. After all, now he didn't have to share the profits with Bellano.

I checked my hair in the rearview mirror. Dark brown and not too long. But I could do with a trim.

Bellano's shop was on Thirty-second Avenue near Lowell Boulevard. It was a barbershop. Not a hair boutique.

There were no hanging plants or FM music or trendy magazines in wicker baskets. There was no chilled Chablis in the refrigerator. There was no refrigerator.

And there were no women.

It wasn't that Joseph and Sal were chauvinists—well, maybe a bit. It was that neither of them knew a damn thing about cutting women's hair. Much less perms, styles, or tints.

A barbershop.

In the middle of the black-and-white tiled floor were two chairs of chrome and red leather, with pump handles and dangling razor strops. A shelf stretched behind the chairs. It was crowded with colorful bottles, narrow necked and smelling of bay rum and witch hazel. Against the opposite wall was a long padded bench with smudged chrome legs. Beside it squatted a barrel-sized floor-model ashtray that stunk of dead cigars. A battered table rested in the corner of the room, its top littered with yellowed copies of the *Police Gazette* and *Sports Illustrated*. There was a TV on a shelf near the ceiling. It had a squashed picture and no sound.

When I walked in, a bell jangled over my head. The mirrors on opposing walls reflected my image a thousand times.

Sal was working on a guy in his chair. The other chair was covered with a white sheet.

Sal nodded at me. I sat on the bench and waited my turn.

When it finally came, Sal had to lower the chair a few inches to get to my head. I was big, and Sal was not. He was in his sixties, with clear blue eyes and thick white hair combed up in front and parted straight and sharp on the side.

"Just a trim," I told him. In a shop like this you don't go into details. You say "trim" or you say nothing at all.

Sal wrapped a tissue-paper collar around my neck and covered me with a blue pin-striped sheet. Then he shook a faint-smelling liquid—maybe just water in a tainted bottle—on my head and rubbed it in with blunt, hard fingers, making me nod back and forth. Sal loved his work. When he was done, he combed it all straight down, jabbing my ears with the comb. Then he started snipping away with long, cold narrow-bladed scissors.

"My name is Jacob Lomax," I said.

"Nice to meet you." Snip snip.

"I'm a private investigator."

"Oh?" Snip.

"I was hired by Joseph the day before he died."

No snip. "Hired?"

"To find Stephanie."

"Has she turned up?"

"Not yet. I was hoping you could tell me something about her that would help."

"Me?" Snip snip snip. "I don't know hardly anything about her. I don't think she ever came in here before last Friday. At least not since she was a little girl. The only other times I ever saw her was Christmases. Over at Joe and Ange's."

"You saw her, though, the day she disappeared."

"Sure, like I said, last Friday." Snip. "Right after Joe got himself arrested." Arrested was a venereal disease to Sal.

"Can you tell me what happened that day?"

"Sure I can. I was here, wasn't I?"

I waited. Sal snipped a few more hairs. When he spoke again, his tone had softened.

"You're still looking for little Steph, right?"

"Yes."

"What is it you want to know?"

"Just tell me everything that happened that day."

Snip. "Oops, damn." He rubbed the back of my neck with his knuckles. "Couple of days it'll grow back, you won't even notice. Let's see, Friday we hadn't been open more than twenty minutes when in come the cops. They took Joe away without even letting him finish the guy he's got in the chair. Can you imagine that? I mean, *I* gotta finish the guy, and I was already busy as hell, it being Friday, which is our second busiest day, next to Saturday."

"What time did Bellano get back?"

"I'm getting to that part, okay?" Sal continued his work—

comb, snip, comb, snip snip—now cutting each hair about a
thousandth of a millimeter.

"Like I was saying, it's real crowded and Joe's not here and
everyone's asking about him. Some of them aren't so much
bothered that he's in jail; they're bothered that they can't
place a *bet*."

"Couldn't you take care of that?"

Sal stopped, his scissors and comb poised behind my head.
We faced each other in the mirror across the room.

"I'm a barber, pal," he said heatedly. "Not a goddamn
bookie."

I believed him. I wondered, though, how he'd managed to
work with a man who *was* a bookie. For twenty years, no less.
And all the while holding back his anger and not blowing up.

Blowing up?

"When did Bellano get back here?"

"Noon," he said, still mad. He laid the scissors along the
bottom of my sideburns and snipped, jabbing the point into
my temple. Thanks, Sal.

"When he came in, it was like he was a hero or something,"
Sal said bitterly. "Everybody was having a good laugh about
it, especially Joe. Until Stephanie came in."

"What time was that?"

He jabbed my other temple to even things out.

"Around one, I guess. Anyhow, she came in upset as hell.
She was crying and yelling all at once. I guess Joe had never
seen her like that, because his mouth was hanging open. Then
he was smiling like he thought it was a joke or something. But
he stopped smiling when she didn't let up."

"What exactly did she say?"

"She was going on about how she'd always believed he was
strong and pure and good, and all the time he'd been
betraying her trust. She said he was nothing but a criminal,
just like the others."

"The others? What others?"

"Hell, I don't know. Anyhow, Stephanie said she was disgusted that he'd been raising a family on illegal money and that he'd been lying to her and that he was a fraud, and on and on. Joe was trying to calm her down, but it was no good. Then Stephanie said something like 'I don't want anything you've paid for with your dirty gambling money, especially not my car,' and she threw her keys at Joe. They landed behind the bottles back here. A couple of guys laughed at that, which I think made Joe mad. Then she says something which even makes *me* mad. She says, 'I hope all of you end up in prison, because that's where you belong.' "

"All of you?"

"I think she meant Joe and me and the customers."

"Why?"

"Probably because she figured everybody in there must be in there to bet on games."

"Oh."

"And I don't even *gamble*," he said with feeling. "I don't believe in it."

"Right. So Stephanie said she hoped you all went to prison. Then what, she ran out?"

"Well, not right away," Sal said. He put down his scissors and pulled his comb through my hair a few times. Finished.

"Did something else happen?"

"Not exactly *happen*. It was Stephanie. All of a sudden she looked scared to death."

"Scared of what?"

"Someone in the shop, what else?" Sal whipped off my paper collar, crumpled it up, and tossed it in the wastebasket.

"Wait a minute. You said she came in upset and angry—"

"And crying."

"And crying. And she and Joseph were talking back and forth and—"

"Mostly she was yelling and blubbering and he was talking, trying to calm her down."

"And suddenly she's scared of someone in the shop?"

"See, it was like she didn't even *see* anyone in the shop when she first came in. As far as she was concerned, it was just her and her father. Then when she said this 'prison' business, she kind of looked around. Then she looked scared. Then she ran out."

Sal brushed hairs from my neck with a whisk.

"Did anyone else notice her being afraid?"

"Joe did. Of course, he figured she was scared of him. He said something like 'Did you see that? She finally realized what she was saying to her father. She'll be apologizing to me tonight, you wait and see.'"

"But you don't think it was Joseph that frightened her."

"Nope."

"Why not?"

He whipped off the sheet and shook hairs onto the floor. Then he used his whisk on me again.

"Because that's not how she acted. She wasn't looking at him; she was looking at the customers. Each one of them, face-to-face. Some more than once. Something about them scared her bad. At least one of them did."

Sal put aside the whisk and got his push broom and started cleaning up around the chair. I stood and dug out a few bills. In spite of Sal's care, hair slivers had fallen down my neck. They itched.

"Who was in here, do you remember?"

"Probably," he said. He rested his chin on the end of the broom handle and stared at the ceiling. "I was cutting Stan Fowler, and Joe was cutting, let's see, I can picture his face, but I can't think of his name. And—"

"Stan Fowler, the appliance guy?"

"That's him. And there were two customers sitting on the bench. One was Gary Rivers. *The* Gary Rivers. And the other was a"—Sal glanced at the door, then lowered his voice—"a two-bit punk named Johnny Toes Burke."

"You're certain those were the customers?"

"Positive. When Stephanie first came in, we were. all looking around at each other, trying to figure out what was going on."

"Who was the fourth guy, the one in Bellano's chair?"

"I've seen him a hundred times. It's on the tip of my tongue."

I gave Sal a card.

"When you remember him, give me a call."

He looked at both sides of the card, then slipped it in his breast pocket.

"I'm telling you, she was scared," Sal said. "Scared to death."

CHAPTER

6

I DROVE home.

I'd been wearing my dark blue suit since Bellano's funeral this morning, and the shirt had gone limp. And itchy from tiny hairs. I showered, put on slacks and a sweater, and opened a Labatt's.

Stephanie had run away, all right, but perhaps not from her father. Not according to Sal. She'd been scared off by someone in the barbershop. Stan Fowler or Gary Rivers or Johnny Toes Burke or the fourth customer, presently unknown. Sal didn't know which one had frightened her. Had Bellano known? Somehow I doubted it, or else he would've told me.

And maybe it wasn't just one man Stephanie'd run from. Maybe it was all of them together, or some combination of the four. I knew a little about the three Sal had named. None of them seemed too scary. At least not to me. One or more of them, though, had scared the hell out of Stephanie.

Perhaps that was why she hadn't returned after her father's death. She was still scared. Hiding. Perhaps with good reason.

For now, though, I was more concerned with *where* she'd run than *why*. I hoped Ken, the hunk, could give me a lead on that.

First, though, food.

I hadn't eaten since my sack lunch with Rachel Wynn. I fixed a sandwich with slices of ham, cheddar, and red onion, also some salsa. It went in the oven, and I waited for the cheese to melt. Maybe I should invest in a microwave. It would be faster. Although this way I had time to drink another beer before dinner.

The Lion's Lair was a few miles west of Loretto Heights, on Wadsworth Boulevard near Hampden Avenue.

It was middle-class pretentious glitz. You could tell by the parking lot. Most of the cars had *X*'s or *Z*'s in their last names.

There was a bouncer at the door. He didn't look like Tom Cruise, though, so he probably wasn't the guy Stacey O'Connor had described to me. This guy looked more like *Deane* Cruz, a guy I'd gone to college with. Deane had been a defensive lineman—strong as a steer and nearly as smart. This bouncer was probably smarter, though, because he didn't have to check my ID to tell I was old enough to drink.

I walked into smoke and dim lights and raucous sounds.

There were as many women as men filling the tables and crowding the bar and rustling around on the small dance floor to some unidentifiable taped noises. It seemed pretty crowded for a Thursday night. Or maybe I was just being old-fashioned. The average age, not counting me, was mid-twenties.

I found an empty stool at the bar next to a couple of college-age girls. I ordered a beer in a bottle. When the bartender brought it, I asked him if Ken was here tonight.

"Ken *who?*" He knew eighty or ninety Kens.

He was a big guy wearing a short-sleeve white shirt and a tie. From the looks of his arms he spent a lot of time in the weight room. In fact, he looked a bit like *Janet* Cruz, Deane Cruz's older sister, who'd attended college with me and Deane and who'd been voted, though not to her knowledge, or Deane's, either, to be the ugliest person on campus, men included.

"That's the funny thing," I said. "I don't remember his last name. A guy who makes the women sigh. He works as a bouncer sometimes. I think he owns a piece of the place."

"Ken Hausom."

"That's him. Is he here?"

"Look around."

"That's another funny thing," I said. "I've never met him."

He cocked his head and looked at me with one eye. "What do you want him for?"

"It's kind of personal."

"Give me a hint."

"Well, okay. I'm from NASA, and we want to hire some of the geniuses he's got working here."

He blinked once. Then his jaw muscles bunched up. He turned and stomped toward the end of the bar, right past a pair of waitresses waiting at the station.

"Carl, I need two Michelobs, a vodka tonic, and—"

"Keep your fucking shirt on," he told her, and flipped up the end of the bar. I thought he might be coming for me, but instead he pushed through the crowd like a rhino through tall grass.

He stopped at a table with three young men and two young women, all nicely dressed. He leaned down and spoke to one of the guys for a moment, then pushed his way back to the bar, with the waitresses telling him to hurry up and him telling them not to get their you-know-whats in an uproar.

One of the guys rose from the table and made his way toward me. I swiveled on my stool to meet him. He was a good-sized character, though not nearly as big as Carl the bartender. I wasn't sure he looked like Tom Cruise. Although he did have dark hair and a smirk.

"Ken Hausom," he said.

I introduced myself and shook his hand. It felt funny, as if there were extra bones. Then I remembered Stacey O'Connor had told me Ken knew karate. The extra bones were calluses from chopping bricks to dust.

"Carl said you were eager to talk to me."

"I'm looking for a girl named—"

"Aren't we all." His bullshit grin widened, and his eyes slid off me and landed on the two young women to my left. I doubted they were old enough to drink.

"Stephanie Bellano," I said.

His attention stayed on the women. They smiled back.

"She's been missing for almost a week. Her parents hired me to find her."

"Buy you ladies a drink?"

"Look, Ken," I said. "I'm in kind of a hurry. There's a special on Channel 7 tonight I'd really hate to miss. It's about how a lot of bars are getting shut down for serving minors."

"What?" He looked at me, the girls forgotten.

"You dated Stephanie last spring, right?"

He studied my face with eyes as hard and gray as ball bearings.

"What do you want?"

"Stephanie Bellano."

He paused just long enough to get his smirk back in place.

"We went out for a few months. So what?"

"So maybe you know where she might have gone."

"I haven't seen her since May."

"That special I mentioned might include the Lion's Lair."

"You know," he said, punching me in the chest with two fingers, "I don't think I like you."

"I can live with that. Now what about Stephanie."

He hesitated, deciding whether to throw me out or walk away or talk.

"I'm telling you I haven't seen her," he said, his voice mean and tight. "Sure, I was balling her back then, but it was no big deal."

"When exactly?"

"Early spring. March or April."

"And after that?"

"After that, nothing. She wanted to get married, so I dumped her. End of discussion."

"Just one more question."

"What's that?"

"Why would a sweet, intelligent girl like Stephanie Bellano want to marry an asshole like you?"

The girl next to me must've been eavesdropping, because she sucked in her breath.

Ken gave me a tight grin.

"There's a very good reason for that," he said.

"What?"

"First, I gotta know. Are you a cop?"

"Private cop."

He nodded. "Then I'll show you."

He turned on his heel and began pushing through the crowd. I grabbed my coat and hustled after him, following a snaky line between the tables. I glanced back to make sure big Carl wasn't following.

When I caught up with Ken, he was already in the long corridor in back. It led past the pay phones and the restrooms to the rear entrance. Ken stopped at the door.

"You're sure you're not a real cop?"

"Positive."

"Okay, then," he said, and opened the door.

I slipped on my coat. I wondered just how illegal this thing was he was about to show me.

He pushed open the screen, and we stepped into the cold, black December air. I followed him across a small, icy paved parking lot—employees only—with four or five cars and a Dumpster. Ken headed toward one of the cars. I was a few steps behind. Suddenly he stopped and spun. I knew in an instant what was going on, but he was much too quick for me.

Or maybe I was just getting stupid. Too many beers for too many years.

His leg went up and around, and his foot caught me in the side of the head.

I staggered back but didn't quite go down. Ken moved toward me in little shuffle steps, one foot before the other, his hands raised loosely in front of him. I considered running back into the bar, but suddenly he was all around me, kicking and chopping and punching from five different directions. I blocked a few but caught the rest, one in a very vulnerable spot that dropped me to my knees, where I was an easy target for a chop to the back of the neck.

Down I went, flat out on the dirty frozen asphalt.

I was awake, barely, but I couldn't move, only lie there and stare at the slush-spattered side of a radial tire and listen to Ken chuckle. He wasn't even breathing hard.

"That's for calling me an asshole," he said.

I tried to wiggle my fingers and toes. I couldn't. I hoped Ken hadn't caused permanent nerve damage. My dancing lessons.

"I'll tell you why Stephanie wanted to marry me," he said, standing over me. "Because she was a good little Catholic girl, that's why. She was such a good little Catholic girl that she wouldn't take the pill, so she got knocked up. That's when I told her to hit the road. You hear what I'm saying?"

He kicked me in the ribs to get my attention. It hurt, but I took it as a good sign. At least I could feel.

"I'll tell you something else. She wasn't even that good in bed."

I heard the back screen door bang open.

"Jesus, Ken, what'd you *do* to the guy?" It sounded like Carl.

"Gave him a lesson in self-defense."

"Who is he, anyway?"

"Some asshole private cop."

"What's he doing here?"

"Eating dirt."

Carl laughed nervously.

"Come on," Ken said, "let's go in."

I heard them move away and close the door. I lay there for what seemed like hours but was probably minutes. Slowly, I became aware of two sensations—pain and cold. Now I could wiggle my fingers and my toes, but I still couldn't get up. Eventually, I knew, the bar would close and people would come out to their cars and somebody would help me. Unless Ken was the first one out. Then I might get run over.

I moved my arm. Then the other one. Then a leg. Nothing to it. I pushed myself onto all fours. What a man.

The dirty ice on the asphalt was melting under the pressure from my knees and soaking my pants. I used a Camaro for a crutch and pulled myself to my feet. My stomach was queasy, and my neck felt as if Ken were standing on it. I let go of the car. See? I could stand all by myself.

I took a step.

He walks, too, folks.

Walk to your car, I told myself. Leave now. Go home. You were stupid and you got suckered and it was your own damn fault, so just forget about it and go home. You shouldn't be mad at him; you should be mad at yourself. Don't even go through the bar to the front. Walk around the building.

Sure.

I opened the back door. I went in.

There were two pay phones on the wall by the men's room. I used one and dialed the number of the other one. Then I turned my back to it and started an intense conversation with the ringing phone—ringing in my ear and ringing on the wall behind me. It rang ten or twelve times before somebody came over and picked it up and yelled over the noise, "Lion's Lair."

"Ken Hausom," I said, covering the mouthpiece. "It's important."

"Hold on."

The guy let the receiver dangle, then went into the crowd for Hausom. I went into the men's room and shut the door, then opened it a finger's width. A few minutes later Ken came down the hall and picked up the receiver.

"Hello?"

I stepped out behind him, grabbed a handful of his hair, and smashed his head into the phone. He struggled feebly. I got one arm around his chest and kept my hand buried in his hair. Then I bashed his face into the phone a couple more times, making the bell ring dully inside the black steel box. He went limp. I took a look at him. His nose and mouth were bloody, and his top incisors were broken, but he still looked like a ladies' man to me, so I rang the phone again. Then I let him slide to the floor.

"Wrong number," I told him, and got the hell out of there before he could wake up.

CHAPTER

7

ON FRIDAY MORNING I felt as if I'd been in a train wreck. But at least I could chew crispy bacon and slurp ice-cold orange juice. Which was probably more than you could say for Karate Ken. Actually, to look at me, you wouldn't even know I'd been beaten up. Other than a puffy red ear, my bruises didn't show.

I showered and dressed without wincing too much. Then I phoned a few airlines. The earliest vacant seat to San Diego was eight o'clock tonight. I bought it with my VISA.

Then I phoned Rachel Wynn—first at home, then at her office. I wondered if she was still mad about my questioning of Stacey O'Connor.

"Good morning," I said.

"I'm just leaving for class." Her voice was cold enough to freeze my ear to the phone. My good ear, too.

"Was Stephanie Bellano pregnant?"

"What?" The ice melted at once.

"You know, with child, in a family way."

"No. I mean, not that I know of. She certainly wasn't showing."

"And you would have noticed if she were seven or eight months along."

"Yes, of course. What are you saying?"

I told her about Ken Hausom. I left out the fight.

"Do you believe him?" Rachel asked, deep concern in her voice.

"I'm afraid I do."

"Then she must have had a miscarriage during the summer."

"Or an abortion."

Rachel was silent for a moment. "I wonder if her parents know."

"I don't know. If I get close to her mother, I'll ask. But first I'm going to talk to her sister in San Diego. I'm flying there tonight."

"Would you . . ."

"What?"

"After you get back, would you call me?"

"Sure."

"I'm really worried about Stephanie."

"Me, too," I said. "Talk to you later."

I *was* worried about Stephanie. She'd been gone a week. She had little money and just the clothes on her back. Was she staying with someone? Was she alone? Was she alive?

My mind was conjuring up worst-case scenarios: Stephanie, battered and amnesiac, wandering the streets; Stephanie, a prisoner of sexual perverts; Stephanie, dead and buried in a shallow grave.

And what scenarios now tortured Angela Bellano?

I locked up the apartment and drove downtown.

It was time to get some input from a real cop. And Patrick MacArthur was that. He'd recently been promoted to head of the Robbery/Homicide Section, which was one step away from captain.

MacArthur and I had become close friends during our days in the police academy. It had probably started the day we'd been paired in hand-to-hand combat. We'd practically beaten each other senseless. Male bonding. He'd been married and

I'd been single, and I think his wife was worried about the bad influence I might have on him. So for the first few years that MacArthur and I were cops, she was continually inviting me over for dinner, pairing me up with one or another of her single girlfriends. She finally found one that liked me. Katherine and I had married a year later.

Of course, a few years after that, Katherine had been murdered. I'd fallen apart, and MacArthur had helped me put myself back together.

Since then, we'd moved apart, MacArthur and I. We were still friends, but in a different way. He had his career and family, and I had, well, whatever it was that I had. He'd moved up to management, and I was still down on the production line. And all of his wife's girlfriends were married.

I got a visitor's tag and permission to go upstairs.

MacArthur was on the phone. He waved me into a chair.

His shirt was powder blue with a white collar, and his tie cost fifty bucks. He'd recently had a manicure. He looked more like a corporate executive than a police lieutenant. He hung up the phone.

"Long time no see, Jake. What's wrong with your neck?"

"What?"

"You're holding your head like a geek."

"I fell down in a parking lot."

"Why doesn't that surprise me?" He shot out his wrist and checked his thin gold watch. "I've got about ten minutes. What's on your mind?"

"Joseph Bellano. Any leads on who killed him?"

"Do you have a personal interest?"

"The day before before he got blown up, he hired me to find his daughter Stephanie."

"Do *you* know where she is?" His voice was pointed.

"You seem anxious about her."

"You bet I am."

"Why?" He was in Robbery/Homicide, not Missing Persons.

"You go first, Jake. What have you found out about her?"

If he were anyone else, I wouldn't be too quick to answer. And of course, he'd pay me back. I filled him in on Stephanie's involvement with Ken Hausom and her apparent fear of the four men at Bellano's barbershop. He frowned and wrote down their names.

"We talked to Bellano's partner, Sal, and he never said anything about this."

"Maybe cops make him nervous."

MacArthur pursed his lips. "And Sal told you he couldn't remember the fourth man's name?"

"Right."

MacArthur pushed the phone at me. "Jog his memory."

"Now?"

"Now."

The phone rang eight times before Sal answered it. He was busy. I asked him if he remembered the fourth man's name.

"Stan Fowler," he recited, "Gary Rivers, Johnny Toes Burke, and Mitch Overholser."

"Mitch Overholser," I repeated. MacArthur wrote it down. "Who is he?"

"I know one thing," Sal said disgustedly. "He's a professional gambler. I got customers waiting."

He hung up.

MacArthur said, "Have you talked to these four?"

"Not yet."

"Good. Don't."

"Why not?"

"Because they're part of a homicide investigation, and I don't want you interfering."

"Hey, I'm the one who just gave you their names."

He pulled back his phone and said nothing.

"Besides," I said, "I'm looking for Stephanie Bellano, not her father's killer."

MacArthur looked out the window separating us from the busy squad room. He was getting ready to tell me something. His eyes locked on mine.

"We're keeping this out of the press to help us sort the cranks from any legitimate leads. So you tell no one."

I waited.

"I mean it, Jake."

"Okay, okay."

He paused before he spoke. "The bomb that killed Joseph Bellano was in Stephanie's car, not his."

"What?"

"His wife told us that his car wouldn't start that morning. He came back in the house, got the keys to Stephanie's car, then went out and blew himself to bits."

"They were trying to kill Stephanie? Why?"

"We've been asking ourselves that, too. In fact, there's some question if the bomb was meant for her."

"I don't understand. You just said—"

"I know, I know. But if you consider her as the target, nothing fits. Method, for one. Bomb in car equals mob hit. The bomb, by the way, has been identified by the lab as a U.S. Army land mine, possibly one—"

"Jesus."

"—possibly one of several stolen last year from the armory at Camp George West, along with some assault rifles and hand grenades. Anyway, whoever rigged it to the ignition was a professional. And professionals don't generally hit college coeds. Which brings up another problem—motive. Why would the mob want to kill an innocent eighteen-year-old girl? She wasn't involved in her father's business. From what we've learned, she didn't even *know* her father was a bookie until the day she ran off. Motive takes us back to Bellano. He *was* a likely target of the mob. At least a target of Fat Paulie DaNucci."

"Then why wouldn't—"

"Wait, let me finish. Another problem with Stephanie as the target is that everyone knew she had run away. Her parents were asking about her all over town. If someone wanted her dead, for whatever reason, a bomb in her car would be chancy at best. Who says she's coming back? Who knows when? The odds are good that someone else might innocently start the car before she did."

"Maybe that's what happened."

"Maybe."

"But you don't think so."

"I have my doubts."

I shook my head. "Am I missing something here? Let's say DaNucci, or whoever, wanted to blow up Bellano. Then why not put the bomb in *his* car, for chrissake?"

"One very good reason."

"What?"

"Angela Bellano can't drive a stick shift."

"Huh?"

"She told us so, and anyone close to her would know. Bellano's car was an automatic. Stephanie's was a stick. If you put a bomb in Bellano's car, maybe you'll get him, but maybe you'll just get his wife when she goes out to buy groceries. Conversely, if you put a bomb in the *other* car, then you're sure to get Bellano. Especially when *his* car won't start."

"Sure, unless Stephanie starts her own car."

"Exactly."

He waited for me to catch up.

I did. "So assuming the bomb was meant for Bellano, whoever planted it knew Stephanie wasn't around."

"And who better to know than the girl herself."

"What? Are you saying you think *Stephanie* is involved in her father's death?"

"It's a possibility."

Not in my mind it wasn't. Of course, maybe that's why MacArthur was a lieutenant and I was self-employed.

"Did you find evidence that Bellano's car had been disabled?"

"Nothing conclusive. There was too much damage. And

this whole thing could just be a case of two wrongs making a right. At least from the bomber's point of view. Let's say the bomb was meant for Bellano but the bomber screwed up and put it in the wrong car. That could've easily happened. Both cars were Ford Tauruses, one black, one dark blue, a year apart. They look pretty much alike. The bomber just got lucky when Bellano's car wouldn't start." MacArthur checked his watch again. He stood. "I've got a meeting." He *was* an executive. "There's one other reason why we think Bellano was the target," he said. He slipped on his suit coat. It was an unusual shade of gray—new, I suppose, for this fashion season. It fit him like paint.

"What's that?"

He came around his desk and faced me eye to eye. We were exactly the same height. Didn't I used to be taller than he was? Either I was slouching, or he was standing up straighter than usual.

"Again, this is not public knowledge."

"My lips are sealed."

"And if by some freak of nature you learn anything new about Stephanie Bellano, you bring it straight here."

"Scout's honor."

He nodded and made a face.

"Bellano's records have been destroyed."

"His records?"

"His bookmaking records. We'd confiscated them along with the records of a few dozen other bookies. Everything was locked and guarded in our property room, which is supposedly secure as a bank. Bellano's records were in there for a few days before they were checked. They were destroyed."

"Just his?"

"Just his. Of course, his were the only ones stored on computer disks. They were destroyed magnetically, not physically."

"Magnetically?"

"With a magnet, or something similar. So it could have been an accident. But we don't think so. And if someone risked getting caught messing with those disks, there must have been some key information on them. Now it's gone. We think whoever wiped out that information also wiped out Bellano."

"I see."

"We're conducting an internal investigation. Somebody will get burned. After you."

He opened the door for me. Then he hustled away through the crowd of cops and victims, perpetrators and suspects. I followed, but not quite as fast. Nobody moved out of *my* way.

I had trouble imagining Stephanie Bellano plotting her father's death. Sure, she'd been angry at him last Friday in his shop. But murder? I also had trouble imagining someone wanting to kill her. How many enemies could a college coed have? Especially ones versed in car bombs.

MacArthur was probably right. Someone had wanted Bellano's knowledge canceled. So they'd erased him and then erased his records.

Although not completely.

Bellano had told me the cops had overlooked one copy of his records, one that was right under their noses. I searched the crowd for MacArthur. He was already gone. If he hadn't been in such a hurry, I would've told him.

Probably.

CHAPTER

8

I FLEW TO SAN DIEGO that night.

It was too late to drop in on Diane Eastbridge, so I spent the night in a downtown hotel. I woke up Saturday morning with a partial view of North San Diego Bay. The toll bridge walked across it on stilts toward Coronado.

I took a shower and ate a room-service breakfast. Then I put on white pants, boat shoes, a purple polo shirt, and perfectly black Ray-Bans. I was cool. Except my summer tan was long gone. I'd probably stand out among the sun-browned locals like a marshmallow in a bag of walnuts.

I drove my rental car north on Cabrillo Freeway to the Genesee Avenue exit. There were lots of palm trees and convertibles and long-legged women, and I wondered why the hell I was living a mile high up in the snow. So I could have a white Christmas? Humbug. I'd rather have a tan.

I checked my map, then realized I'd gone too far. I made a couple of turns before I found Diane's street.

I hadn't phoned ahead. If she was hiding Stephanie, she'd lied about it to her own mother, and she sure as hell wasn't going to admit it to me.

Diane's address was one of eight units, which formed a horseshoe surrounding a courtyard of red tile. There were plants in huge terra-cotta pots. An old guy in khaki pants and a Hawaiian shirt was sweeping up a few dead leaves with a stiff broom.

"Good morning," I told him, and walked over.

Up close his skin looked as rough as hide. It was laced with a thousand wrinkles from too much sun.

"I'm looking for Diane Eastbridge."

"She's home," he said, nodding. "Unit F, right over there."

"Are you the manager?" I asked.

He stopped sweeping and leaned on his broom, showing me skinny, leathery forearms.

"I *own* these units, fella."

Big deal. "I wanted to surprise her and her sister."

He looked me up and down, then squinted at me with a half smile.

"You from out of town?"

I guess my disguise hadn't fooled him. I took off the Ray-Bans.

"That's right. I'll only be here a short time, and I wanted to drop in on them. Are they both home?"

"I didn't even know she had a sister."

"Isn't there a young woman staying with her?"

"Nobody's staying with her. Just the kids."

I crossed the courtyard and knocked on F. A moment later the door was opened by Diane Eastbridge. The last time I'd seen her she'd been in black. Now she wore a green tank top, blue shorts, and sandals. She was prettier than Stephanie—at least Stephanie's picture. But there was a strong family resemblance. It was mostly the pouty lips and the dark bedroom eyes.

"Yes?" She was frowning. She didn't know me, and I obviously wasn't selling anything.

"My name is Jacob Lomax. I'm a private investigator from Denver. Your father hired me to—"

"My father is dead," she said with finality.

"I know, and I'm sorry. The day before his death he asked me to find your sister."

"I'm not surprised. It's him she ran away from, and I don't blame her one bit. Wait a minute—Did my mother send you here?"

"No."

"Then why don't you leave us alone. Steph will come home when she's ready. Good-bye." She started to close the door.

"Her life may be in danger."

The door stopped, half-open.

"Stephanie didn't run away from your father," I said. "She ran away from someone else. Someone she feared."

"What are you saying?"

I looked over my shoulder. The leather-skinned owner was quietly sweeping clean tiles and keeping an ear pointed our way.

"Could we talk inside?"

Diane hesitated, then opened the door and unlatched the screen. I followed her in.

The rooms were small. The furniture had cane legs and floral-printed cushions. I could see through an arched doorway into the kitchen. A young girl was eating a bowl of cereal at the table. Her older brother, about ten or so, sat across from her and chuckled into a copy of *Mad* magazine. It used to make me chuckle, too.

"Won't you sit down," Diane said.

I sank into the sofa. On my right was a table with a glass top and wicker legs. There was a picture in a red-plastic frame showing Diane hugging her two children. In front of them was a big English sheepdog. Maybe Diane's ex-husband had taken the picture. I hadn't seen a dog. Maybe he'd taken that, too.

Diane sat across from me and leaned forward. When she spoke, her voice was low. She didn't want the kids to hear.

"Why do you think Steph is in danger?"

I'd already decided not to tell her about the bomb having been in Stephanie's car. And it had little to do with my promise to MacArthur. I described Stephanie's exit from the barbershop, then named the four customers.

Diane didn't know any of them. She'd heard of Stan Fowler, but only because he'd been in business for years and had flooded the Denver media with his ads.

"Do you think one of these men is after Stephanie?" She looked worried.

"Possibly. Anyway, Stephanie believes one of them is."

"But why?"

"I don't know."

"My God, do you think it has something to do with my father's death?"

"I don't know that, either. Has she made any contact with you since she left?"

Diane shook her head no. "I assumed she was staying with a friend."

"She's not. And I've talked to all of her friends. Except one named Chrissie, whom she apparently met during the summer. Do you know her?"

"No. But if it was during the summer . . ."

"What?"

"Steph and I and my parents used to go to Big Pine Lake for two weeks every summer. Maybe she met Chrissie there. In fact, I think Steph stayed at the lake for several months last summer and worked part-time. My father believed in work."

"Where did she work?"

"I don't know. I'm not even certain she did."

We were quiet for a moment. I could hear one of the kids running water in the kitchen sink.

"What did you mean," I asked, "when you said you didn't blame Stephanie for running away?"

"From our father."

"Because he was a bookie?"

"What?" She looked as if she were ready to laugh. "Hell, no. That might've been the best thing about him. It brought in a lot more money than his stupid barbershop."

"Then what?"

"Because he was a goddamn tyrant."

"That surprises me."

"It does? Did you know my father?"

"More or less. He seemed like a soft-spoken man."

"Oh, he was soft-spoken, all right. Speak softly and carry a big stick."

"He beat you?"

"No, no, nothing like that. He never laid a hand on me or Steph. But he made sure everything in that house was done his way. *Exactly* his way." She shook her head, a pained smile on her face. "Do this," she mocked. "Don't do that. You can wear this, you can't wear that. You can go out with this boy, not that one. Jesus, he damn near suffocated me." She smiled meekly and shook her head, then glanced up at the ceiling and beyond. "Sorry, Dad," she said. She looked at me. "Anyway, that's why I left. I came out here, got a job, met a man. He gave me two wonderful kids. Then *he* took off. Maybe *I* suffocated *him*."

Again, we fell silent.

"Mom, we're done."

The boy stood in the doorway. He was slim and tentative, but I could see the resemblance to his grandfather Joseph.

"Did you do the dishes?" Diane asked him.

"Yes. Are we still going to the beach for shells?"

"Pretty soon."

The beach. Sigh. Back in Denver people were crunching around on studded snow tires. The boy retreated through the kitchen. I heard a back door open and close.

"Did you know Stephanie was pregnant?"

Diane looked shocked. "You're not serious. *Stephanie?*"

"She got pregnant early last spring. Sometime between then and now she either had a miscarriage or an abortion."

"I don't believe it. I would have heard something. My God, my parents would've freaked out." She shook her head. "An abortion? No. My mother would've told me, I'm certain."

"Maybe your mother didn't know."

"But how . . ."

We were both thinking the same thing—Big Pine Lake.

"Maybe it happened at the resort," Diane said. "Maybe she's *hiding* up there. Except that's probably the first place my father would've checked."

"Probably. I'll take a look, though."

I heard the back door open and close. The boy and the girl stood in the doorway, pails in hand. It was time to go to the beach.

I flew back to Denver that evening. It was cold and snowing. The Olds ice-skated all the way from the airport to Holy Family rectory.

I was told at the door that Father Carbone was rehearsing a wedding. I found him next door, at the church. He stood before the altar with half a dozen nervous young people in street clothes. I sat in a pew and waited.

Twenty minutes later the practice was finished, and the kids filed out, smiling. Father Carbone saw me and came over. I stood and met him in the aisle.

"Any word on Stephanie?" he asked.

"I'm still chasing leads."

"Her poor, dear mother."

"Yes. She's why I'm here. I need to talk to her. The last time I tried, she broke into tears and I got tossed out by a large character named Tony."

He smiled with one side of his mouth. "That was probably Anthony, her brother."

"I want them to know I'm on their side. Perhaps a word from you . . ."

"Of course," he said. "I'll see them tomorrow after mass. Is that soon enough?"

"It's fine."

We started toward the door.

"Father, did Stephanie tell you last June that she was pregnant?"

He kept walking. His mouth had opened slightly, then immediately snapped shut.

"Was that the 'trouble' you mentioned?"

"I told you before, Mr. Lomax, I am bound by the seal of the confessional."

"I know. Hypothetically, though, if a young, unmarried Catholic girl confessed to you that she was pregnant, what would you advise her to do?"

He shook his head, his face neutral. "It's impossible to answer that. It would depend on the individual and on the circumstances. And I'm not going to engage in a game of twenty questions."

He led me through the vestibule to the outer doors. He stopped. He wasn't leaving; I was.

"A young girl's life may be at stake."

"I understand that."

"I'm trying to help her."

"Yes. Yes, I'm certain that you are, Mr. Lomax." He put his hand on the door, ready to push it open and kick me out. "If such a girl came to me," he said, looking at the door, not at me, "I would probably first inquire about the father of the unborn child."

"And if the father was a louse, if he just dumped her and left her to deal with it alone?"

"I'd suggest that she talk with her parents."

I doubted that Stephanie had told her parents or anyone else about her pregnancy.

"Father, what if this girl came to you months later and told you, I mean, confessed to you that she'd had an abortion."

He turned and faced me with tired eyes and pain in his heart.

"Then I would help her pray to God for forgiveness."

CHAPTER

9

FATHER CARBONE had only confirmed what I'd already suspected: Stephanie had had an abortion this summer. Probably at Big Pine Lake.

Before I started snooping around up there, I wanted to talk to Angela Bellano. I couldn't do that until tomorrow. No use wasting tonight, though. So I went home, unpacked my suitcase, and changed from my airline-traveling clothes to my barhopping clothes.

I wasn't looking for a good time. I was looking for Johnny Toes Burke.

My leads to Stephanie's whereabouts were nearly gone. Pretty soon I might have to start looking at *why* she'd run and hope that would give me a clue as to where. Apparently she'd run from one or more of the four customers in her father's shop. Johnny Toes Burke was the only one I knew personally.

I hadn't seen Burke in several years, so I had no idea where to find him. But by my fifth saloon I'd learned that he lived in an apartment in Aurora and hung out at a place on East Evans called Terry's. Also, he was now working for Fat Paulie DaNucci.

I got to Terry's at ten.

The clientele was visibly drunk. They were a mix of blue-collar workers, frayed-white-collar workers, and nonworkers who tried to act as if they were rolling in dough. They wore zircon rings, gold-plated chains, and polyester shirts open to show off their hairless chests. So did their women.

I squeezed up to the bar. One of the bartenders told me that Johnny Toes hadn't been in yet tonight. I bought a beer and waited.

My man came in around eleven.

He was wearing a lime-green suit and a hooker on each arm—one white, one black, both about six feet tall in heels, which put them a few inches taller than Johnny Toes even in *his* heels. He limped up and down the bar, showing off his toys for the night. Actually, the black one wasn't too bad looking. He bought a bottle of cheap champagne and took his women to a table in the back, limping all the way.

Johnny Toes limped because he didn't have any toes on his right foot.

He had various explanations, depending on whom he was trying to impress. They ranged from "wounded in 'Nam" to "hit by a shark near Acapulco." The truth wasn't quite as exciting, but then it usually isn't. When Burke was a teen, he'd been caught shoplifting at J. C. Penney's. The store dick slapped him around, then tossed him out. Johnny showed *him*. He kicked in the store's huge, heavy front window. Poor Johnny. The bottom part of the glass broke inward, and the top part dropped like a guillotine, slicing off the end of his foot.

I walked over to his table.

He and the ladies were laughing it up. Johnny frowned when he saw me. The ladies kept smiling. Of course, they were getting paid for it.

"Hi, Johnny."

"What're *you* doing here?"

It had been six years, but he remembered me. I'd been in uniform then. My partner and I had busted him coming out of a convenience store. He'd just robbed it. We broke his arm taking away his gun.

I put my beer on the table and sat down.

"I just want to talk. Introduce me to your girlfriends."

"My name's Doreen," the white girl said. She had bleached-blond hair, blood-red lipstick, and false eyelashes long enough to knock the ash off my cigar, if I'd been smoking one.

"Shut up," Johnny told her.

Doreen pouted.

"I don't have to talk to you, Lomax," Johnny told me. "You ain't a cop anymore." He smirked. "In fact, I heard they kicked you out after your bitch got killed. Something about you hiding in a bottle."

I smiled.

The black hooker sat back. She'd seen that kind of smile before, probably on the face of her pimp just before he used his razor to put that scar on her upper arm.

"She wasn't my bitch, Johnny, she was my wife. And you're right, I'm not a cop anymore. But I am capable of shoving this beer bottle up your ass and kicking you until it breaks."

His Adam's apple went up and down in his skinny neck, and his hand moved inside his coat. If he was carrying a gun, it was too small to make a bulge.

"I'm not afraid of you," he let me know.

"Take it easy," I said. "We're all friends here."

I reached over for the bottle of champagne and poured some in each of their glasses. The hookers relaxed. Johnny Toes didn't. He was keeping an open mind.

"Looks like you're in the chips, Johnny. Fine booze, good-looking women. Did Fat Paulie give you a raise?"

He smirked.

"Or did you get a bonus for putting a bomb in Joseph Bellano's car?"

"Try to prove it," he said, and smirked again. This time, though, it was forced. He'd like me to think he was a cold-blooded killer. He wasn't. He was just a lizard.

"I'm not interested in Bellano," I told him. "I'm looking for Stephanie."

"Who?"

"You know who. Bellano's daughter. She's been missing for a week."

"Life's a bitch," Johnny Toes said, and sipped the bubbly.

"Why did she run away?" I asked him.

"What? How the hell should I know?"

"You were in Bellano's shop last Friday. Stephanie came in angry, and she ran out scared to death. You remember, don't you?"

His eyelids drooped like an iguana's.

"I might."

"I think she was afraid of one of Bellano's customers."

"Afraid of me?" Johnny Toes looked about him in mock innocence. "You gotta be kidding. I'm a sweetheart, ain't I, girls?"

He hugged his whores, and they laughed.

"I don't mean you, Johnny. You couldn't scare Bambi."

He gave me his meanest look. Well, okay, maybe Bambi.

"I meant the other three customers," I said. "What do you know about them?"

"You expect me to remember who was in there?"

I named them.

"Sure I've heard of Stan Fowler," he said. "*And* Gary Rivers. But I wouldn't recognize either one of them."

"*The* Gary Rivers?" the white whore said. "I've seen him on TV."

Johnny Toes glared at her.

"What?" she wanted to know.

"Shut up," he said.

"I can't even *talk*? You said we were going to party."

"This *is* a party."

"Excuse me for interrupting," I said, "but what about the third customer. Mitch Overholser."

Johnny Toes glanced at me. He sipped his cheap champagne.

"Sure, I know Mitch."

"How?"

"Ask *him*. Look, Lomax, who gives a damn about Bellano's daughter. I'm sure none of *these* guys did. If they wanted anything from Bellano, it wasn't his little girl. It was his books." Johnny Toes licked his scaly lips, flicking his tongue like a gecko. "I wished I had them myself," he said. "But I heard the cops got everything."

"Why would you want Bellano's books?"

"His client list and the accounts receivable? Are you kidding? Bellano had a successful business going there, and I'm not talking about his barbershop. If a guy wanted to make some easy money, all he'd need would be Bellano's books. He'd have a working business plus a list of guys that owed him money."

"You'd need something first, though."

"What's that?"

"You'd need to get Bellano out of the way."

"That goes without saying," he said. "Speaking of which, why don't you get out of *our* way." He put his arms around his women of the evening. "We're trying to have a party here, and you're talking about dead people."

I didn't tell Johnny Toes what MacArthur had told me— Bellano's records had been destroyed. At least the cops' copy. There was another copy, though. And I was beginning to wonder if they might contain a clue, if not to Stephanie's whereabouts, then to Bellano's killer.

And so early Sunday afternoon—after I'd checked with Father Carbone by phone but before I visited Angela Bellano—I made a side trip.

I took Interstate 25 south, then I-225 east between the snow-covered embankment of Cherry Creek Dam and the snowy fields of Kennedy Golf Course. I got off the highway on Parker Road, drove another mile or so to a small shopping center, and parked in front of MicroComp Computer & Software Center.

There were some Christmas wreaths painted in the windows. Also a few arcane signs: "Sale on Clones!" "30% Off All Hardcards!" "Special on Laptops!"

It was close enough to Christmas for the store to be open on Sundays. I pushed through the glass door.

It was a big place, crowded with computer displays. Each one was separated from the carpet by a static-free mat. There were customers scattered here and there. Some stared at video screens and tentatively tapped on plastic keys. The rest nosed through racks of books and packs of software.

A salesman approached.

He was around thirty, with bushy hair, thick glasses, and buck teeth. His corduroy sports coat was older than my Olds. The elbows, though, were nice and shiny.

"Help you, sir?"

"Is Zeno around?"

He eyed me suspiciously. "Sure."

I followed him across the showroom, then through a door.

The back room had a concrete floor and bright fluorescent lights. There were worktables with keyboards and video screens, some fitted with small black canopies to cut out the glare. The walls were lined with metal shelves loaded with electronic gizmos. There were two guys in the far corner huddled before a computer. They were talking about bad chips. I didn't think they meant food. A woman worked alone by the near wall.

"Someone to see you, Zeno."

"I'm busy," she said. Then, "Hey, Jake!"

Eunice Zenkowski, known to all as Zeno, smiled up at me from a worktable spewed with the guts of a computer, which lay open before her like a dissected android. Zeno was wearing her usual blue jeans, beat-up white tennies, and dark long-sleeved shirt rolled up over her skinny white arms. She had a narrow, bony face; thick dark eyebrows; and thin, colorless lips. She had pale fuzz on her upper lip. She also had a crush on me. At least she used to.

"How you doing, Zeno?"

"I'll be doing better when I figure out how the owner of this machine managed to crash three hard disks in one month. So what's up? Did you just stop by to say hi? Or are you finally ready to join the computer generation?"

"Not exactly," I said, and looked over my shoulder. The salesman was hovering nearby.

Zeno told him, "It's okay, Milton. Jake's a friend."

"Oh." Milton lingered a moment longer, then returned to the front of the store.

After the door closed behind him, Zeno said, "Milton's the jealous type."

I looked at her and smiled. Two small dots of color rose to her pale cheeks.

"You and Milton? Hey, that's great."

"I guess it's okay," she said, avoiding my eyes, squirming in her chair like a snagged trout. I let her off the hook.

"Zeno, I need your help with something."

Her colored dots went away.

"You *are* going to buy a computer."

I shook my head no. "A friend of mine, recently deceased, has some files in his home, probably hidden in one room, probably computer related. I want you to help me find them."

"What do you mean, they're hidden?"

"Before he died, he told me the police had searched the room for his files and—"

"The police?"

"Don't worry. We're not going to be doing anything illegal. Anyway, the police overlooked one set of files, and it was 'right under their noses.' His words."

"Gee, Jake, I'll help if I can. But you're supposed to be the expert at finding things, not me."

"The trouble is, I'm not sure what I'm looking for."

"I see. I don't suppose you know what kind of system your friend was running."

"System?"

She sighed. "Computer and software, Jake."

"No. Does it matter?"

"It might. I'm familiar with some more than others. When do you want to do this?"

"Now. That is, if you're not too busy."

She waved her hand at the mess on the table. "This can wait. Let me get some things."

I waited while she packed a small case with tools, disks, and gadgets, then followed her to the front. She told Milton she was going with me on a consulting job.

We left him burning with suspicion.

CHAPTER

10

IT STARTED TO SNOW on the way to Angela Bellano's house. Icy flakes swirled in the wake of the car ahead of me. They melted when they hit the warm windshield of the Olds. Zeno took off her gloves and scarf and unzipped her bulky parka.

"Can we have a little music?" she asked, opening the glove compartment.

"The radio's over here."

"I was looking for your tapes."

"You don't need tapes with a radio."

"Geez, Jake," she said, reaching for the knob, then, "What, only AM?"

"Sorry."

"Geez."

She went through the dial from one end to the other, a high-tech kid with a low-tech toy.

I thought about the first time we'd met, nearly four years ago.

She'd been a senior in high school, and her little sister, Darla, had been ten. Their mother had recently been killed, run down by a stolen car filled with kids on a joy ride. Zeno's father, Paul Zenkowski, was devastated by the loss. He began to hit the bottle pretty hard. He was an air force sergeant stationed at Lowry, and after being caught drunk on duty one too many times, he was in danger of losing his stripes.

Meanwhile, his dead wife's sister, a genuine bitch named Gwendolyn, was trying to get the courts to give Zeno and Darla to her, citing Paul's incompetence.

Paul wasn't incompetent. He was just drunk. But Gwendolyn's husband, a cut-rate attorney from Pueblo, seemed to have a fairly strong case. So Paul got an attorney. The attorney hired me to get some dirt on Gwendolyn. It's distasteful work, but I was new in the business, and I took what I could get.

What I got were some excellent photographs of Gwendolyn and her husband and their next-door neighbors playing Ping-Pong in the living room. It was an exciting match. Many innovative techniques. Both couples were naked, and the only equipment they were using were the paddles.

One look at the blowups and Gwendolyn dropped her case. Zeno and her sister and their father were left alone to get on with their lives. Of course, the girls weren't told the sordid details, only that nice Mr. Lomax had helped them out.

I parked in front of the Bellano residence. It was snowing more heavily now, blanketing the sidewalks, which had been shoveled this morning.

When Angela Bellano opened the door, Zeno and I were still stamping snow off our feet.

"Father Carbone told me you were coming," she said, letting us in. There was no joy in her voice. Why should there be? Her husband was dead, and her daughter was missing.

I introduced Zeno as "my associate, Eunice Zenkowski."

Angela took our coats and led us through the living room. Empty of mourners, it seemed larger than the last time I'd been here. The sofa and chairs had muted patterns and carved walnut legs. The Christmas tree looked futile.

We sat in the kitchen. It was filled with warmth and cooking smells, even though there was nothing on the stove or in the oven. I heard a toilet flush in another part of the house.

"Would you like coffee?" Angela asked.

As she was pouring it, a man came through the kitchen door. He was in his late forties, with pockmarked cheeks. He wore a white shirt and a navy-blue V-neck sweater, both extra-large, both barely large enough. He was the same guy who'd tossed me out the last time I was here.

"You again," he said.

"Me again."

"Tony, he's here to help, remember," Angela said. "Mr. Lomax, this is my brother, Tony Callabrese."

I started to stand, but he waved me back without offering to shake hands.

"Give me some more coffee," he asked Angela. Then he leaned against the counter, where he could sip it and look down at me.

"Diane called me last night," Angela told me. "She said you'd flown out there to find Stephanie."

"Yes."

"She said you seemed nice."

Tony blew air out his nose and folded his arms.

"I wonder, though," Angela said, "why Joseph didn't tell me he'd hired you."

"I don't know. Maybe he thought you wouldn't like him bringing in an outsider."

"I know *I* don't like it," Tony put in.

"If it would help find my baby . . ."

"Well, what good has he done so far?" Tony looked at me. "What *have* you done, big shot?"

He'd like to get something started so he could toss me out again. It was his hobby. When I spoke, it was to Angela.

"So far, I've talked to her friends at college, her teachers, her boyfriend, and—"

"Boyfriend?" Angela looked surprised. "She never told me she had a boyfriend."

She never said she was pregnant, either. But I decided to

spare Angela that. At least for now. "Stephanie met him last spring," I said, still aware of the stiffness in my neck. "An unpleasant young man. Ken Hausom."

Angela frowned. "Is he a student?"

"No," I said, and let it go at that. "Mrs. Bellano, do you know a girl named Chrissie?"

"I . . . no."

"Apparently Stephanie met her during the summer. Diane suggested it might have been at Big Pine Lake."

"Oh."

"Were you there this summer?"

"Yes. Every summer for years. Joseph would rent a cabin on the lake for two weeks. The . . . the girls loved it. This year, and last year, too, Stephanie stayed up there after we left. Joseph had gotten her a job. It was only temporary, just for the summer."

"Where?"

"At the clinic in town. She was a receptionist."

"I see. Did she stay in the cabin all summer?"

"No, that would've been too expensive. Besides, it was too big for one person. After Joseph and I left, Stephanie stayed in a rooming house."

"Do you have the address?"

"I'll get it."

She left the kitchen. Zeno and I sat in silence. Tony watched us. Angela Bellano returned. She handed me a slip of paper with an address and a name—Mrs. Henderson.

"She's the owner," Angela said. "But we've already called her. Stephanie's not there."

I nodded and slipped the paper in my pocket.

"Mrs. Bellano, Sal told me when Stephanie ran out of your husband's shop she was scared to death."

She nodded. "Joseph said she looked frightened. He was surprised. He was surprised by her yelling, too. And hurt."

"Sal didn't think it was your husband who'd scared her."

"What do you mean?"

"He thought it was one of the other four men in the shop. Stan Fowler, Gary Rivers, Mitch Overholser, or Johnny Toes Burke. Do you know any of them?"

"Gary Rivers? The one on the radio?"

"Yes."

"I think I've heard Joseph mention his name. And I'm pretty sure he was at the funeral."

"What about the others?"

She shook her head. "I don't know."

"I know this Johnny Toes."

I looked at Tony.

"By reputation, I mean. He's a weasel."

"Did Joseph have dealings with any of these men?"

Tony shrugged and looked at Angela.

She said, "I don't know. Of course, maybe they were bettors."

"That's one thing I'd like to find out," I said. "Which is why I brought Miss Zenkowski with me."

Tony and Angela looked at Zeno. Zeno looked embarrassed. She'd been sitting quietly, invisibly, watching our little soap opera. Now she was in it.

"Mrs. Bellano, when the police confiscated your husband's records, did they search the entire house?"

"No. Just his den."

"I see. He told me there was another set of records right under their noses. I wonder if you would let me and Miss Zenkowski look for them."

"Well, I guess it would be all right."

"Wait a minute," Tony said to me. Then to his sister, "Ange, you're not going to let this guy poke around in Joe's things, are you?"

"If it will help find Stephanie—"

"How could it, for chrissake? You don't know this guy from Adam. He could be *anybody*."

"Tony, please, it's okay. I—"

"No, it's *not* okay. I got a bad feeling about this guy, I don't care *if* Joe hired him. I think maybe he's got something up his sleeve."

Angela shook her head and pushed up from the table. I stood, and so did Zeno.

Angela said, "Follow me, Mr. Lo—"

"No." Tony stepped in front of me. "I won't allow it."

Angela turned on him. "This is *my* house, Tony, you hear me, *my house*. I say what goes on in here." Tony blinked, then backed off, hurt. Angela reached for his hand. "Tony, it's okay if they look. It can't hurt." The grieving widow comforting the macho brother. She turned back toward me. "Mr. Lomax. Miss uh . . ."

"Zeno," Zeno said.

"Please follow me."

Angela Bellano led us through the dining room and down a carpeted hallway, past a couple of bedrooms and a bathroom. The air felt close. Not stale or musty, just used, lived in. There was a room at the front corner of the house. The door was closed but not locked.

Angela pushed it open and motioned us in. She stayed in the doorway, unwilling to tread on hallowed ground.

"This is Joe's room," she said. "This is where he worked when he wasn't at the barbershop. The computer was something we bought for Stephanie a couple of years ago. She hardly used it, so Joe took it. Mostly it was just something to play with. If you need anything, I'll be in the kitchen."

She left. I closed the door.

The walls were white, broken only by a few framed photographs. Family portraits. Against one wall was a couch that folded out into a bed. Next to it was a rocking chair. There were a desk and chair next to the front window. On the desk was an ultra-sleek-looking computer and printer. Zeno snorted.

"What?"

"Obsolete equipment," she said.

"Can you work it?"

"*Work* it?" She made a face at me and shook her head. "Yes, Jake, I can *work* it. It's an IBM clone, no problem." She opened the little doors on the computer's disk drives to show me they were empty. "But first we need something to put in here."

We searched the room.

There was a small bookcase between the desk and the table—half a dozen books on the stock market, a few on computers, and some two-week-old issues of the *Wall Street Journal*. Bellano had told me he dabbled in stocks. There were no floppy disks in sight. I flipped through the books looking for hidden compartments, and Zeno searched the desk. I pulled the cushions off the couch and folded out the bed. We pulled off the mattress. Nothing.

" 'Right under their noses,' he told me."

Zeno sat before the computer, opened her bag, and took out a few disks. She shoved one in the left-hand slot and switched on the computer.

"Let's see what he's got," she said.

The machine hummed for a while, then beeped to let us know it was ready. Zeno typed in some instructions. The monitor displayed a few lines:

```
S  SYSTEM BOARD
S  640KB MEMORY
S  KEYBOARD
S  MONOCHROME ADAPTER
S  2 DISKETTE DRIVE(S) AND ADAPTER
S  1 HARD DISK AND ADAPTER
S  PRINTER ADAPTER
```

"That might be it," she said.

"What?"

"A hard disk."

"What?"

"See, right there."

"I see it. What the hell does it mean?"

"Geez, Jake. Okay, most newer systems have a hard disk and one floppy drive. This is an older system—two disk drives and no hard disk. But the diagnostics routine shows a hard disk, so Mr. Bellano or someone had one installed after it left the factory. But I don't see a hard drive, do you?"

"Is this a quiz?"

"Okay, okay. There's no exterior hard drive, so it must be a hard card—a miniaturized hard disk installed *inside* the main unit. Let's see."

She typed in a few more commands.

"There we go. We show drives 'A,' 'B,' and 'C.' 'A' and 'B' are the two floppy drives, and 'C' is the hard disk. Let's see what he's got on there."

Zeno tapped some keys, and the screen displayed this:

```
PROGRAMS      <DIR>
STOCKS        <DIR>
GAMES         <DIR>
```

"He's got everything in three subdirectories," she said. "Here's PROGRAMS." She typed "cd/programs," then "dir," and the screen filled with things like:

```
CURSOR     .COM
DBASE      .SYS
PORT       .TST
WP         .EXE
WPHELP     .FIL
```

"These are all of his program files. Let's look at the subdirectory labeled STOCKS."

Now we got lines like:

```
CHEMEX     .NOV
CHEMEX     .DEC
KERMCGEE   .JAN
KERMCGEE   .FEB
KERMCGEE   .MAR
```

"File names," Zeno informed me. "It looks like each one is a company name and a month."

"Let's look at the GAMES subdirectory," I said.

It looked more interesting:

```
ANDREWS    .BAS
ANDREWS    .BSK
ANDREWS    .FBL
ASOTTI     .BAS
ASOTTI     .BSK
ASOTTI     .FBL
BROWNE     .BAS
```

"Proper names," Zeno said. "With extensions. BAS might mean BASIC."

"I'd say it means baseball. BSK is basketball. FBL is football. Can we look inside all these files?"

"Now?"

"Is there a problem?"

"How much time do we have?"

"I don't want to overstay our welcome," I said.

"Then I'd better copy this subdirectory and work on it at home."

"Go ahead."

Zeno began transferring data onto a blank diskette.

"Okay," she said finally, removing the diskette.

"Now, can you wipe out the GAMES subdirectory on the hard disk?"

"Wipe out? You mean delete the files?"

"That's what I mean."

"Sure. But are *you* sure?"

"Yes." Bellano was gone, and his sins might as well join him. His widow had enough to grieve over.

"I can delete the files, Jake, but with a little work a computer person could probably retrieve them. Unless I reformat the hard disk. But that would destroy *all* the subdirectories."

"Then do it."

The process took about ten minutes. When it was done, Zeno typed, and the screen looked like this:

```
C> dir
  Volume in drive C has no label.
  Directory of C:
    File not found
C>
```

She looked up at me. "All gone."

"Good. Let's go."

Angela Bellano met us in the living room.

"Did you find anything?"

"Possibly. Zeno's going to work on it."

Angela got our coats. I told her I'd be in touch.

CHAPTER

11

IT WAS STILL SNOWING. Zeno helped me brush snow off the Olds. Then I drove her toward MicroComp. The streets were slick where they hadn't been sanded. Zeno told me it might take a while to print out all of Bellano's files, since her personal printer was relatively slow.

"There's a high-speed printer at work," she said.

"I think you should do it at home. I'd rather we kept this to ourselves."

"Okay."

"How long will you need?"

"I don't know exactly. I'll do some tonight and tomorrow after work. Maybe by tomorrow night."

"That's fine," I said. "What about dinner tonight? I'm kind of hungry."

"Milton's taking me out."

"Oh. Good."

"You're welcome to come along."

"Thanks, anyway."

When I got home, it was dark. It was still snowing, and I was still hungry. I didn't feel like eating alone, so I phoned Rachel Wynn. After all, I'd promised her we'd talk after I'd returned from San Diego. No answer. Maybe Milton was taking her out, too.

I opened a beer, then dumped a can of chili in a pot. I turned on the TV to catch the results of the Bronco game. I'd been so busy during the week, I'd forgotten to get down a bet.

Lucky you, said the sportscaster. Bears 42, Broncos 17.

I went back to the kitchen, stirred my chili, and opened another beer. The TV sounds droned from the next room. After the sports, I half listened to the weather. Heavy snow in the city and more in the mountains. Travelers' warnings. Chain law in effect. Some of the passes were closed. After the weather came a special report. I heard a word that caught my attention.

Bellano.

I stood in the doorway and watched.

The screen was filled with Bellano's bombed-out garage. The voice-over alluded to this as file footage, not news; there'd been no new developments in the murder case. This was a special series. Part one of seven.

The narrator's face came on the screen. Gary Rivers. It said so underneath.

I'd heard him before on the radio, but I'd never seen him. His talk show was a hot item, if you go for that kind of thing, which I don't. He got listeners stirred up over all sorts of things, from gun control to parting your hair on the wrong side. One thing, though, he generally did his homework. Now it looked as if he were pushing into a more lucrative market.

"Gambling is not a harmless pastime," he said, then paused dramatically. "It can kill."

Rivers went on to describe the many ways that gambling destroys lives and families.

Rivers had a good voice, but I wasn't sure he had the face for television. Sure, he was good-looking—even features, perfect hair, strong jaw, and a nice suit. But his expression was too stiff, too controlled. He looked like a mannequin.

On second thought, he was *perfect* for television.

"Tomorrow night," Rivers said, "I'll have part two of my series, 'Gambling in Colorado—Sport? Or Sickness?' Back to you, Bob."

I went back to my chili.

I wondered if Rivers had been the one who'd scared Stephanie. I also wondered what a hip character like him had been doing in a neighborhood barbershop in North Denver. Researching his series on gambling? Maybe I'd ask him.

In fact, if I didn't find Stephanie soon, I'd talk to all four customers. Not that I thought they'd confess to anything, at least not directly. But maybe they'd tell on each other.

Rivers wouldn't be hard to find. Neither would Stan Fowler or Johnny Toes Burke, for that matter. In fact, the only one of the four customers that I still knew nothing about was Mitch Overholser. Well, not *nothing*. I knew he was a gambler.

I opened another beer and got out my phone book. There were three bookies I knew in the city, but Eddy Natiele was my main man. I called him at home. After all, this was Sunday.

I didn't know what bookies did on Mondays. Maybe shoveled snow off their driveways. But Tuesdays they collected from the losers. Wednesdays they paid off the winners. Thursdays through Saturdays they took bets. And Sundays they stayed home with their families.

I apologized to Natiele for bothering him at home.

"No problem. What's up?"

"Do you know a player named Mitch Overholser?"

"Sort of. Why?"

"Tell me about him?"

"I've taken a few bets from him. But he usually wants more action than I can safely handle. I mean, without laying a lot of it off with another book. I'll tell you what, though. Me and most guys I know have shied away from him lately. He's been getting slow about paying when he loses."

"That can be dangerous," I said.

"Not as much as you might think, Jake. None of us use leg breakers."

"Except Fat Paulie DaNucci."

"Well, him, yeah. But that's a different league. Of course, I do know a book or two who's sold his overdue markers at ten cents on the dollar to guys like DaNucci, guys who *enjoy* beating up some poor slob for his last few bucks. None of my friends, though. We'd just stop taking bets from the guy and swallow the losses."

"About Overholser . . ."

"Right, I digress. Mostly, he's a gambler, and not a very good one. I heard he lost his job, his house, and his family. I don't mean he dropped his family on a bet; they took off. Of course, given the right odds, he might've tried it."

"What does he do when he's not gambling?"

"Last I heard he was working, if you can call it that, at his brother-in-law's used-car lot on West Colfax."

"What's the name, do you know?"

"Honest Somebody-or-other."

"That figures."

"Harry's," Natiele said. "Honest Harry's."

It was still snowing Monday morning.

Getting up to Big Pine Lake today looked doubtful. Even getting around the city didn't look too good. The radio said the "snow law" was in effect, which meant that on specified streets the city was towing away cars stuck in the path of snowplows. The owners had to pay for the tow and the impound. On *unspecified* streets, if they were plowed at all, your car only got buried under a five-foot drift.

The radio began listing school closures. I didn't hear Loretto Heights, but I tried Rachel Wynn at home first. She answered on the second ring.

"Playing hooky today?" I asked.

"No, in fact, I was just about to leave. Have you located Stephanie?" Her voice was hopeful.

"No."

"Oh, I thought maybe that's why you'd called."

"Just thought I'd give you an update," I said. I told her about my visit with Stephanie's sister, Diane, and about Big Pine Lake. "Maybe I can find this girl Chrissie up there."

"You're not going to drive up today, are you?"

"I doubt it."

"Good, because the roads are terrible. It took us over four hours to drive down from Vail last night, and it looked like things were getting worse."

"Ski trip?"

"What? Oh, yes. My friend Pat and I spent the weekend up there."

"How nice."

She paused. "Are you being sarcastic?"

"I don't think so. Only . . ."

"What?"

"Is Pat a Patricia or a Patrick?"

"Good-*bye*, Mr. Lomax." She hung up before I could tell her that skiing is bad for the knees.

But then, so is sitting around the house all day. I had to get out and about. Big Pine Lake was out of the question, though, at least for today.

I pulled out the phone book and called Honest Harry's. No answer. It's tough to sell cars when they're covered with snow. I phoned radio station KNWZ and asked for Gary Rivers. He wouldn't be there until later, I was told. His show was from noon until three. I called Stan "the Man" Fowler's TV & Appliance Center. Open for business.

Fowler's place was just off Bryant Street in the northern shadows of the Sixth Avenue viaduct, an area of warehouses and wholesalers. It was still snowing when I got there, though not heavily.

I pulled into the nearly empty parking lot.

There was a guy bundled up like an Eskimo riding a little tractor with a plow on the front and doing his best to keep part of the lot cleared. I nosed the Olds up to a pile of snow packed tight by the plow. Then I pushed through the double glass doors of Stan "the Man's."

Although I'd never met Fowler, I was irked by his nickname.

See, the *real* Stan the Man, Stan Musial, was one of my childhood heroes. He was one of the greatest hitters of all time. And he was one of the few ballplayers I'd ever heard of who could *see* the seams on a baseball as it came hurtling at him at ninety miles an hour—actually *see* those little red stitches and tell by their rotation whether he was being delivered a fastball or a curve, then react accordingly, all in less than half a second, and drive it into the gap for a double. Now *that's* "the Man."

The store was about two blocks long.

The block on my right was jammed with pastel rows of washers, dryers, stoves, and refrigerators. The block on my left was filled with television sets, all tuned to the same channel. John was telling Marsha that he was running off to Rio with Carlotta, the maid.

A salesman approached.

"Looking for a new TV?"

He was a small middle-aged guy with razor-sharp lapels, cuffed pants, and a bow tie. His mustache was hardly worth the effort. "Whatever you want, we've got, and don't worry about price, because we can finance."

"I'm looking for Stan Fowler."

One corner of his mouth turned down.

"He's busy right now," he said. "Can I help you?"

"Sorry."

The other corner turned down. "This way," he mumbled, another sale lost.

I followed him along a row of pink dishwashers and through a cluster of avocado stoves to a door marked Employees Only. He held it open for me. We stepped into a cement-floored expanse of crates and boxes. A forklift whispered toward us. We got out of its way, then walked around two beefy dudes wrestling with a blue refrigerator the size of an outhouse.

The salesman knocked on the door of an office with no roof. He went in and I stayed out. There was some mumbling and some angry ass chewing. It ended with, "All right, all right, Roberson, send the son of a bitch in."

I guess he meant me.

Roberson came out, looking a few inches shorter than when he'd gone in.

"Mr. Fowler can see you now," he told me, then slunk away.

I went in and closed the door. The office had thick carpeting and expensive, if tasteless, leather chairs. The desk was huge, with gaudy fittings. It looked like a whorehouse for elves.

"Howdy," Fowler said, standing, smiling. "Stan Fowler." He stuck out his hand and I shook it.

Fowler was a big man, a few inches taller than I and a good seventy pounds heavier, but a lot of that was from gin and roast beef. His face was flushed, with a web of purple capillaries on his cheeks and across his thick nose. He had the piercing blue eyes and thickly lacquered dark blond hair of a TV evangelist. His suit and vest were brown, his pinky ring was gold, and his Rolex was fat. I'd give odds the watch was fake, if only because I wouldn't trust Stan the pseudo-Man as far as I could spit.

"Jacob Lomax," I said. "I hope I'm not interrupting."

"That depends, Jake, my friend." He sat back on his leather throne, making the air hiss out of the seat. "You buying or selling?"

"I'm a private investigator," I told him, "working for the widow of Joseph Bellano. Her daughter Stephanie has been missing for over a week and—"

"You're not here to buy a stove?" There was an exaggerated look of innocent surprise on his beefy puss.

"I thought you might be able to help me since you were one of the last people to see her."

"How could I, my friend? I don't even know this Stephanie whoever."

"Stephanie Bellano. You—"

"Bellano. Doesn't ring a bell." He smiled at his stupid little joke.

"You knew her father, Joseph."

"That's bullshit, my friend. I've never heard of him."

"You were sitting in his barbershop a week ago Friday when Stephanie came in, made a big scene, and ran out. She was scared witless of somebody in there."

Stan was staring at me with narrowed eyes.

"There was you," I said, "Gary Rivers, Mitch Overholser, and Johnny Toes Burke. Plus Joseph and Sal."

"I don't know what you're talking about, my friend."

"You were there, Stan."

"I don't know what the *fuck* you're talking about, my friend."

"I'm not your friend, Stan. None of my friends are liars."

His face got dark.

He pushed himself up out of his chair, slowly, threateningly, giving me a chance to run for my life. I stood up. He stalked past me to the door.

"Frank! Wayne! Come here!"

Frank and Wayne were the two oxen I'd seen working out with the refrigerator. They appeared on Fowler's threshold with their sleeves rolled up over heavy arms. I glanced around the office for a weapon.

"Jake here has lost his way," Fowler said. "Show him out to the front. So long, Jake."

I tried not to look relieved.

"Talk to you again real soon, Stan. And oh, by the way. You wouldn't make a pimple on Musial's butt."

"What?"

Frank and Wayne led me out to the showroom. I looked around for Roberson. I spotted him in the distance, surrounded by television sets, waiting for his day to improve. He perked up when he saw me approach.

"Change your mind about a new TV?"

"No, Mr. Roberson, I just wanted to apologize to you."

"Huh? For what?"

"Getting you yelled at by your boss."

"Oh, that." He looked past me toward the far-off swinging doors. "Forget it."

"No, really, I'm sorry. It was my fault. If I'd've known Fowler was such a loud, obnoxious bastard, I— Oops, I guess I shouldn't be talking that way about your boss."

"Forget it," Roberson said with a small smile on his tired face.

"I worked for a guy like Fowler once," I lied. "He acted like he owned me just because he signed my commission check. If I hadn't needed the money so bad, I would've told him to shove it."

"I hear you."

"What makes guys like that tick, anyway?"

"Beats me," Roberson said.

"Take Fowler, for instance. Now he's probably a pretty evenhanded guy to begin with, right?"

"Hah." Roberson looked over my shoulder and lowered his voice. "If you only knew."

"What?"

He shook his head. "Never mind."

"Don't worry, I've probably heard it before. Guys like us, we've seen most of it, right?"

"Tell me. And Stan Fowler uses every trick in the book."

"No kidding. What, for instance?"

Roberson nodded toward the end of the row, and I followed him around the side of a big-screen Zenith. John was still explaining to Marsha about him and Carlotta and Rio.

"Counterfeits," Roberson said. He patted the Zenith. "Like this baby here, which sells for fifteen hundred and comes with a three-year warranty. The trouble is, it's made in Mexico, worth a couple hundred at best, and Mr. Zenith never laid eyes on it. We get the customer to waive the warranty, which we convince him he's never going to need, anyway, and knock off three or four hundred bucks. The set might last three years or three months. Whatever, Fowler's profit is around five hundred percent."

"Clever. He must be rolling in dough."

"You'd think. But he's not. Business is not good. I don't care *what* the government calls it, we're in a depression. Plus Fowler's got personal problems."

"Really?"

Roberson nodded. "His wife's an alcoholic. Practically a shut-in. Of course, he probably drove her to it. I mean, everyone knows he likes to hit the bars and pick up young chicks. He tells his wife he's playing poker with the guys. He's playing 'poke her,' all right."

When I got outside, there was half an inch of new snow on the Olds. I brushed it off, wondering if Stan Fowler had ever been to the Lion's Lair looking for "young chicks." Chicks like Stephanie Bellano.

CHAPTER

12

AT A QUARTER TO THREE I was sitting in the reception area of radio station KNWZ, 730 on your AM dial.

It was pleasant. The room was pleasant, and so was the receptionist. She'd taken my message to Gary Rivers. Then she'd brought me coffee in a Styrofoam cup. Sugar, no cream. I sipped it and looked at her legs. Pleasant. I listened to piped-in muted voices—Rivers and a caller named Al. They were arguing on the air. Something about gambling.

The show ended at three.

A few minutes later Rivers came into the reception area. "Mr. Lomax?" he said.

I stood and shook his hand. He was about five nine, shorter than he looked on TV. Thinner, too. He wore a crewneck sweater with no shirt underneath, faded Levi's, and running shoes. I guess you don't have to dress up for radio.

"Carol said you had some information about Joseph Bellano."

"Not exactly. I want to talk to you about his daughter Stephanie."

"Oh. Okay, but"—he checked his watch—"I'm in a bit of a rush, and the traffic with this weather . . ."

I waited.

"My office," he said.

I followed him down a carpeted hallway. There was smoked glass on our left, allowing a dim view of plush offices. There were doors with brass doorplates. General Manager. Program Director. News Director.

Rivers's door was blank. His office was small and generic. The window offered a southwestern view from twenty stories up. On a clear day you could probably see all the way across town to the tiny black spire of Loretto Heights. Today, though, you could see snow and a few partially obscured downtown buildings.

Rivers sat with me on this side of the desk, in an armless chair like mine.

The desk and chairs were durable, not pretty. Since the turnover rate was high among radio "talent," why waste money on expensive furnishings? Besides, these guys weren't about to complain; most of them were glad just to be working. Some of them, including Rivers, were *very* glad. Their incomes ran to six figures.

"I've been hired by Mrs. Bellano to find Stephanie."

"Stephanie still hasn't come home?" He looked surprised and concerned.

"No."

"God, poor Angela."

"Do you know Stephanie's mother?"

"No. Nor Stephanie, for that matter. But Joseph talked a lot about them."

"I didn't know you and Joseph were friends."

He nodded. "You see, for the past few months I've been putting together a series on gambling in the state. It's just now airing on Channel 5. Actually, I started toying with the idea almost a year ago—talking to bookies, gamblers, and so on. That's when I met Joseph. He was easier to talk to than most. And he'd been around longer, too. So I tried to stay close to him. In that respect, we were friends."

Some friend. Rivers had used film of Bellano's death site for his own commercial purposes. Oh, well, that's show biz.

"You were in Bellano's shop," I said, "the day Stephanie ran away."

"Yes. In fact, that was the first time I'd ever seen her."

"Sal told me she looked scared to death."

"She *was* scared," Rivers said. "She'd said some things to her father that she instantly regretted."

"Sal thinks she was scared of one of the customers."

"One of the customers?"

"Yes."

"Well, I wouldn't know about that," Rivers said. "What I do know is that when she came in the shop she was out of control, crying and yelling her head off, calling Joseph a liar and a criminal. She said she hoped him and all of us gangsters would end up in prison where we belonged."

"We?"

"She pointed a finger at each one of us, me included. Joseph was as surprised as any of us. At first he thought it was funny. Then he got angry. He told her to shut up. He said he'd talk to her after work. It sounded like he meant more than just talk. That's when she ran out. Joseph joked about it with everyone in the shop. He said Stephanie would be home with an apology before dinnertime."

"She didn't come home, though."

"No."

"And she didn't come home even after her father was killed."

A frown blemished Rivers's face. He was thinking.

"I see what you mean," he said. "If she'd run for fear of her father, she'd have returned by now." He frowned some more. "If only I could remember . . ."

"What?"

"The other men in the shop."

"Stan Fowler, Mitch Overholser, and Johnny Toes Burke."

"Johnny . . . that's right, I remember now." He stared very hard at the wall behind me. He *was* thinking. "That's too much of a coincidence," he said, looking at me. "I know something about Johnny Toes Burke. He works for Fat Paulie DaNucci."

"So I've heard."

"God, do you think the *Mafia* is responsible for Stephanie's disappearance?"

"It's possible. The odds are they killed Bellano."

"We've got to find her," Rivers said.

"We?"

"Yes. If Stephanie is hiding from Burke and DaNucci, then she may have information. Valuable information."

I saw the light behind his eyes. A new TV special was in the making.

"If they find her before we do," he said, "her life won't be worth two cents."

"We?"

"Yes, we. I feel personally involved. Joseph Bellano was my friend."

"He's also a news story."

Rivers gave me a hard look.

"I know what you're thinking—that I'm just interested in the news value. Okay, I admit it, that's part of the reason. Stephanie may know things that would surprise us all."

"Surprise? Don't you mean entertain?"

Anger crossed his face. Then he smiled. "Perhaps I do. In any case, I'd like to help. I *can* help."

"How?"

"That's up to you," he said. "I've got a lot of connections in this town and access to information most people don't have. And I've done a fair bit of investigating, too." He looked smug.

Then he looked at his watch. "Christ, I'm going to be late." He got out one of his cards. There was nothing on it but his name. Ah, success. He turned it over and wrote down three phone numbers.

"The first one is the office, the second is my home."

"And the third?"

"Oh. My car."

"Why doesn't that surprise me?"

"Please," he said, "call me if you want any help."

He ushered me out of his office and down the hall to the reception area. He opened a closet and put on his jacket. It was black and bulky and hip. He said good-bye to Carol, then held the door for me. I hesitated.

"I've got to make a call. Do you mind if I use this phone?"

"Help yourself," Rivers said. "Got to run."

I know. "I'll be in touch."

Rivers hurried out. Carol the secretary turned her phone toward me. I smiled at her and called my answering machine.

"I didn't quite finish the interview," I told the recording of my voice, "because he had to leave. No, I don't think he'll be free until tomorrow. Goddamn it, I— Oops." I gave Carol a sheepish grin. "Sorry," I whispered to her. "Look," I said to the beep telling me to begin my message, "I'm here with his secretary. Maybe she can give us what we need. I *know* we're on deadline." I hung up.

Carol looked at me expectantly.

"I hate to bother you with this," I said.

"Are you interviewing Mr. Rivers?"

"For the *News*," I said, getting out my notepad. "*TV Dial*. There's just a few background questions I missed, and my editor's screaming deadline at me. Would you mind?"

"Not at all."

I flipped through the pad as if searching for a blank page. They were all blank.

"How long have you known Gary?"

"I was here when he started. Almost two years."

"Really? I'll bet you know him better than most."

"I suppose so," she said with some pride.

"Is he hard to work for?"

"*I* don't think so."

"*You* don't. Are you saying that others do?"

She took a little breath through her cute nose.

"Not everyone understands Mr. Rivers," she explained. "He's extremely talented and dedicated. A perfectionist, you know? If things aren't just right, well, he lets people know about it in no uncertain terms."

"He gets angry."

She nodded apprehensively. "Sometimes, very much so. But maybe you shouldn't print that."

"Why? Everyone gets angry now and then."

"Yes, but Mr. Rivers . . ."

"What? He wouldn't like me to print it? Or do you mean he gets angrier than most?"

She paused. "Both," she said, then added quickly, "but really, he's been a lot more low key for the past few months, since, well, you know. Since the tragedy."

"What tragedy?"

"He didn't tell you? No, I guess he wouldn't; it's still too painful. He and his wife suffered a death in the family."

"I'm sorry to hear that."

"It was just terrible. Especially under the circumstances."

I sat on the corner of her desk. "What do you mean?"

"Well," she said confidentially, "Mr. Rivers had been under a lot of stress. His ratings were okay, but overall the station's ratings were down. There was a lot of pressure on *everybody*. Also, Mr. Rivers was starting to produce specials for television. Of course, you know about that."

"Of course."

"Anyway, the strain was getting to him. He and the general manager had a tremendous argument. The manager forced Mr. Rivers to take time off from work. Mr. Rivers *really* blew up then. But he had no choice. And it was during that time that the tragedy occurred. His wife was so distraught that Mr. Rivers had to take her down to Colorado Springs to stay with her parents. As far as I know, she's still there. Mr. Rivers, though, has managed to carry on. He really is extraordinary."

"This argument between Rivers and the general manager, when was that?"

"Four or five months ago."

"What was it about?"

"I have no idea."

Later that evening I got a call from Zeno. The printouts were ready.

I drove to Aurora. The snow had nearly stopped, and the streets were scraped and sanded. I turned off East Iliff Avenue into Zeno's apartment complex. Milton buzzed me up. He let me in and tried to look aggressive. His thick glasses and buck teeth, though, weren't much help.

"Zeno's in the kitchen," he said.

I took a step, and he put his hand on the sleeve of my coat, then quickly withdrew it.

"Yes?"

"Zeno, ah . . ."

"What is it, Milton?"

"Zeno's my girlfriend."

"Yes?"

"Well, I . . . just wanted you to know that."

"Oh. Oh, I see."

"As long as you know."

"Sure, Milton. Look, Zeno and I are just friends, you know? Like cousins or something. You're the only man for her. She told me that."

"She did?"

"Scout's honor."

"Oh." He blushed. Love.

"I won't be a minute."

"Sure," he said.

Zeno was making cookies, which surprised me. Her hands were covered with goo.

"Hi, Jake. They're right there."

At one end of the counter was a stack of fan-folded, green-barred computer paper. I flipped through the sheets, fifty or more, each filled with rows and columns of names and numbers.

"Do you want the disks, too?" she asked.

I thumped the stack with a finger. "Is this everything?"

"Yes."

"Then destroy the disks."

"You mean erase them."

"Whatever you call it, Zeno."

"Are you sure?"

"Absolutely. Do it tonight, okay?"

"Sure, Jake."

"Great. Now what do I owe you for all this?"

"No charge," she said, and smiled coyly.

"Baloney. You work, you get paid."

"Call it a favor, then."

"A favor. All right, I owe you. A big one, okay?"

"Okay, Jake."

When I got home, I filled a squat glass with ice and Jack Black. The computer sheets were separated by perforations, but I didn't bother to pull them apart. I began reading through them. It was all pretty elaborate. More so than usual for a bookie. Maybe Bellano had been carried away by his new computer toy.

He'd arranged his records in two sections: bettors and games.

The games were separated by week and by sport—baseball, basketball, and pro and college football. Each week had a column for team name, point spread, bettor's name, bettor's choice, and amount wagered. The last column listed plus or minus amounts, depending on whether Bellano was to collect or pay. At the bottom of this column was a total. It was a plus. I guess bookies don't lose. The worst week I could find, from

Bellano's standpoint, was a profit of four hundred dollars. The average was around four grand, give or take. The best week I found—last year's Super Bowl—was twenty-nine thousand. I estimated that Bellano had taken in close to a quarter of a million this year. Assuming all his players paid off. There's the rub.

I turned to the sheets listing the bettors.

Some of these individuals had an entire sheet to themselves. Some had more. Most of them bet a hundred or two a week. There were a few heavy players, though, a couple of which still owed Bellano some hefty sums.

The heftiest of all was Stan the appliance man Fowler. He'd been betting three or four grand a week with Bellano for the past two years. According to these records, Fowler owed the late Joseph Bellano ninety-eight thousand dollars. Serious money. Perhaps enough to kill for.

I found Gary Rivers here, too. Over the past ten months he'd managed to win a few thousand dollars. In fact, Bellano had died owing Rivers eight hundred bucks. I wondered if Rivers had been gambling for research purposes. Or maybe he was simply a gambler. If the public found out, would it hurt his career?

I found Mitch Overholser. Surprise, surprise. He was the second-biggest loser of the bunch, owing Bellano forty-six grand. Of course, with Bellano dead, he didn't owe a dime.

I didn't find Johnny Toes Burke. Gambling wasn't one of his vices. I wondered if car bombing was.

CHAPTER

13

AFTER BREAKFAST TUESDAY MORNING, I put on my gloves and stepped out on the balcony.

The snow had stopped during the night. It was a foot deep on the wooden deck. The barbecue grill was a large white lump in the corner. I brushed it off. Then I removed the black lid and the crosshatched grill and began wadding up sheets of Bellano's computer records. I stuffed them in the bottom with last summer's ashes. After I'd replaced the grill, I soaked the pages in charcoal starter fluid and dropped in a match.

The pages made a good blaze. Bellano's guilt went up in smoke. The only pages I'd saved contained data on Stan Fowler, Mitch Overholser, and Gary Rivers. These I locked in the safe.

Then I bundled up and went out to start the Olds.

Interstate 70 was snow packed and sanded as it took me west out of Denver. It started snowing lightly near Idaho Springs, and it continued all the way to the turnoff for U.S. 40. By the time I reached Berthoud Pass, it was coming down hard enough for me to use my windshield wipers. Once over the pass, though, things got better. The snow stopped, and the road leveled and became fairly straight. It took me north through a wide, flat valley. Hills marched along either side. The white fields and pastures were blemished only by a scattering of buildings and straight strands of barbed-wire fence.

I drove through towns that were barely towns—Hideaway Park, Fraser, Tabernash.

I stopped in Granby to ease my bladder and stretch my legs.

Then I left U.S. 40, which turned west, and took U.S. 34 north toward Rocky Mountain National Park. The highway skirted a couple of big lakes, then took me into Big Pine. The town lay within the park boundaries. The waters of Big Pine Lake lapped at the town's toes. During the summer, anyway. Today the lake's edges were crusty with ice.

I cruised down the main street of Big Pine.

It was noon on a Tuesday, but most of the stores were closed. This was a summer resort town. There was no skiing here. Just the lake for fishing and boating and the park for hiking and camping. I drove around town until I found the address Angela Bellano had given me two days ago.

It was a ninety-year-old, two-and-a-half-story frame house with a peaked roof and gables. I parked the Olds in the street and went up the shoveled walk. A thin, icy breeze stung my ears.

The woman who answered the door fit the description Angela had given me of Mrs. Henderson. She was less than five feet tall. She wore a high-collared, long-sleeved dress and a shawl. She had hard gray eyes, steel-framed glasses, and gray hair pulled back in a severe bun. Her mouth was thin-lipped and ready to tell me to hit the road.

"What is it?" she asked in a voice as crusty and cold as the ice on the lake.

I introduced myself and held up my card to the screen door. Mrs. Henderson wasn't impressed. In fact, her eyes never left my face. Maybe I should get new cards, ones with holograms that you could turn from side to side and see me in action, fighting injustice and saving the day.

"I was hired by the Bellano family to find their daughter Stephanie," I said. "She's been missing for a week and a half."

"Missing?" Her look softened a bit.

"She ran away, and she may be hiding. Could we talk inside?" Come on, I'm freezing my buns out here.

"And her parents don't know where she is?"

"I'm afraid not."

"Those poor people must be worried sick."

Apparently Mrs. Henderson hadn't heard the bad news about Joseph Bellano. "They are," I said. "Any information you can give me would be most appreciated."

"Are you a policeman, then?"

Mrs. Henderson didn't seem to mind standing in the open doorway in the freezing breeze. Meanwhile, icepicks were jabbing the back of my neck.

"A private detective, ma'am."

"Do you have any identification. I mean, besides *that*."

She pointed her nose at my pathetic card. I showed her my driver's license, Social Security card, library card, and a couple of credit cards. I would have showed her my P.I. license, but in this state there's no such thing. If you want to be a private investigator, just hang up a sign. I didn't even have a sign.

She unlatched the screen and let me in.

"Close the door," she said, "and wipe your feet."

I did as I was told.

"I haven't seen Stephanie since she left here in August," Mrs. Henderson said. She stood in the middle of the foyer and made no move to show me any farther into the house. There were leaded glass doors on her right and left, both closed, both covered with lace curtains. Behind her was a staircase with a heavy carved banister.

"Was Stephanie your only tenant?"

"I don't have tenants, sir," she snapped. "I have boarders."

"Of course, that's what I—"

"Stephanie was one of eight. From May to October, Big

Pine is quite attractive to the tourists. Most of the rooms in town stay full. My house is no exception. Naturally, in the winter it's a horse of a different color. With the exception of me and Mr. Johnson, who occupies a room in the rear and performs necessary maintenance duties, the house is empty."

"You said there was Stephanie and seven others. All women, I presume."

"Of course."

"Would you remember their names?"

"*Would* I? Or *do* I?"

"Do you remember if one of them was named Chrissie?"

"Chrissie Smith," she said without hesitation.

Smith. That's a big help. "Were Chrissie and Stephanie friends?"

"It's possible they became friends. They were about the same age, and I had them in rooms next door to each other all summer."

"Was Chrissie here on vacation?"

"I would assume so."

"Do you know where she was from?"

Mrs. Henderson put a bent finger to her lips. "Eastern Colorado, I believe. Yes. She told me she lived on a farm near the Kansas border."

"How near the border?"

She curled her finger into her fist and stuck it on her hip.

"Are you being brassy with me, young man?"

"No, ma'am."

"Near" might be fifty miles. Fifty times roughly two hundred miles of common border equaled ten thousand square miles in which to find one girl—last name Smith—who may or may not know the whereabouts of Stephanie Bellano.

"What did Chrissie look like?" I asked.

"She was a plain-looking girl, if you'll pardon my saying so. Seventeen or eighteen. Brown eyes and long brown hair. It went partway down her back."

"You have a good memory."

"Hmph."

I asked her how to get to the clinic where Stephanie Bellano had worked.

She told me, then said, "The doctor's name is Rahsing, but he may not be much help."

"Why not?"

"Because he wasn't the doctor when Stephanie worked there."

"Who was?"

"Doc Early. But he died a few months ago."

I found the clinic at one end of a small shopping area, which also included the Big Pine Grocery, Winchell's Donut House, and the Lake-View Laundromat. There was an antiseptic smell in the clinic's waiting room. No one was waiting. The door to the back was blocked by a receptionist's desk. No receptionist.

I called out, "Hello," and a minute later a woman appeared in the doorway.

She was short and busty, a pretty woman somewhere in her thirties, with an oval face, oversized glasses, and dark hair pushed back behind her ears. She wore nurse's whites under a green cardigan sweater.

"May I help you?"

"I'd like to see the doctor."

"He's with a patient. Are you in any pain?"

"Not to my knowledge."

She frowned.

"It's a personal matter."

"Then you'll have to wait," she said, and was gone.

I sat on a clean green vinyl couch and picked up the top copy of *Reader's Digest* from a foot-high stack.

I'd already skimmed through all the jokes and the wise sayings, and I was halfway through "Life in These United States" when a woman and a young boy came through the door. They were followed closely by a man in a white smock.

The boy's eyes were red from recent tears, and his arm was in a sling.

"You're a very brave young man," the doctor said. "A sprain like yours can be quite painful. Come back in a few days and we'll take a look at it."

The boy and woman walked out, and the doctor turned to me.

"Yes, sir?"

I stood. "Doctor Rahsing?"

"Yes, sir, I am."

He was a small, dark man, with the facial features and lilting voice of an East Indian. I introduced myself.

"Are you ill, Mr. Lomax?"

"No, it's nothing like that. I wonder if I could ask you a few questions."

"Concerning?"

"Your predecessor."

"Dr. Early," he said. "I'm afraid I never met the gentleman. He was murdered, you know, a terrible thing."

"No, I didn't know. What exactly—"

He held up his hand and shook his head. "I'm not familiar with the details. You see, I've only been here for a month, and that horrible event happened last October. Have you been to the police? I'm sure they can tell you all about it. Now if you'll excuse me, I have another patient waiting."

He started to turn away.

"Was your nurse working here at that time?"

"Yes, of course. Miss Phipps has been here for a number of years. But as I said, the police—"

"May I speak with her, Doctor? It's very important. I'm working for the parents of a girl who worked at this clinic last summer. Stephanie Bellano. She's missing."

"Oh, dear."

"Yes."

"Please wait here," he said, then went to the back.

Nurse Phipps came out a few moments later.

"Dr. Rahsing said you're here about Stephanie Bellano?" It was a question.

"Yes, she's run away. There's a chance she came up here."

"Run away?" She looked genuinely concerned. "No, I . . . I haven't seen her since August."

"How long have you worked here?"

"Six years. Six and a half."

"Were you here all summer with Stephanie?"

"Yes."

"What exactly did she do here?"

"Clerical work. She sat at this desk and answered the phone, scheduled appointments, helped patients fill out forms, and so on. There was plenty to do. You see, we get a lot of tourists up here during the summer, and they keep us busy. Mostly minor things—fishermen impaling themselves with hooks, water skiers banging into the docks, hikers twisting ankles, things like that. For the past four or five summers Dr. Early hired part-time help."

"How did Dr. Early die?"

She blinked, then looked away. "He . . . he was murdered. Shot to death."

"Did they catch whoever did it?"

"No."

"How did it happen?"

Nurse Phipps shook her head, as if she didn't want to talk about it. Then she said, "He surprised a burglar."

"At his home?"

"No, here. The man, or whoever it was, was apparently after drugs. We keep them locked up in the back. The place was all torn up when I—"

"*You* found him?"

She nodded grimly.

"I knew something was wrong when I unlocked the door in the morning," she said. "I mean, I could *feel* something.

When I went to the back, I— There were pills and bottles scattered on the floor, and Dr. Early was lying on his back. His chest was covered with blood. I checked for vital signs, but there was nothing, and . . . he was so *cold*." She looked at me as if she wanted me to do something about it.

"It must have been traumatic for you," I said.

She said nothing.

"You called the police then?"

"Yes. They, I mean, he, Chief Grogan, said he'd been shot twice in the chest, probably with a rifle. I think that's what the sheriff's investigators finally determined."

"Did they arrest anyone?"

"No. They *say* it was probably a transient, a drug addict."

"You sound like you don't believe that."

"I—"

"Nurse Phipps." Dr. Rahsing stood in the doorway behind her. "I need your assistance, please. Now." He turned away without waiting for a response.

Nurse Phipps started toward the door.

"Could we talk later?" I asked.

"I don't know."

"What time do you get off work?"

"Six, but—"

"Is there a restaurant open this time of year?"

"There's the Trail's End."

"How about we meet there at seven?"

"I . . . I don't know."

"I'll buy. We need to talk about Stephanie."

"I don't know if there's much I can tell you."

"You can tell me about her abortion."

CHAPTER

14

THE TWO-STORY RED-BRICK BUILDING looked like a school, but it was Big Pine's mayor's office, courtroom, police department, and jail.

The cops occupied one room with three beat-up metal desks, a locked gun rack, and an idle fan on a tall chrome stand. Some yellowed WANTED posters were tacked to the walls for dramatic effect.

Chief of Police Daryl Grogan was the only cop on duty today. He was middle-aged, fat, and bald. His uniform sleeves were rolled up to his elbows to show off his red thermal underwear. He looked like a TV cowboy's sidekick. But I got the feeling he could take care of business.

"I'm here all by my lonesome, so I could use the company," he'd told me after I'd introduced myself and he'd poured me some coffee in a cracked cup. "One of my officers is down sick with the flu, and the other took the day off to go buzzing around in his snowmobile. You ever *been* on one of them damn things?"

"Not on purpose."

"Well, they're a nuisance, and they ought to be outlawed. What exactly are you after, Mr. Lomax?"

"Information on the murder of Dr. Early."

"You mind if I ask why?"

I told him about Stephanie Bellano.

"You saying there might be a connection between her disappearance and Doc Early's death?" he asked.

"I don't know. For her sake, I hope not. I'm just trying to cover every angle. Do you remember the details of the murder?"

"I would hope to shout. Except for a petty theft now and then, we mostly handle drunk-and-disorderlies and dog bites. Doc Early was the first person ever been murdered in this town since I've been chief, and that's been seventeen years."

"When did it happen?"

"Not quite two months ago. October fifteenth, to be exact. Betty Phipps found him. She called me, and I went over there with one of my officers. There wasn't much for us to do. I confirmed that Doc was dead; then I sealed off the area and called the county sheriff. Them and the Colorado Bureau of Investigation are equipped for homicides and crime scenes and such, and I'm not. I sure as hell wasn't going to clomp around and screw up any evidence."

"Miss Phipps told me they never caught the killer."

"That's right."

"Any suspects?"

"Nope."

"Motive?"

"Oh, it *looked* like a burglary, and it *looked* like Doc walked in on the burglar and got shot."

"You think it was something else?"

"I think it *might* have been something else."

"Like what?"

"Don't you want to know 'why' first?"

"Okay. Why?"

"For one thing, he was shot twice in the chest. You ever heard of a surprised burglar shooting anyone *twice?* Hell, most of them don't even carry guns."

"I thought everyone carried a gun these days," I said.

"Yeah, well, maybe. But how many of them carry M-16 rifles?"

"What?"

"That's what Doc Early was shot with. The CBI identified the slugs and the shell casings. You ever heard of a burglar crawling in through a window with a combat rifle strapped to his back? I haven't."

"What did the sheriff's report say about that?"

"They said it was a murder committed during an interrupted burglary. Officially, I said the same thing, because there wasn't any evidence that pointed to anything else."

"You're not convinced that's what happened, are you?"

"No, I'm not. And neither were they, but you gotta go with the evidence."

"Let's say it wasn't a burglar."

"Okay, let's," he said.

"Then why would someone want to kill Dr. Early?"

"Yes, indeed. You want some more coffee?"

The first cup had left paving material on my tongue.

"Sure," I said.

After he'd filled our cups, he said, "Doc Early wasn't your typical highbrow doctor. He liked to hunt, drink, and play poker with the boys. All of which is okay. But there was something else he was getting into which was *not* okay. Actually, I didn't *know* he was getting into it, but I heard he was; namely, taking bets from guys around town on baseball games and football games. In other words, being a bookie."

"The town's doctor was a bookie?"

"Like I said, I just *heard* that's what he was doing. What I did know was that the doc was always trying to raise money to keep the clinic going. It gets some money from the county and some from the patients themselves, but mostly it's run on a shoestring and a prayer. So I figured if Doc Early was operating a bookie joint, it wasn't for personal profit, it was to help finance the clinic. Still, that sort of thing is serious business. Too big for me to look the other way, even if Doc *was* my good friend. Which he was. So I warned him. I told him what I'd heard and that pretty soon I'd be taking a real close look at things and I'd damn sure better not *find* anything or this town would be looking for a new doctor. Which seems kind of ironic now, doesn't it?"

"Do you think his murder had to do with gambling?"

"Not necessarily. What I'm saying is that Doc Early didn't always play strictly by the rules. If he thought he could get away with something, he might be inclined to do it. Which is not to say that he wasn't a damn good doctor. He was. But it's possible he broke one rule too many and crossed the wrong person and got shot for it."

He clucked his tongue and shrugged: That's the way it goes.

"You don't seem too worried," I said.

"About what?"

"Dr. Early's killer living in your town."

"Not likely."

"What makes you so sure?"

"Because I'm *from* this area, Mr. Lomax. I was born not thirty miles from where you're sitting, and I know just about everybody who lives anywhere near here, and I can tell you two things for certain. Number one, there are plenty of gun enthusiasts around here, but only two or three of them, myself included, know how to operate an M-16 rifle, assuming they could even *get* a weapon like that. And number two, *no* one around here, and again I include myself, is shrewd enough or experienced enough to kill someone and make it look like an interrupted burglary, right down to stealing the proper drugs."

"I see."

"Of course," he said, waving his hand as if to discount everything he'd just said, "maybe it really *was* an interrupted burglary."

"But you don't believe that."

"Not for a minute," he said.

I was tempted to agree. And I wondered if it was merely a coincidence that both Dr. Early and Joseph Bellano had been killed with military weapons.

The Trail's End restaurant consisted of one very large square room, brightly lit by ceiling lights shaped like wagon wheels. There were about twenty tables, most of them empty, all with Formica tops and paper place mats. Each mat featured a map of Colorado, which is the perfect state for that since it's *shaped* like a place mat. There was a counter by the door with a cash register, a little bowl of mints, and a toothpick dispenser.

I chewed a toothpick and waited for Betty Phipps.

She came in five minutes later, exactly at seven.

Her greeting was polite, cool. She was friendlier to the waitress, whom she knew by name. The three of us walked to a table in the corner, away from the scattering of diners. The waitress smiled knowingly; Betty was having a dinner date.

We removed our coats, hung them over the backs of our seats, and sat down. The waitress put down full water glasses and plastic-encased menus, then left us alone.

Betty had changed from her nurse's clothes to a skirt and sweater. They were somewhere between brown and green, the exact color of her eyes, which were slightly magnified behind her oversized glasses. She'd also put on perfume. It smelled nice.

"You look very nice."

"How did you know that Dr. Early aborted Stephanie's pregnancy?" she asked, her voice low. So much for sweet talk.

"It wasn't too tough. She was pregnant in April and unpregnant in August, and in between she worked for the only medical doctor in this town."

"Oh."

"By the way, did the townsfolk know that Early *did* that sort of thing?"

"You make it sound like something . . . dirty."

"Me? You're the one keeping your voice down."

Betty glanced at the few diners, who all were busy with their meals. Busier now, it seemed, since she'd looked at them.

"I would think that everyone knew," she said to me. "But not everyone approved. We got nasty phone calls now and then. Anonymous, of course."

The waitress returned and took our orders—sliced turkey for Betty, beef stew for me, plus a basket of rolls and two salads with ranch dressing.

"Did anyone ever threaten his life?"

Betty looked shocked. "No. I mean, not that I know of. And I don't think he would have kept something like that a secret."

"Did you know he was a bookie?"

"What?"

She'd spoken loud enough to raise a few heads. I looked at them, and down they went.

"Dr. Early took bets from people," I said quietly, "and charged them a ten percent commission."

"That's a lie." There was anger in her eyes. And maybe fear.

"It's true."

She pushed back from the table as if to rise.

"I came here to talk about Stephanie Bellano," she said, "*not* to listen to you slander Bill Early."

"That's not my intention."

"What *is* your intention?"

"To find Stephanie before something bad happens to her."

She held my eyes a moment longer, then looked away.

"Listen, Betty, since Stephanie's abortion, she's disappeared and both her father and her doctor have been murdered. I don't think those events are unrelated."

She started to speak but closed her mouth when the waitress showed up with our salads. Betty scooted her chair back in place, picked up a fork, and poked at a slice of tomato. She put down her fork.

"I'll help you if I can," she said.

"Thank you." I took a bite of salad. The dressing wasn't bad. "Why were you so surprised that I knew about Stephanie's abortion?"

"Because she wanted desperately to keep it a secret. She was terrified her parents might find out. She made me and Dr. Early swear not to tell anyone."

"She must have had a lot of trust in the good doctor."

"He *was* a good doctor. I don't mean just technically good. He was a kind and good man."

I wasn't too sure of that, not after talking to Chief Grogan. But I let it pass.

"Tell me about the abortion."

"There's nothing to tell. Dr. Early performed it, and I assisted. It was simple, relatively painless, and there were no complications. Stephanie was back at work at the front desk a few days later."

"Just like that?"

"Yes. She was in her first term—it's a simple matter, really. She was depressed, of course. The poor girls usually are. Some get over that phase of it sooner than others."

"And Stephanie?"

"She was still upset when she left here in August." Betty looked guilty.

"How many abortions did Dr. Early perform each month?"

"You make it sound like a production line. It wasn't like that at all. In fact, it was fairly rare."

"How rare?"

"A few per year, perhaps more. Dr. Early took little money for this, only what the girls or their boyfriends could afford."

"How did Stephanie get her job here?"

"Dr. Early hired her."

"Did he know her father?"

"Yes."

"Did you know him?"

"We were introduced."

"Did you know that *he* was a bookie?"

"I didn't ask," she said disgustedly.

I was thinking that if Dr. Early had been a novice bookie, as Grogan had implied, then who better for him to learn the trade from than Joseph Bellano?

"Who took care of Early's books? I mean for the clinic."

"He did most of it. I helped him. I do it all now."

"Were there payments other than those directly from patients?"

"Yes. There were donations."

"And everything was entered in the books?"

"Yes."

"I'd like to look at them."

"Oh . . . Well, I don't know if—"

"Tonight, if possible."

CHAPTER
15

AFTER I PAID for our dinner, I drove Betty Phipps to the Big Pine Medical Clinic.

She unlocked the front door, and we stepped into the dark foyer. When she flipped the switch, the overhead fluorescent lights sputtered for a few moments before they kicked on.

"Dr. Rahsing might not approve of this," she said.

"Does he need to know?"

She hesitated. "No."

I followed her to the back. There were a couple of examination rooms with sinks, cabinets with glass doors, and narrow black padded tables. There was one fairly spacious office with a big old wooden desk and a group of file cabinets. Betty pulled open the bottom drawer in one of the cabinets, lifted out a ledger, and set it on the desk.

"We put everything in here," she said. "It's kind of a mess, because we used it for payments as well as the daily log."

"Let's start with June," I said.

I leaned next to her, close enough to smell shampoo on her hair. She opened the book and flipped a few pages. Then she moved for me to look.

The columns listed date, patient name, treatment, and payment, if any. Most of the treatments were for cuts and scrapes, coughs and colds, with a few broken bones thrown in for good measure. There were also entries that listed only the date, the payment, and "anonymous." There were half a dozen of these each week. The payments ranged from ten to fifty dollars.

"Are you familiar with these entries?" I asked, putting my finger on an anonymous payment.

She barely glanced down. "Of course."

"How do you explain them?"

"What do you mean? They're donations."

"Get real."

"Well, they are," she said, her eyes wide with innocence. "Lots of people like to give to worthy causes and not—"

"Betty, cut the bullshit, okay?"

She set her jaw.

"Dr. Early was making book, and these entries are his profits, right?"

She said nothing.

"Look, Betty, it's just between you and me."

She looked down at the book. When she nodded her head, it was so slight I almost missed it.

"But he didn't keep any of it for himself," she said. "It all went for the clinic."

"How did he take bets?"

"On his private phone in here."

"Were all the bettors local people?"

"Yes. They were all men Dr. Early knew personally. He tried to be as careful about it as he could." She sighed. "I didn't like what he was doing, and I'm not certain he did, either. But it was for the clinic."

"How did Joseph Bellano figure into this?"

"He showed Dr. Early what to do."

"How to be a bookie?"

"Yes."

"Why?"

"Why? They were friends. Mr. Bellano brought his wife

and two daughters up here each summer and rented a cabin by the lake. It's a small town. He and Dr. Early got to know each other. Mr. Bellano knew the situation at the clinic and how tough it was to make ends meet. I know he donated some money of his own. And he showed Dr. Early how to make money on gambling. Other people's gambling."

"And Dr. Early reciprocated by hiring Stephanie Bellano."

"Yes. But we really did need the extra help during the summer."

"I see."

I looked through the rest of June. Except for the ubiquitous "anonymous donations," there was nothing that caught my eye. I turned the page to July. Here I found an entry for Stephanie Bellano: July 10, complete physical exam, no charge.

"Was this Stephanie's abortion?"

Betty Phipps nodded. My eyes moved down a few lines, and I saw an entry for one Christine Smith: July 12, complete physical exam, $150.

"Was this an abortion, too?"

Betty looked at the entry. "Yes."

"Do you remember this girl?"

Her brows went together. "Vaguely. She was in her late teens, average size. I think she had long brown hair."

Here was my Chrissie.

"Do you have her address?"

"I'm sure we do. In the patients' log."

She got it from the file cabinet and opened it on the desk. It was a three-ring binder filled with Xeroxed forms showing the vital statistics, ailments, and treatments of every patient under Dr. Early's care.

We found Smith, Christine. The entry stated that she was in excellent health and that the physical examination had proceeded without incident. Also listed were her age, height, weight, and the color of her hair and eyes. It fit the description Mrs. Henderson had given me. There was also an address listed. Wray, Colorado.

"Is this address genuine?"

"Genuine?" Betty looked at the page. "That's my handwriting. We always require some form of identification. I believe I saw her driver's license."

I turned back to the ledger and skimmed through the remainder of July. I wasn't sure what I was looking for—a familiar name, I suppose. I was about to turn the page when I noticed an entry dated July 31:

> Sex: male.   Age: 6 months.   Weight: 17 lbs.
> Length: 26 in.   Hair: black.   Eyes: blue.
> Infant was dead on arrival—sudden infant
> death syndrome.

The baby's name was Thomas Rhynsburger. I pointed out the entry to Betty.

"I remember this," she said, "although I didn't work that day. When I came in the next morning, Stephanie was extremely upset. She'd been here when the parents brought in their dead infant. It would've been upsetting to Stephanie in any case, but coming so closely after her abortion . . . well, it was almost too much for her to handle."

"Were the parents local people?"

"No. Dr. Early told me they were tourists from out of state."

"Did the coroner verify the cause of death?"

"Dr. Early was the coroner."

I turned the page to August. More cuts and breaks and anonymous donations. Nothing out of the ordinary; that is, for your average country doctor who moonlights as a bookie. I turned to September. More of the same. Except for an entry on September 3. On that date someone had given the clinic ten thousand dollars.

"What's this?"

"I . . . I don't know." She looked away.

"Come on, Betty. You know about the nickel-and-dime stuff. You sure as hell know about this."

She shook her head. "I don't, honestly. Of course, I saw it. I asked Dr. Early what it was for. He told me not to worry about it. I knew . . . I guessed there was something . . . unusual involved, but I didn't press the matter."

"Unusual? You mean illegal?"

She said nothing.

"That's a lot of money. More than a simple wager."

"I know," she said gravely. "I don't know what it was for."

I skimmed through the rest of September. Nothing unusual. I turned to October. More of the same. Except that after October 15 there were no more anonymous donations. The bookie joint had shut down that night. Permanently.

Betty put away the book, turned out the lights, and locked up. I drove her to the Trail's End, where we'd left her car. It was the only car in the lot, cold and lonely looking. The restaurant was already closed for the night.

"I really appreciate your help," I said.

"Do you think you'll find Stephanie?"

"Eventually. I'll talk to Christine Smith."

Betty nodded. She stared straight ahead and made no move to get out of the car. We sat in silence, with the Olds rumbling patiently. I wondered if she was waiting for me to get out and open the door. It was a long drive back to Denver, and it was getting late.

"Would you . . . like to get a drink?" I asked her.

She turned and looked at me. "Yes."

"Okay. Do you know a good place?"

"Yes."

She drove her car through town and onto a road that took us halfway around the lake. She stopped before a cabin. It was one of a few dozen, most of which looked boarded up for the winter. I parked behind her.

The small living room had pine walls and pine furniture with blue cushions. There were dried flowers in vases and paintings of flowers on the walls.

I helped her build a fire in the large stone fireplace. We sipped brandy. I told her what it was like to be a private eye, and she told me what it was like to be a nurse in a small town. Her boyfriend of four years had left her last spring. She assumed he was living in Denver.

She asked me if there was a woman in my life. I thought of my dead wife. I told her no.

We went to bed. There were no groans or whispers. Near the end she moaned once, softly, and then we both shuddered and clung to each other like the last two people on earth.

In the morning she fixed us breakfast. We talked about how close it was getting to Christmas, about how pretty the mountains and the lake looked under the cold morning sun—about everything but last night.

I washed the dishes while she got ready for work.

Outside it was clear and cold, and the snow squeaked underfoot. We started our cars, then let them run while we scraped frost off the windshields. I tried to think of something clever to say. She beat me to it.

"It's been nice to know you."

I made the long, cold drive back to Denver.

CHAPTER

16

I GOT HOME about noon.

I emptied a can of Progresso Extra Zesty Minestrone into a saucepan, turned on the heat, and phoned Angela Bellano. I didn't have to ask if Stephanie had come home. Angela asked first:

"Any news?"

"I've located the girl Stephanie met in Big Pine—Chrissie Smith."

"Has she seen Stephanie?"

"I'm sorry, I didn't mean that I've talked to her. I've just learned where she lives. In Wray."

"Oh. When are you going there?"

Wray is about ten miles west of the point where Nebraska and Kansas meet on the Colorado border. Given the present road conditions, I figured it was at least a four-hour drive, probably more. And I'd already spent the morning on the road. My legs were stiff. Besides, Stephanie had known Christine Smith for only a few months. I had no real reason to believe that Stephanie was staying with her; it was just one more slim lead. But *if* Stephanie was staying with a girlfriend on a ranch in Wray, she was no doubt safe and sound. I could take it easy this afternoon and drive up there first thing in the morning. Stephanie could spend one more night away from home and it wouldn't hurt a thing. Except a mother's heart.

"I'm on my way," I said.

Before I left, I clipped a gun to my hip. Stephanie might be on a ranch. Ranches meant ranchers. And ranchers meant guns. At least *I* thought they did. I was just trying to fit in.

I took I-25 north to I-76, which led me northeast out of the metro area, beyond the fringes of suburban sprawl.

After an hour I was in the midst of vast, open land. There were a few humps and bumps, but mostly it was flat and white. The snowfields were occasionally broken by houses and barns, outbuildings and fences. The horizon was an indistinct line of white and gray.

A few hours later I reached Fort Morgan and turned onto State Highway 34 heading due east.

The wind had picked up. It blew snow across the highway, making it slippery. What few cars there were crept along at a cautious pace. Of course, a few jerks in four-wheel drives with fat studded tires would periodically blow by and temporarily blind us sensible types in clouds of cold powdery snow.

It was nearly six when I got to Wray.

There were few lights on as I cruised down the main street. The Conoco station at the end of town was an island of cold white fluorescence in the dark landscape. The old geezer running the station wore coveralls, a red parka with greasy sleeves, and an orange hunting cap with the earflaps turned down. He filled my tank and checked my oil. Then he told me how to get to the address I showed him.

The house was a mile or so from the center of town.

It was a rambling single-story ranch-style brick built in the fifties. It looked like a typical suburban dwelling. Except that the backyard was thirty acres of snow surrounded by a barbed-wire fence. My tires crunched over gravel and crusty snow as I pulled into the long, dark circular drive.

The porch light went on before I'd shut off the engine. When I climbed out, cold air stung my face. A couple of dogs started barking from inside the house.

The woman who answered the door was wrapped in a bulky

sweater, which I guessed she'd knitted herself. She was around forty, with long dark hair, a thin jaw, and tired but kind eyes. A pair of golden retrievers crowded in front of her and barked ferociously. Their tails, though, swung like metronomes.

"I'm sorry to bother you at this hour," I said. I told her who I was and what I did for a living. "I'm looking for Christine Smith."

She pulled the dogs back and quieted them down.

"I'm Chrissie's mother. Is there something wrong?"

"Not as far as I know. I was hired by a family in Denver to find their daughter, Stephanie Bellano. I was hoping she might be staying with Chrissie."

"Chrissie . . . isn't here right now," she said.

"Right now, hell."

A man appeared behind Mrs. Smith. He wore a robe and slippers. His hair was mussed, his face was pale, and his nose was red.

"She doesn't *live* here anymore. And just who the hell is *this*, Alice?"

"He's a detective from Denver," Alice Smith said. "He's looking for a friend of Chrissie's."

"Well, you know where to send him," he said, and sneezed.

"Go lay down, hon. I'll bring you some tea."

"I can make my own damn tea." He turned his back on us. "And close the door. You're letting in the cold."

Alice Smith hesitated for a moment.

"Please come in."

The house was furnished in beige-on-brown neotacky American. There were clear plastic covers on the lampshades and on the arms of the stuffed chairs. The coffee table held a sculpted ashtray the size of a canoe. It was clean and shiny. I stood in the warmth of the living room and let the dogs sniff my pants cuffs.

"You'll have to excuse my husband," she said quietly. She nodded toward the kitchen and the sound of a kettle banging on the stove top. "He's feeling under the weather."

"I understand. He said your daughter doesn't live here anymore."

"Of *course* she lives here," Alice Smith said with feeling. "This is her home as much as it is mine and Bob's. I keep her room up, and she can stay here or come and go as she pleases. She's practically a grown woman, you know."

"I see." What I saw was hurt. Her little girl had moved away.

"Where does Chrissie li—, er, where is she staying now?" She folded her arms under her breasts and lifted them in a sigh.

"Over at Reverend Lacey's place."

"If he's a reverend," Bob shouted from the kitchen, "then I'm the goddamn Roman pope! Where the hell are the tea bags?"

"Excuse me a moment."

Alice Smith went to the kitchen. She and Bob spoke in voices too low for me to understand. Their tones, though, were plain enough—his, anger laced with frustration; hers, sweet solace. In a few minutes she was back, another line in her face, another strand of gray at her temple.

"He really is feeling poorly," she said. "Now this girl you're looking for . . ."

"Stephanie Bellano."

"There was a girl who came here last week asking for Chrissie. No, it was week before last. I didn't get her name, though. I did tell her where Chrissie was."

I showed Alice Smith my photos of Stephanie.

"That's her," she said.

"Was she alone?" Obviously Stephanie hadn't driven her own car, and I hadn't talked to anyone who'd lent her one.

"She was," Alice Smith said. "In fact, now that you mention

it, when she left here, she walked clear down the driveway to the road."

She'd hitchhiked from Denver, I thought. And with the number of weirdos out there, it was probably fortunate she'd made it this far.

"You said Chrissie is staying with Reverend Lacey."

"Yes. His place is twenty-five, thirty miles from here."

"Is it a church?"

"Well, not exactly. It's more like a commune. They've got some livestock and some acreage of wheat and corn and beets."

"Is he an ordained minister?"

"He—"

"Hell, no," Bob Smith said, coming out of the kitchen, rattling his cup and saucer. He sat down on the couch, sipped his tea, and made a face. "Oh, he does Bible readings and calls his place the Church of the Something-or-other, but he's no goddamn minister."

"Bob, please."

"Well, he's not, no more'n I am." He looked up at me. "This Lacey character showed up four or five years ago when old Roy Smalls died and his wife put the place up for sale. It wasn't much of a place to begin with, so Lacey bought it for a song. He hung out a sign and called himself a church. Which, when tax time rolls around, is a pretty damn good idea."

"Bob . . ."

"Anyhow," Bob said, waving aside his wife's warning, "*Reverend* Lacey, as he calls himself, opened his arms and his place to every drifter, *pre*vert, and drug addict in the state, or I should say, in Denver, because that's where most of them come from."

"Bob . . ."

"What?"

Alice Smith sighed at her husband, then turned to me.

"Most of Reverend Lacey's followers are young people from

the city, and *some* of them are there to try to overcome drugs. He gives them a roof and a bed and food to eat. In return, they help him work the land."

"Help?" Bob Smith snorted. "I'll bet you a dollar Lacey never gets his hands dirty."

"Why is your daughter staying there?" I asked. "Did she have a drug problem?"

"Jesus God, no."

"No," Alice Smith said. "Like some of his other followers, she was going there to . . . well, as she told it to me, to get away from modern society."

"Modern society?"

" 'Responsibility' is more like it," Bob Smith said. "Most of them are city kids running away from something. Lacey isolates them out on his place, which gives him plenty of cheap labor."

"Now, Bob, that's not necessarily true."

"It *is* true," he said angrily, standing, spilling tea in his saucer. His robe hung crookedly on him, giving him a comical appearance. Nobody laughed. "And if Christine ever figures that out," he said, "well, then maybe we'll have a daughter again. Right now we don't." He looked at his wife, daring her to argue. She didn't. He hung his head, then turned his back on us and mumbled, "I'm going to bed."

We stood for a moment in silence. I asked her for directions to Reverend Lacey's place.

"When you go there . . . if you see Chrissie . . ."

"Yes?"

"Would you . . . tell her we both said hello."

Alice Smith's directions took me south and then west on a snow-packed county road. I hoped I didn't meet anyone head-on, because the plow had left room for only a car and a half.

My headlights picked up barbed-wire fences. They ran along both sides of the road and made me feel as if I were in a long, narrow animal pen. Beyond the wire was darkness. Every few miles the fences were interrupted by gates, beside which stood oversized mailboxes. I could read the names without leaving the car.

I nearly missed Lacey's gate, though, because it didn't have a mailbox. There was a wooden sign wired to the gate:

The CHURCH of the PENITENT
Rev. J. LACEY

No Trespassing!

I turned in the narrow drive, sliding through deep ruts of snow. I stopped at the gate. There was a heavy chain wrapped around the metal gate and post. There was also a padlock the size of my fist. I shut off the lights and climbed out.

The sky was beginning to open. A few brilliant stars poked through. The moon, though, was still a fuzzy wad of gauze. My eyes gradually adjusted to the feeble light.

The Church of the Penitent was a shadowy snowfield dotted with small, vague black shapes. They were either cattle, stunted trees, or nameless demons. In the distance, perhaps half a mile from where I stood shivering in the black night air, were tiny warm dots of yellow light. Windows.

The only sounds were the rumbling of the Olds and the grumbling of my stomach.

My options were limited. I could pick the padlock, drive up to the house, and beg for something to eat, hoping the punishment for trespassing in the night wasn't crucifixion. Or I could go back to town and try to find a motel that was close to a bar.

No contest.

CHAPTER

17

THE NEXT MORNING I stood in the tiny shower in the Columbine Motel until I'd used up all the hot water. The other guests didn't mind. There weren't any.

The motel was on the outskirts of Wray. It was a dumpy six-unit affair with a vacancy sign that hadn't been taken down in years. Last night, after I'd checked in, I'd found a bar and drank shots and beers with a couple of good old boys who raised hogs north of town. By closing time, when I stumbled out to my car, I'd almost gotten used to their smell.

The shower had somewhat eased my hangover. But when I stepped outside into the clear, crisp morning air, the sunlight went through my eyes like a needle.

I found a café up the street and chowed down on ham, eggs, home fries, and coffee.

Then I drove to the Church of the Penitent.

The sky was royal blue, and the fields flanking the road were startlingly white, with tiny dancing points of brilliance. I turned off the snow-packed road into the snow ruts of the church's driveway. The gate was still chained shut.

I climbed out, picked the padlock, and pushed open the gate. Then I drove through and stopped. I closed the gate behind me. It was the neighborly thing to do.

I followed the ruts in the snow toward a complex of

unpainted wooden structures, a few hundred yards distant. The dark demon shapes I'd seen last night were discernible now—cattle lethargically trampling the snow into narrow, muddy paths.

I didn't see any people.

The main house was a hodgepodge of additions tacked on to a central building, which I guessed had been the original farmhouse. Beside it was a propane tank the size of a submarine.

The other buildings were all to my right, separated from the main building by trampled snow and mud. There were a big two-story barn, a long, low chicken coop, and a foggy-windowed greenhouse. There were several other structures, which were probably garages and storage sheds. Or maybe that's where they kept the grain for the demon cattle. There was one other large building, nearly as big as the barn, which stood apart from the others. It had a high peaked roof. There was a crucifix over the door. The building looked newer than the others, but its unpainted wood was beginning to show the weather.

I pulled alongside the main house and stopped. A young woman stepped out of the chicken coop. She carried a covered basket. Before she closed the door, I could see the ugly red-and-brown birds behind her.

She stopped short when she saw me. Then she hurried into the main building.

I shut off the Olds and got out.

Before I took two steps through the slush and mud, the side door of the house burst open and out came two men. They were both in their twenties and dressed in blue jeans and flannel shirts. The first one, though, was bigger. His hair was pulled back in a ponytail. He had a beard and a long-handled ax. The latter he carried at port arms.

"Who are you?" he demanded.

I told him. "I'm looking for Stephanie Bellano."

The men glanced at each other.

The big one said, "You'll have to talk to Reverend Lacey about her. But he's in town now. So you can just turn right around and leave." He motioned with the ax. The sunlight danced on its keen, clean edge.

"When will he be back?"

"You heard him," the other guy said. "Get out of here." He felt brave standing behind his pal with the ax. Hey, who wouldn't?

"Why don't I just wait here for the reverend," I said.

The big guy shifted his boots in the snow. Apparently he wasn't quite sure what to do without Lacey around.

"Maybe if you come back in an hour or—"

He stopped at the sound of a truck engine. I turned to see a large pickup roaring toward us from the distant gate and throwing equal amounts of snow and mud from all four tires. It was an old International Harvester with different-colored front fenders and a winch on the bumper. It slid to a stop a foot behind my Olds.

"Looks like your waiting is over," the smaller guy said to my back. I didn't like the way he said it.

Reverend John Lacey clambered out of his truck. He was clean-shaven and tall—a rawboned man in his late forties with steely blue eyes and shocking red hair that was clumped on his head in thick curls. His arms were a bit too long for his coat, and his wrists stuck out, hairless and hard as ball bats. His patched khaki pants were tucked into high-top lace-up boots. He covered the distance between us in a few long strides.

"Who *is* this man?" he bellowed, rattling the windows in the house. Before either of the young men could answer, he turned his glare on me. "Who *are* you, and what are you doing here?"

"My name is Jacob Lomax and—"

"And how did you get through my locked gate?"

"I unlocked it."

He stiffened, pushing his already adequate height up another inch or so. Then he smiled. Barely. It was more like an unstraightening of his hard, thin lips.

"An honest thief?" he said.

"I'm not a thief, Reverend, I'm a private investigator."

"Is that supposed to *mean* something?"

I opened my mouth to give him a cute answer, but he cut me off.

"What do you want here?" he demanded.

"I'm looking for Stephanie Bellano."

"She's not here."

"She *was* here, though, wasn't she?"

He nodded yes. "But she left a few days ago. You two"—he said suddenly over my shoulder—"help Judith put everything away. And I mean everything."

For the first time I noticed a young woman in the truck. She got out. Then she and the two men carried sacks into the house. Probably flour and dried beans. Several men and women watched from the windows.

"Where did Stephanie go?"

Lacey turned his long, lean face to the side and aimed one hard blue eye at me. "Why do you want to know?"

"Number one, her father hired me to find her. And number two, her mother is worried sick."

Lacey spread his large hands with the palms upward. They were shiny with calluses. I guess Bob Smith had been wrong about Lacey not doing any work.

"Stephanie is of age," he said, his tone as condescending as if it had come from the pulpit. "She no longer need answer to her earthly father."

"You're right about that. Her earthly father was blown to bloody bits by a car bomb."

His mouth parted, then immediately clamped shut.

"Look, Reverend, it's important that I find Stephanie."

"It sounds as if she's in danger."

"She may be."

"And how do I know that *you're* not the danger?"

"Phone her mother."

"And how would I know that this woman *is* her mother?"

"You don't trust anyone, do you?"

"I trust in God."

"Right."

He squinted at me.

"I told you that Stephanie isn't here. Now what *else* do you want to know?"

"Could we talk inside?"

He hesitated a moment, then walked toward the house. He wiped his boots on a straw mat and led me through the door.

We were in the kitchen, an enormous room with wide wooden counters scrubbed bone-clean. There were a pair of old gas stoves side by side, a large refrigerator, and a freezer the size of a coffin. Iron pots and pans dangled from hooks on the wall. One end of the kitchen was taken up by a table that could seat twenty. There were two doorways leading into other parts of the house. I got the feeling some of Lacey's followers were just out of sight. The only person in the room with us was the girl I'd seen leaving the chicken coop. She was heating water on one of the stoves.

Lacey motioned me toward the table. He sat at the head, his usual spot.

"When did Stephanie leave here?"

"Day before yesterday."

"Tuesday?"

"Yes."

"What happened?"

"Well, I was going into town, and she asked if she could ride with me. She wanted to use the telephone." He waved his hand as if to show me the entire house. "We don't have one. In any case, I gave her some coins, left her at the drugstore to make her call, then went across the street to the hardware store."

"Who did she call?"

"I don't know. A man."

"How do you know it was a man?"

"When I went back to get Stephanie, she said she'd called someone in Denver. She said he was coming to town to pick her up. *He*. She said she preferred to wait at the drugstore rather than come back home with me. So I left her there."

"You just left her?"

"I tried to change her mind, of course. But she was firm. I certainly couldn't *force* her to come with me."

"You could've waited with her."

"I *could* have done any number of things, Mr. Lomax, but I didn't. I had work to do, and I came home. It's not as coldhearted as it sounds. Young people come here, stay for a while, then leave. Some stay longer than others. Some not long at all. In fact, just this morning I drove a young man into town so he could get a ride back to Denver. His name is Dexter. I'm afraid he's a drug addict."

I was trying to think who Stephanie could have phoned. Father Carbone? Her uncle Tony? No. Either way, Angela would've known and told me. Of course, maybe the good reverend was lying through his teeth.

"How do I know Stephanie's not still here?"

"Because I just told you."

"I heard your words, Reverend. But how do I *know*?"

He managed to look at once amused and mildly offended. "Why would I lie about that?"

"I'm not sure."

"Perhaps you'd like to search the premises," he said with some sarcasm.

"Good idea."

He rose from his chair and glared down at me. "Or perhaps I should just throw you out on your ear."

He was just about big enough to do it. And if he couldn't, he had plenty of help in the next room.

I stood.

"Let me put it this way, Reverend. Stephanie is listed with the Denver police as a missing person. Denver cops are friendly with your cops. If I leave here now, I'll be back with the sheriff and a search warrant and a truckload of deputies who'll track mud all over your house."

Lacey could barely stand *one* stranger nosing around, much less an army of cops. He gave me what passed for a smile.

"Would you like the guided tour?" he asked amiably, "or would you rather just wander to your heart's content?"

"I'd like you and Chrissie Smith to show me around."

"Of course," he said without hesitation. "Sarah, would you please get Chrissie?"

"Yes, sir."

Sarah left her boiling pot and hurried from the kitchen. I asked Lacey how many people lived here.

"People tend to come and go. Right now there are eight, not counting myself—five men and three women." He gave me a look of mock servility. "Shall I line them up for your inspection?"

"Why not?"

His face reddened, and cords stood out on his neck.

"Careful," I said. "Anger's one of the seven deadly sins."

Just then Sarah entered the kitchen with Chrissie Smith. Chrissie looked a bit like her mother. Her hair hung down her back in a long brown braid.

"I will oblige you, Mr. Lomax," Lacey said, back in control of himself, "so that you may soon quit this place, never to return." He turned to face the young women. "Please bring everyone to the kitchen. Mr. Lomax wants to check under their fingernails."

The girls gave each other quizzical looks. Then Chrissie went back through the doorway. Sarah went outside. Lacey and I stood alone in silence for a few moments. One by one his followers came into the kitchen. They were all in their teens and twenties and dressed in plain, practical, patched clothing. Two of the five men looked fit enough to work on a ranch. The rest looked like city kids masquerading as settlers. None of the women wore makeup.

"What's going on, Reverend John?" one of the men asked. He had a scraggly beard and a runny nose.

"Mr. Lomax has threatened to bring the police unless we let him search our home for Stephanie Bellano."

There was a chorus of loud protest, which stopped at once when Lacey raised his hand.

"Chrissie, you and I will show him around. Then we'll show him the way back to town. The rest of you please stay here."

At this point I felt fairly certain that they were neither hiding Stephanie nor holding her against her will. Still, I was obliged to snoop. Professional ethics.

Lacey and Chrissie led me from the kitchen to the "social room." There were a number of uncomfortable-looking chairs and benches. A wood-burning stove was wedged into the big stone fireplace.

My two guides showed me the separate sleeping quarters for the men and women. The bed frames looked handmade—crude but sturdy, sort of like summer camp. I looked in the closets. Few clothes, all neatly hung.

Lacey had his own room and his own bath. I looked under the bed. No dust bunnies.

They led me back to the kitchen. I realized I hadn't seen a stereo, television set, radio, or telephone. I mentioned this to Lacey.

"We have plenty to do, Mr. Lomax, without being reminded of the sins of the world."

When we got to the kitchen, we found most of Lacey's flock sitting at the table drinking coffee from heavy mugs.

"Let's get back to work," Lacey told them. He started to lead me outside.

"Wait." I nodded toward a closed door. "What's that?"

"The canning cellar," Lacey said.

He opened the door, flicked on a light, then led me down the creaky wooden stairs. The cellar was a single room, much smaller than the house above. Much cooler, too. The overhead bulb threw harsh light on the concrete floor and walls. Most of the wall space was taken up by shelves. These were loaded with mason jars of fruits and vegetables swimming in their own juices.

I followed Lacey back up the stairs and outside. Chrissie joined us.

"I'll move my truck," Lacey said, "and you—"

"First we check the other buildings."

He hesitated, then gave me a slight bow. "As you wish."

The three of us headed toward the chicken coop. I turned to Chrissie.

"Did you tell Stephanie about this place when you met her in Big Pine?"

She looked at me, then at Lacey. He nodded his permission.

"Yes," she said.

"Did you talk to her at all between then and the day she showed up here?"

"No."

We checked the chicken coop. It was full of chickens. It stunk. Lacey closed the door and led me toward the greenhouse.

"When exactly did Stephanie arrive here?" I asked him.

"Friday before last. It was fairly late at night. She'd walked up from the road, and she was cold and wet. We took her in, of course. A few of the women helped her out of her clothes and into a hot tub and then to bed."

"Did you ask why she'd come?"

"I *knew* why she'd come. She was afraid, and she was seeking sanctuary. I gave it to her. She was safe here."

"Who was she afraid of?"

"I don't know. She didn't say, and I didn't ask."

I looked at Chrissie. Her eyes were as wide and innocent as a doe's.

"I don't know, either," she said.

"The next morning I explained the rules to Stephanie," Lacey told me. "No drugs, no alcohol, no sex. We work and we pray and we help each other, the way God intended. I told her she was welcome to stay as long as she liked. She stayed until last Tuesday."

Lacey led me into the greenhouse. It was filled with plants and warm, humid air.

"Did you ever try to contact her parents?"

"No," Lacey said. "Stephanie is a woman, not a child. That was her decision to make. And I certainly didn't *prevent* her from contacting her parents. Or anyone else, for that matter."

Lacey watched me search the barn. It was warm with a heavy animal smell. There was clean straw spread on the floor. The half-dozen stalls were neat and empty. I climbed the ladder to the loft. Nothing but bales of hay.

Lacey showed me to the other structures: garage, woodworking shop, storage sheds. As expected, there was no sign of Stephanie.

The only building left was the chapel.

There were two rows of high-backed wooden benches facing a raised pulpit. The ceiling was high, and so was Lacey's optimism—there were enough seats for fifty people. The only window was behind the pulpit. It would allow Lacey to attack from out of the sun, like a Japanese fighter pilot.

I followed them outside. Chrissie went into the house. Lacey led me to my car.

"Did you know Chrissie had an abortion this summer in Big Pine?"

He paused. "Yes." He pulled open the door to his pickup.

"Did you send her there?"

"No. I . . . I was against it."

There was something in Lacey's face that surprised me—pain. When he spoke, it was sadly.

"Chrissie told me she'd been treated by a doctor there a few years ago while on vacation. She trusted him. And she didn't want her parents to know."

"Why didn't she want the baby?"

Lacey stared at the distant horizon, a sharp line of white and blue.

"She wanted to stay here, Mr. Lomax," he said slowly. "And we do not yet have the resources to maintain nonworkers."

"You mean babies and pregnant women."

"It was . . . Chrissie's decision," he said.

He climbed in his truck, started the engine, and backed out of my way. I turned the Olds around and drove to the gate. Lacey followed. He locked the gate behind me. I drove away, watching him in the rearview mirror. He stood motionless by the entrance to his church—a tall, strong, troubled man.

Then the road curved, and he vanished.

CHAPTER

18

I DROVE BACK to Denver, which gave me five hours to think about Reverend Lacey's story. There wasn't that much to think about.

Thirteen days ago Stephanie had shown up at the Church of the Penitent, seeking safety. Two days ago she'd left. With a man, according to Lacey. Someone she'd phoned in Denver.

The possibilities were limited; there were few men in Stephanie's life.

There'd been her father, of course, but he could no longer be reached by telephone. There were Father Carbone and Uncle Tony. But they certainly wouldn't hide her from Angela. There was Ken Hausom. Had Stephanie decided she'd had enough of the hard life on the church-farm and was now ready to reunite with the father of her aborted child? Somehow I doubted that. And there were the four customers.

Something about them tugged at my mind.

I'd been assuming all along that Stephanie had fled the barbershop for fear of her life. What if there'd been another reason? Maybe she'd been involved in something that I had yet to discover, something concerning her father. What if she'd known there would be an attempt on his life? Or as MacArthur had hinted, what if she'd helped set him up?

That was hard to swallow. But it would explain a few things.

She'd disappeared to establish an alibi. Sure, she'd been scared when she'd reached the church; she'd been afraid of arrest and prosecution. She'd waited there as long as she could stand it—no TV, no telephone, no way of knowing what was happening back in Denver. Finally, she'd risked a call to her man. He'd told her that the deed was done, that everything was okay, and that he was coming for her.

Possible. Not likely, though.

But I was running out of "likely"s.

It was late afternoon when I got home. The sky was dark and cloudy, and I was hungry. I hadn't eaten since breakfast. I bought a bucket of Kentucky Fried Colonel and walked it upstairs to my apartment. Then I opened a beer, munched a chicken part, and phoned Father Carbone.

He'd not heard from Stephanie.

I phoned Angela Bellano.

"I traced Stephanie to a religious commune near Wray," I told her. I described my talk with Reverend Lacey and Chrissie Smith and my search of the farm.

"Could she be in Denver now?"

"It's possible. Let's keep a good thought." Easy for you to say, Lomax.

"By the way," she said, "two police detectives were here today. They searched Joe's room again for his records. They asked if anyone had been there."

"Yes?"

"I'm afraid I told them about you and your associate. I hope that wasn't wrong. I didn't know if I should lie or not."

"Don't worry about it." Great. Police harassment was definitely in my near future. "I've got a few leads to check out. I'll be in touch."

I ate some more chicken and drank some more beer. The "few leads" I'd mentioned to Angela were mostly just one: Ken Hausom. I planned on catching up with him tonight at the Lion's Lair. The problem was he wouldn't be happy to see me. He might not want to talk. In fact, he might want to beat me severely about the head and face.

Maybe I could distract him with a beautiful woman.

I phoned Rachel Wynn. I told her I hadn't yet found Stephanie but I was getting closer.

"I could use your help tonight," I said.

"How?"

"I want to talk to Ken Hausom, but he's very angry with me."

"So you want a bodyguard."

"Exactly. What time should I pick you up?"

"Well . . . we're eating dinner right now. Give me an hour."

"We?"

"What? Oh. Pat and I."

Oh, fine. "I suppose Pat will want to tag along."

"Possibly."

Rachel Wynn lived in Lafayette Circle in South Denver. The house was an old frame with new paint. It sat amid giant leafless elms. Their black fingers scratched at the overcast night sky.

Rachel answered the door with her coat on.

"Shall we go?" she said, not asking me in.

"Sure. Where's Pat?"

"Pat was tired. She went home."

She. Things were looking up.

On the way to the Lion's Lair I told her about the Church of the Penitent and Reverend John Lacey. I explained how Stephanie had phoned a man in Denver, then waited for him to pick her up. I told her Ken Hausom was my choice for the "man."

"You only have Lacey's word that she called anyone."

"I know."

"Do you believe him?"

"I don't have much choice. I searched his place from top to

bottom. There was no sign of Stephanie. The fact that he let me search at all just about told me she wasn't there."

"Maybe she was someplace where they knew you wouldn't find her."

"Like where?" I said. "The hidden room behind the secret panel? We're talking about a farmhouse here, not a medieval castle."

"So get sarcastic."

"I'll work on it."

It had been a week since I'd been to the Lion's Lair. It had been crowded then, and it was crowded now. We found a pair of stools at the bar. The nearest dozen or so guys gave Rachel the eye. Some more blatantly than others. She didn't seem to notice.

"What would you like?" I asked her above the crowd noise.

"Nothing with ice in it. I see a bar rag hanging out of the ice machine."

I ordered two Miller Lites from Carl the bartender. I don't think he recognized me until I asked him if Ken had come in yet.

"No." He managed to look angry and worried at the same time.

We sipped our beers and watched the people. It was too loud for meaningful conversation.

"Dammit," Rachel said.

"What?"

"See those two girls over there? The ones sitting with that big fat guy? They're both students of mine, and they're both under twenty-one."

"Do you want to go talk to them?"

She grimaced. "I don't want to make a scene. I'll talk to them tomorrow. But it bothers me that they're with an older man."

I watched the two pretty young girls leaning over their drinks with smiles on their faces, listening to a seasoned hustler feed them a line. It was probably similar to the line he fed his customers at the appliance store.

"I can take care of that," I said. "Save my seat."

I squeezed between tables until I stood behind the man. The girls looked up at me.

"Your wife's looking for you, Stan," I said.

Fowler turned around so fast he almost fell out of his seat. His face was flushed with booze and embarrassment. Then anger.

"Lomax. What're you doing here?"

"Your dear, sweet wife would probably want to know the same thing about you, Stan. Aren't you going to introduce me to your new girlfriends?"

The young ladies weren't smiling anymore. "Excuse us," they said in unison, rising. They took their drinks into the crowd.

Stan got up and grabbed his coat from the chair. He was leaving, his cover blown.

"Did Stephanie Bellano go for your line as quickly as those two?"

"I don't know what you're talking about." He knew.

He turned to leave. I grabbed his arm.

"You met her in here, didn't you, Stan?"

"Let go of me before I knock you on your ass."

I let go, but not for that reason. I'd just seen Ken Hausom walk through the door.

"We'll talk, Stan."

He walked away, pushing through the crowd toward the door.

Meanwhile, Ken was making his way down the bar, slapping hands and saying howdy. He had his eye on the only empty stool, the one next to Rachel. I got there as he prepared to deliver *his* line. His smile was wide enough for me to see the temporary caps on his front teeth. They looked like Chiclets.

"Hi, babe. Is this seat—"

"Yes, it's taken," I said, stepping up close to him so he wouldn't have room to demonstrate his karate kicks.

His lip dropped over his shiny fake teeth.

"You're dead meat," he said, almost too low for me to hear.

"Can we talk first?"

"I could've crippled you last week, but I went easy. This time will be different."

Rachel looked at me questioningly.

"Look, Ken," I said, "I just want to talk to you about Stephanie. Now I've been to Wray and—"

"Let's take it outside," he said, "where we've got more room."

"I don't want to fight." I didn't, either.

"I don't blame you," he said, "but you don't have a choice."

"Will you cut the macho routine for a minute?"

We both looked at Rachel.

"You can fight him later, Ken, but—"

"Thanks a lot," I said.

"—but first we need to see Stephanie Bellano."

"What?"

"We need to make sure she's all right," Rachel said. "Her mother is worried to death. You can understand that, Ken, can't you? We're not going to take her away from you. We just want to talk to her. Okay?"

Ken had been looking at Rachel as if she were speaking Portuguese. He turned to me with one side of his mouth pulled up in a question.

"She with you?"

"We came here together," Rachel said.

"What the fuck's she talking about?" Ken asked me in all sincerity.

"I traced Stephanie to a farm in Wray," I said. "I was told she left there a few days ago with a man. I figure that man was you."

Ken shook his head and smiled with his mouth closed. "Must be some other man."

"You're lying," Rachel said.

"Hey, fuck you," Ken told her. Then he poked me in the chest with two fingers, hard as wooden dowels. "And you, you're coming outside with me now, or I'm going to take you right here."

"He knows where Stephanie is," Rachel said angrily. "He's a damn liar."

"Rachel, please, my ears," I said.

"Oh, brother. So now what?"

"Me and Lomax go outside," Ken told her. "And when I'm finished with him, you and I can get better acquainted. Tell you the truth, I *prefer* getting it on with older women."

"Get it on with this," she said, and slapped her beer bottle down on the bar.

"Do your students know you act this way?" I asked her.

"I'm leaving."

"We're all leaving," Ken said.

Rachel and I moved through the crowd toward the door, Ken following. Rachel touched my arm.

"You're not really going to *fight*, are you?"

"Not if I can help it."

When we got out to the front parking lot, Ken turned around, ready to do me in. I put one arm around Rachel and stuck my other arm out, palm forward.

"Hey, wait a minute, okay? At least let the lady get out of the way. And let's go around the side of the building. You want a cop to drive down the street and see us? Here," I said, handing Rachel my keys. "Wait in my car. This won't take long."

"What are you going to do?"

"Reason with him."

"Let's do it, Lomax," Ken said, his breath foggy in the cold air.

Rachel walked toward my car.

I followed Ken between parked cars toward the side of the building. But I kept my distance. I didn't want him demonstrating his little spin kick. We kept an eye on each other all the way around the corner of the building.

There was a yellow arc light about halfway toward the rear. It was fastened high up on the outside brick wall. Ken stopped under it and turned around. He grinned. The light made his teeth look like fangs. He went into a karate stance—one leg forward, hands up, fingers curled. Then he shouted something like "Heeyiiah" and shuffled toward me.

I took the gun out of my belt holster. I'd been carrying it since yesterday when I drove to Wray. It's a small piece, a Smith & Wesson Chief's Special with a two-inch barrel. Still, it *is* a .38. I showed it to Ken.

"Hee-ya, yourself."

He stopped and blinked. "Oh, fuck."

"That's right, Kenny."

"Oh, fuck, don't shoot." His hands were still up, but his fingers had lost their karate curl.

"Where's Stephanie Bellano?"

"Oh, fuck, don't shoot me."

"Come on, Kenny, it's cold out here, and my trigger finger's starting to cramp. Where is she?"

"Stephanie? I told you, man, I don't know."

"You drove to Wray and brought her back here."

"No, man, honest to God. I've never been to Wray in my whole fucking life."

"You're starting to make me mad, Kenny." I raised the gun so he could look down the barrel.

"No! Look, Jesus, I'm telling you the *truth!* I don't know where she is. I haven't seen her since May. Honest to God. Okay, look, if this is about child support, if she's carrying my kid and she wants money, fine. Is that what this is about? I mean, I can pay. Whatever she wants."

"It's too late for that," I said.

I guess he'd misinterpreted my statement, because he screamed, "NO!" Then he turned and ran for his life.

I walked back to my car.

Rachel had the doors locked and the engine running. She let me in. The air was warm. It smelled faintly of her perfume.

"Are you okay?"

"Oh, just peachy," I said, and pulled out onto Wadsworth Boulevard.

"You look . . . strange."

"I've got a bad taste in my mouth."

"So . . . what happened?"

"Nothing."

"You didn't fight?"

"No."

"Well, thank God for small favors."

"Right."

"What about Stephanie?"

"Ken doesn't know anything," I said. "He hasn't seen her since May."

"How do you know he's not lying?"

"I know."

"How?"

"Trust me, okay?"

"So where is she?"

"I don't know. I need a drink. You want to join me?"

"You *need* a drink?"

"Okay, I *want* a drink."

CHAPTER

19

I TOOK SIXTH AVENUE west to Simms Landing.

Rachel and I walked through the restaurant, past the bar, and down some steps into the lounge. It had lots of heavy ropes and ships' fittings. The ocean's only a thousand miles away.

The piano player wasn't too loud, which was nice. The nicest part, though, was the view. We sat high up on the western edge of the city. The windows faced east over a vast carpet of tiny lights. Beyond the city stretched the plains, black as the void.

The waitress brought our drinks—one scotch, one vodka with a twist. Rachel asked me what I was going to do now about finding Stephanie. I told her about the four customers in Bellano's shop and the possibility that Stephanie had run from one of them.

"I'm going to take a closer look at all four," I said, and sipped my scotch.

"Do you think Stephanie may have phoned one of those men from Wray?"

"It's possible."

"That doesn't make sense," Rachel said. "If Stephanie ran from one of them, she wouldn't call him, would she? Or wait for him to come pick her up?"

"I don't know. But right now I've got nothing else to go on. Stephanie knows something about one of those men. Or he knows something about her. When *I* know it, then maybe I'll know where she is."

We were silent for a moment. The candlelight from the jar on the table made her eyes dance.

"Do any of them seem likely to you?" she asked. "I mean more likely than the other three."

"Right now my money's on Stan Fowler. That was him trying to hustle your two students tonight."

"That bastard," she said, as if they were her children. Which, in a way, they were.

"Yes, he is. There's a good chance he met Stephanie in the Lion's Lair. I'm just speculating, but if he somehow found out she was pregnant, then threatened to tell her father—"

"Why would he do that?"

"For sex."

"God." She'd looked disgusted. Then she downed part of her drink and shook her head. "How can you do this?"

"What?"

"This kind of work. I mean, where you have to *deal* with people like Stan Fowler and that other one. Ken."

"It's a living."

She didn't smile. "Have you considered another occupation?"

"Sure."

"What?"

"Astronaut."

"I'm serious."

"So am I. The pay's good, the view's spectacular, and you only have to work a few days a year."

"Very funny."

"Well, what about you? Do you always want to be a teacher?"

"No."

"What, then?"

"Seriously?"

"Seriously."

"Astronaut."

"See?"

She was smiling now. "Really, though, how did you ever become a private investigator?"

"Well, I was a cop first, and then I sort of fell into it."

"You were a policeman? Somehow I can't picture you in a uniform."

"Are you kidding? I was quite the dashing figure."

"I'm sure. Were your parents proud of their son the policeman?"

"Well, they'd both died when I was still in college."

"Oh. Oh, I didn't mean to . . ."

"No, it's okay. Actually it was a blessing when my mother passed away. She'd fought cancer for years. My father never got over her death, though. His health declined until he finally died of a heart attack. At least he went quickly."

"I'm sorry for your loss," she said.

I nodded. "Anyway, after college I kicked around for a few years, moved here and there, tried this and that. I finally tried being a cop."

"Why?"

"I guess it seemed like the thing to do at the time. Maybe I wanted to help."

"Help whom?"

"I don't know. Just help."

"Why aren't you still a policeman?"

"I changed."

"Not completely," she said. "Even I can tell that much."

"What?"

"You still want to help."

"I suppose. But on a smaller scale."

We were silent for a few moments. Her smile was long gone.

"The other three men who were in the barbershop," she said finally. "Are they as sleazy as Fowler?"

"They've all got points in their favor," I said. "Johnny Toes Burke is probably the most evil of the four. If you believe in that concept."

"I certainly do."

"Plus Johnny Toes works for a gangster who had reason to kill Joseph Bellano. It wouldn't surprise me if Johnny Toes had a hand in the car bombing. Then there's Gary Rivers. I think he'd do just about anything to further his career. Or protect it, for that matter. He volunteered to help me find Stephanie."

"He what?"

"Probably to use it in his next special: 'Runaway Girls' or 'Daughters of Dead Bookies.' "

"Not funny," she said.

"Sorry. The fourth man, Mitch Overholser, is the only one I haven't talked to. Maybe tomorrow."

Rachel was frowning and picking at the small paper napkin under her glass.

"What is it?"

"I was just thinking," she said. "If Stephanie's in Denver, she must know by now that her father's been killed."

"That's true."

"Then why hasn't she come home? Or at least contacted her mother?"

"That worries me, too. I can think of only two reasons, and neither one is very heartwarming."

Rachel nodded. "Either she doesn't want to, or she can't."

We finished our drinks. I asked her if she wanted another. She didn't. It was a school night. I drove her home and walked her to her door. I was hoping she'd ask me in for coffee.

"Thanks for the drink," she said.

"My pleasure."

"Call me, won't you? If you learn anything at all about Stephanie. Or . . ."

"Yes."

"Or if I can help."

"Sure thing."

I went home.

On Friday morning the sky was patchy blue, and the temperature had shot up to thirty-one. I had to wear shades to see my way down West Colfax, past motels and restaurants and lots filled with cars, new and used.

Honest Harry had a cracker-box office with a peaked green roof and forty used cars. The special of the month stood above the rest of the wrecks on a knee-high stand in the corner of the lot—a four-year-old black Firebird with a cracked side window and smooth rear tires. There was only one salesman. But then, I was the only customer. He finished telling the shag boy to wipe *all* the snow off the cars; then he walked over to me.

"Time to trade in the old heap, eh?" he said, nodding toward my primo-condition, fully restored, aqua-and-white Series 98 pride and joy, with Rocket V-8 engine, Jetaway HydraMatic drive, power steering, dual horns, courtesy lights, padded dash, Deluxe steering wheel, and electric clock—with *hands* on it, for chrissake, not digits—plus a heater that could roast marshmallows.

"Thank you, no," I told him. "I'm looking for Mitch Overholser."

"You found him."

He was in his late thirties, with thinning brown hair, horn-rimmed glasses, and a weak chin. He would've been about my height if he stood up straight. I guessed he'd recently lost some weight; his overcoat, though expensive, was one size too big.

"I want to talk to you about Stephanie Bellano."

"Who?"

"Joseph Bellano's daughter."

Overholser squinted at me. "What are you, a cop?"

"Private detective. I was hired by Joseph."

"Say, now, wasn't that something about Joe? Got blown up in his own car." He made a clucking sound, as if Bellano had merely lost his license.

"Why don't we go inside and talk."

"Let's don't," he said. "Inside is my brother-in-law, Harry, counting his money and looking out the window to see if I'm earning him more."

"Then let's sit in one of these cars. I'm cold."

We sat in a big white Lincoln. Overholser started the engine and turned on the heat.

"Only eighty thousand miles on this baby," he said, "and she runs like a dream."

"You were in Bellano's barbershop the day his daughter disappeared."

"I was?" He blew into his hands and rubbed them together. There was a wedding ring on his middle finger and a faint dent where it used to fit on his ring finger.

"Two weeks ago today," I said. "She came in the shop mad as hell, then ran out scared to death."

"Oh, sure, I remember now." He put his hands on the wheel as if he were ready to drive. "So?"

"She hasn't come back."

"So what's that got to do with me?"

"That's what I'd like to know."

"I don't get you," he said matter-of-factly.

I watched him closely.

"Why is Stephanie afraid of you?"

"What?" He let go of the wheel and turned in his seat to face me. "Afraid of *me?* You've got to be kidding. I'm a *father*, for crying out loud. A family man. Well, sort of. My wife took the kids. Ex-wife. But I've got a *daughter*, for crying out loud, exactly the same age as Stephanie."

"How do you know exactly how old Stephanie is?"

He blinked once. Then he licked his lips and smiled.

"Very good," he said. "Okay, I know Stephanie. She and

my daughter were friends in high school. She's probably been over to my house a half-dozen times."

"Is she there now?"

"At my house? Why, hell, no. Say, what're you getting at?"

"What do you think?"

"Look, I don't know anything about Stephanie. Sure, I heard she'd run away, but that's all. Joe called me the day after she ran out of the barbershop. Called my wife, too. Ex-wife. Neither one of us had seen her. That's all there is to that."

I was inclined to believe him. Then I remembered he sold used cars.

"What can you tell me about the other men who were in Bellano's shop that day?"

"Who remembers?"

"Stan Fowler."

"Never heard of him."

"Gary Rivers."

"Never heard— Wait, the TV guy? He was in there?"

"Didn't you recognize him?" I asked.

"I guess not."

"What about Johnny Toes Burke?"

"What about him?" Overholser's voice had hardened.

"Do you know him?"

"I know who he is. I owed his boss money once." He worked the muscles in his jaw. "Never again," he said.

"Bad news, right?"

"You wouldn't even believe it."

"Then I don't blame you for feeling desperate."

"Desperate?"

"About the possibility of Bellano selling your markers to Burke's boss, Fat Paulie DaNucci."

"What markers? What the hell are you talking about?"

"When Bellano died, you owed him forty-six thousand dollars."

He pressed his lips together so hard they wrinkled.

"Who told you that?"

"I saw Bellano's records."

"Impossible. He'd never show *anybody* his records."

"I've got a copy."

"No way," Overholser stated with utmost confidence. "The police took the only copies, and they were destroyed."

"How do you know?"

"Because . . ." Again, the wrinkled lips.

"The cops are keeping that to themselves, Mitch. How did you find out?"

He said nothing.

"Or did you have something to do with it?"

He looked scared. Then smug. He slowly shook his head from side to side.

"Those records are gone forever," he said.

"Forever, Mitch? Try ten seconds."

Which was about how long it took me to remove the computer sheets from my coat, unfold them, and show him his. I'd brought them along for theatrical purposes. It worked. Overholser's jaw dropped down to the orchestra pit. He reached for the sheet. I slapped his hand away.

"Maybe I'll give this to Fat Paulie," I said. "He can split with Angela Bellano whatever he squeezes out of you."

I opened my door.

"Wait."

He put his hand on my arm, and I shook it off. I climbed out. So did he. We faced each other across the roof of the Lincoln. He looked desperate.

"Look, I'll buy that from you myself," he said quickly. "Don't take it to Fat Paulie."

"Buy it with what, Mitch?"

"I'll pay you whatever he would. Ten percent? Okay, twenty. That'd be about—"

"I don't want money."

"What, then?"

"Where's Stephanie Bellano?"

"I don't know. I swear."

"Why did she run out of her father's shop, Mitch?"

"I don't—"

"Who was she afraid of?"

"I'm telling you I don't know."

I think I believed him. Which meant he was of no further use to me. Except . . .

"Who destroyed the cops' copy of Bellano's records?"

"I . . . don't know."

"Fine. You want these to go to Fat Paulie?" I held up the sheets.

"No, God, no. Look, I can raise the money. As much as you want. The whole forty-six. I just need some time, that's all."

"Tell Paulie." I turned to leave.

"No, wait!"

I took a few more steps.

"Isenglass," he said.

I turned and faced him.

"His name is Isenglass. He's a property clerk for the cops. I paid him to wipe out Bellano's computer disks."

"Why?"

"So no one would get hold of my markers."

"Like Fat Paulie."

"Him or someone like him."

"I see." I started to leave.

"Wait. What about the sheets?"

"Oh, these? Maybe I'll tear yours up."

"*Maybe?* But you said—"

"Look, Mitch, I'm still pretty angry with you, you know."

"Why? What'd I do?"

"You called my car a heap."

CHAPTER

20

I DROVE east on Colfax.

I felt certain Overholser didn't know Stephanie's whereabouts. If he did, he would've traded her for his markers—anything to avoid the attention of Fat Paulie DaNucci. After all, he'd hardly hesitated to trade his partner.

And now I was ready to do some trading—Overholser for information. I was sure Lieutenant MacArthur would be interested in Mitch Overholser. Particularly so if the cops were still working on the theory that whoever had destroyed Bellano's records may have also destroyed Bellano. I put MacArthur on the top of my list of phone calls, just ahead of Gary Rivers's secretary and Stan Fowler's wife.

Colfax carried me past the Auraria campus, across Speer Boulevard and Cherry Creek, and into downtown.

As I passed Bannock Street, I glanced back to my right at the front steps of the City and County Building. They were assembling the traditional Christmas display, a conglomeration of lights and painted wooden figures. Angels and elves. Mary and Santa. Rudolph and Jesus.

Something for everyone.

I turned right on Broadway, heading for my office.

I hadn't been up there in a week and a half. By design. It's either too cold to take off your coat, or else the heating pipes

bang so loudly you can't think. By now there'd be bills and
junk mail piled on the dusty floor, and the answering machine
would be filled with sales pitches and wrong numbers.

I drove past without even glancing up at the windows.

When I got home, I phoned MacArthur. I asked him how
the Bellano murder case was going.

"Slowly," he said. He didn't want to talk about it.

"Have you found out who destroyed Bellano's records?"

"We're down to two suspects. No surprise, they're both
property clerks. They're also both scared, both claiming
innocence, and both clamming up under advisement from
their attorneys."

"Is one clerk named Isenglass?"

He paused. "Why do you ask?"

I told him about Mitch Overholser. He asked me where to
find him. I told him that, too.

"On another matter," I said, "have you turned up any leads
on Stephanie Bel—"

"What?" he said, away from the phone. Then, "Sorry, Jake,
got to run. Thanks for the information."

He hung up.

"You're welcome."

I started to call the office of KNWZ. There were a few
questions I wanted to ask Gary Rivers's secretary. But
someone knocked before I got through. I put down the phone
and went to the door.

Two men stood on the landing. The one with the gun was
Johnny Toes Burke. The other one I'd never seen before. He
looked as if he'd been abandoned by his parents and raised by
gorillas.

"Can we come in?" Johnny Toes asked. He pointed the
snout of his ugly black gun at my stomach.

I backed away from the door.

They stepped in. The big guy closed the door and locked it.
There was something about him that was much scarier than

Johnny Toes Burke, and he wasn't even waving a gun. It wasn't just his size, either, although his overcoat could've covered my Olds. It was his eyes. They were as emotionless as a shark's.

"Who's your girlfriend?" I asked Johnny Toes.

The big guy didn't like that. He moved around Johnny Toes, much faster than I thought he could, and stiff-armed me in the chest with the palm of his hand. It knocked me back against the couch. I sat down.

"As you can see," Johnny Toes said, limping over to the couch, "Bruno doesn't like jokes."

"His mother named him Bruno?"

"I mean it, Lomax, don't screw around. Just hand them over and we'll be on our way." Johnny Toes looked nervous. He really *did* want to be on his way. I had a feeling he would never have come here alone, gun or no.

"Hand what over?"

"Bellano's records," Bruno said. His voice sounded as deep as a diesel. It rattled my teeth.

"What makes you think I have them?"

"A little birdy told us," Bruno rumbled.

I wondered if it had been Mitch Overholser. He could've phoned Johnny Toes and struck a deal.

"She said you made a copy," Johnny Toes said.

"She?"

"Angela Bellano. We went there yesterday and showed her a couple of badges. She let us search Joe's den. Then she told us about you and your friend Zeno. We talked to Zeno last night. She didn't believe we were cops, and she wasn't too cooperative. At least at first. But then—"

I stood up.

"What did you do to her?"

Johnny Toes stepped back and pointed the gun at my face. Bruno didn't budge.

"We didn't hurt her," Johnny Toes said. "Just scared her a little bit. She told us about the records. We know you've got the only copy."

"What's so important about those records?"

"What do you think? Bellano's markers are like money in the bank. All a guy's got to do is go collect. That is, if he's got enough muscle. Now let's have them."

"I'll trade you."

"You're in no position to be cutting deals, Lomax."

"What do you wanna trade for?" Bruno asked.

"See there, Johnny? A businessman. What I want is Stephanie Bellano."

"Her again?" Johnny Toes said. "Didn't you ask me about her before? And didn't I tell you I don't know nothing from nothing about her?"

"Where is she?"

Johnny Toes turned to Bruno. "This guy's got a one-track mind."

"Do you know where Bellano's kid is?" Bruno asked him.

"Now *you*, for chrissake?"

"Do you?"

"Fuck, no."

"He doesn't know," Bruno said to me. I believed he was right. "Give us the records."

"Sure thing."

I walked past Bruno toward the kitchen. He grabbed my shoulder to stop me before I got to the table. My .38 was lying on top in its holster. Beside it, draped over a chair, was my overcoat. What was left of Bellano's records was stuffed in the pocket.

"Outside," I said.

Bruno picked up my gun, emptied the shells in his pocket, and tossed the gun into the sink.

"Go ahead," he said.

I led them out onto the high snowy balcony. It had snowed some more since I'd last been out here, so I had to dig down into the barbecue to get to the soggy ashes.

"Here you go," I said, holding out a handful of gray mush. Johnny Toes looked confused. Bruno looked pissed.

"I burned them," I said.

"What?"

"They were of no further use to me. I thought they'd lead me to Stephanie, but they didn't. So I destroyed them."

"You're lying."

Johnny Toes's finger was white on the trigger. I wasn't sure if it was from the cold or from tension. Either way, I didn't think he'd shoot me. At least not out here. There might be witnesses. The top balcony of this old house was visible to a score of apartment windows across the alley plus half a dozen backyards.

"Inside," Johnny Toes said.

I closed the door behind us and invited them to search the apartment.

"You can even peek in my safe."

"Where is it?"

"In the bedroom closet."

Bruno went looking for the bedroom. Johnny Toes kept me company in the kitchen.

"What zoo did *he* escape from?" I asked.

"Who, Bruno?" He grinned from ear to ear. "Bruno's handy to have around."

"Yeah, well, you'd better not miss any of his feeding times, or he'll have you for lunch."

"I can handle Bruno," he said seriously.

"Sure you can."

Bruno returned.

"There's a safe like he said. It's locked."

"You hear that, Johnny? I keep my safe locked."

Bruno stepped over and tossed me against the wall as if I were a toy he no longer found amusing.

"Slow down, Bruno," Johnny Toes told him.

Bruno stared at me with dead pig eyes.

"How'd you like to take a dive off that balcony?" he asked.

"Come on, Bruno." Johnny Toes sounded scared.

"You know, Bruno, if you frighten me too much, I might forget the combination."

"Open it," he said.

"You heard him, Lomax," Johnny Toes put in, as if he were still in charge.

I could've just pulled the remainder of Bellano's records from my coat. Of course, that might not have satisfied them. Also, there was a principle involved: I didn't like being forced. And I didn't like the idea of handing the pathetic Mitch Overholser over to them; he had enough problems. But most of all, there was another gun in the safe.

They followed me into the bedroom. Bruno had yanked some of my clothes out of the closet looking for the safe, and they were scattered on the floor. The safe, a two-foot cube that weighed over a hundred pounds and that Bruno could've probably tucked under one arm and carried home, was wedged in the back corner of the closet. I bent down, spun the dial, and worked the combination. I pulled open the door and reached in.

Bruno yanked me back out of the way. Then he squatted before the safe while Johnny Toes kept his gun on me.

"Well, he's got this . . ."

Bruno took out the .357 Magnum, ejected the shells in his hand, and skidded the gun under the bed. He dropped the shells in his pocket with those from the .38. He probably saved them for snacks. It would explain his disposition.

". . . and an envelope with maybe a thousand bucks and some insurance papers and the title to his car." He looked up at me. "You need a *safe* for this crap?"

"A guy can't be too careful."

"Where's Bellano's records?" Johnny Toes said, poking me in the back with his gun.

"He ain't got 'em," Bruno said, rising to his feet and stuffing the envelope with my mad money in his coat, "or he would've had 'em in the safe."

Bruno started toward the door.

"Maybe he hid them somewhere else," Johnny Toes said.

"He wouldn't hide 'em," Bruno said, "not when he's got a safe."

"How do we know for sure? Why don't we do like we did to the other two?"

Bruno turned and looked down on Johnny Toes. The small man didn't know whether to point his gun at me or Bruno. He swallowed hard.

"We need to be sure," he said nervously.

"I *am* sure," Bruno said. "*You* want to be sure? Okay." He looked at me. "Come here."

I didn't have much choice. I walked over to him.

"Turn around."

I turned around and faced Johnny Toes. Bruno slugged me over the right kidney with such force that I dropped to my knees, gasping for breath.

"Did you have Bellano's records?"

I managed to say, "Yes."

Bruno picked me up from behind by the collar.

"And where are they now?" he asked politely.

"I burned them."

He slugged me again, and down I went, this time on all fours.

"You what?"

"Burned" was all I could get out. He punched me again so hard I heard him grunt.

"Jesus," Johnny Toes said.

I was on the floor now, curled up on my side.

"Where are they?" Bruno asked me kindly.

". . . burned."

He booted me in the tailbone. I nearly threw up on Johnny Toes's Italian loafers.

"Jesus," Johnny Toes said again. He didn't have any more stomach for this than I did.

My face was pressed to the floor. I could see my empty Magnum under the bed with the dust balls. My second gun, also empty, was in the kitchen sink, about a hundred miles away. I didn't have a third gun. Maybe I should give that some thought.

"Where are the records?" Bruno asked me once more.

Enough. The hell with Overholser and the hell with the records. ". . . burned . . . everything . . ." I was trying to tell him that I'd burned everything except the pages in my coat.

"Satisfied?" Bruno asked Johnny Toes.

"Jesus, yes. Let's get out of here."

They let themselves out the front door.

I pulled myself to my feet and managed to get all the way to the bathroom before I threw up. I felt only slightly worse than when Ken Hausom had stomped me behind the Lion's Lair.

However, there was a big difference between Ken and Bruno. With Ken, you could get even. He'd understand. He might not like it, but he'd understand. Bruno, no. With a guy like Bruno, you had two choices. Forget what he'd done and stay out of his way. Or kill him.

I flushed the toilet. Then I leaned on the sink with one hand and threw water in my face with the other. I rinsed out my mouth. Good as new.

I hobbled out to the kitchen. The lower half of my body trembled. It felt as if it'd been run over by a bus. I hoped Bruno hadn't broken the tip of my spine. I carried Bellano's records to the bedroom and locked them in the safe.

Then I got the .357 Magnum from under the bed.

I phoned MicroComp. Milton answered and told me Zeno was home sick. He sounded angry and upset.

"Just . . . leave her alone," he said.

I drove to Zeno's apartment. It hurt every time I lifted my foot to the brake pedal.

Zeno didn't answer until I'd buzzed for several minutes.

"Who . . . who is it?" Her voice sounded small and scared through the speaker.

"Zeno, it's me, Jake."

"What . . . what do you want?"

"Are you all right?"

"Please, go away."

"I'm not going away, Zeno. Let me in."

Silence.

"Zeno?"

"Are . . . are you alone?"

"Yes, I'm alone. Do you want more people?"

The door buzzed, and I pulled it open. I went up the elevator and knocked on Zeno's door. She opened it on the chain, then let me in.

She was wearing a ratty terry-cloth bathrobe and slippers. Her eyes looked puffy. Her hair was matted to one side of her head, as if she'd just gotten out of bed.

"Are you all right?"

She looked at the floor and shook her head no. I noticed a faint smell in the room. Metallic—familiar, yet totally out of place.

"Zeno, tell me what happened."

She crossed her arms and hugged herself. A tear started down from each eye.

I put my arms around her. "It's okay now, babe, you can tell me."

"Oh, God, Jake." She buried her face in my chest and began to sob. Her thin body shook beneath her robe like a small frightened animal. I had to shift my feet, because it hurt to stand. After a few minutes, Zeno pushed back from me and wiped her eyes with the cloth belt of her robe.

"I . . . I thought they were going to kill us."

"Johnny Toes Burke and Bruno."

"They didn't give their names. One was skinny and shifty looking. The other was a hulk."

"What did they do?"

She took a breath and let it out with a shudder.

"They came here last night," she said. "Milton and I were watching television. I don't know how they got into the building, because they didn't buzz. They knocked on the door, and I opened it without thinking. I mean, I thought it must be one of the residents. They started pushing us around. Milton yelled at them to leave, and the little man hit him with his fist. It made Milton's mouth bleed. Poor Milton. I . . . I can't face him."

"It wasn't your fault, Zeno." It was mine.

She hugged herself. "They wanted the copy of Joseph Bellano's computer records, and they threatened to hurt us if I didn't give it to them. They'd already talked to Angela Bellano and the people at MicroComp, so they knew you and I had made a copy. I didn't know how to lie to them, Jake. I mean, they already knew. I told them I'd given you the printout, then erased the disks. They didn't believe me. That's when . . ."

"What?"

"The big man . . ."

"Bruno."

"Bruno. He said he knew how to make us talk, and he left. He came back ten minutes later with a can of gasoline."

That was the smell.

"They tied our hands behind us with towels and shoved us down on the couch and splashed gas all over us. And then . . . and then Bruno took out a lighter and flipped on the flame and started waving it around us and said that if I didn't tell him where my copy was, he'd set us both on fire. God, Jake, he would've done it, too. I could see it in his eyes. The other man, the smaller one, he was scared, too. Milton started crying and begging him not to do it. I . . . I guess that convinced them, because they untied us and left."

"Did you call the police?" I asked, my voice amazingly calm.

Zeno shook her head. "They said if we did they'd come back and . . . finish the job. Jake, I'm afraid to go out or even answer the door. Those two men, if they came back . . ."

"They won't bother you again, Zeno. Ever."

She didn't look convinced. "And Milton . . . he . . . doesn't want to see me again."

"Did he say that?"

"No, but . . ."

"Hey, Zeno, that man *cares* about you."

I went to the kitchen, lifted the phone, and called Micro-Comp. I told Milton that Zeno needed to see him, and that he should probably take the rest of the day off and get his butt over to her apartment on the double. I hung up.

"He's coming," I said.

She gave me a weak smile and a kiss on the cheek.

I left.

CHAPTER

21

I DROVE straight from Zeno's to Johnny Toes's apartment. I drove slowly. I needed time to calm down. If I got my hands on him right now, I might not let go until it was too late for both of us.

He lived in a cheesy low rise near Havana and Jewell. I'd gotten his address last week when I'd first gone looking for him. I assumed he hadn't moved since then. His name was still on the mail slot, and the box was full of envelopes. It hurt to climb the stairs, but I made it to the second floor. I walked along the outside balcony to Johnny Toes's number.

It hurt to raise my leg too high, but I did it, anyway. Then I kicked in the door.

The place had enough velour to warm the heart of the meanest pimp. There were erotic paintings on the walls and pillows on the floor. The room smelled of stale marijuana. I turned the apartment upside down. Johnny Toes wasn't home.

When I came out, there were a couple of guys and a young woman standing on the balcony, staring at me.

"I'm calling the cops," one guy said.

"So call them."

I stomped down to my car and drove to Terry's. No one there had seen Johnny Toes for days. No one there knew a

bruiser named Bruno. I drove around to several more bars
and got the same story—no Johnny Toes. My pulse, though,
had settled down to normal. I was thinking more clearly now.

I was thinking of Fat Paulie DaNucci.

If Johnny Toes worked for DaNucci, then he'd terrorized
Zeno and Milton under orders. It was DaNucci who wanted
Bellano's records. And it was probably DaNucci who'd been
responsible for the bomb that had killed Bellano. I wondered
if DaNucci was the "man" Stephanie had called.

One thing, though, was clear: DaNucci was the com-
mander. Johnny Toes and Bruno were merely soldiers.

It was time to go to the top.

It was two-thirty Saturday morning.

I stood in the dark with the garbage cans. The toes of my
shoes were just beyond the cone of yellow light thrown from
the fixture over the rear door of Giancio's Italian Restaurant.
My fingers and toes ached from the cold. I shuffled my feet
and clapped my hands. It woke up my kidneys, which were
still convalescing from Bruno's pounding.

I'd spent the afternoon and half the evening making calls
about Fat Paulie DaNucci. What I found was that he spent a
lot of time at his restaurant. The place closed at ten, and the
poker game started at ten-thirty. Just DaNucci and some of
his pals. They usually broke up around two, by which time
they'd had their fill of cigars, Sambuca, and seven-card stud.

When I'd arrived an hour ago, there'd been five cars in the
parking lot. Not long ago, they'd begun to leave, a few
throwing headlight beams my way. One, in fact, had touched
my pant leg and turned me to stone.

Now the lot was empty save for one car—Fat Paulie
DaNucci's shiny black Cadillac.

Suddenly the back door of the building opened. Two men
stepped out. One was big and tall; the other was big and fat.
They both wore dark overcoats. The fat one wore a hat.

"Mother o' God, it's cold," he said.

"Why don't you go back in, Mr. DaNucci? I'll get the car heated up."

"Forget it, Vinny. Let's just go."

They walked toward the Caddy. I stepped out of the shadows behind the fat guy. He started to turn, and I poked the muzzle of the Magnum under his ear.

"Hey—"

"Freeze, Paulie. No pun intended."

Vinny had already spun around and yanked out his piece and was pointing it our way. I hid behind Fat Paulie.

"Tell him to lose the gun, Paulie, or you're going to be deaf in one ear."

"Let him go, motherfucker," Vinny told me.

"Relax, Vinny. This dumb shit only wants my money. Ain't that right, you dumb shit?" Fat Paulie didn't sound frightened, as I'd hoped. He sounded irritated. "It's in my pants pocket, dumb shit. You want me to take it out for you? Or are you queer besides being dumb and you wanna reach in there yourself and play with me first."

"Get in the car."

"What for?"

"We're going to talk."

"About what?"

"Move it, Paulie."

"Drop down, Mr. DaNucci. I'll ice this son of a bitch."

"Put away the gun, Vinny," Fat Paulie said. "You're forgetting something, right?"

Vinny frowned, his one eyebrow dipping down to form a heavy, hairy black V.

"Right, Vinny?"

"Oh, yeah, right." Vinny put away his gun.

"Right," Fat Paulie said.

Obviously there was something going. I didn't know what it was, but I didn't like it. I waved my gun, and we all went around to the left side of the car. Vinny climbed in the driver's seat. Fat Paulie and I squeezed in the back.

"Keep your hands in front of you," I told Vinny. "If you even *look* back here, I'll shoot your boss. Start the car."

"Now, Mr. DaNucci?"

"Not yet."

They knew something that I didn't, and it was beginning to make me nervous.

"First let's hear what Dumb Shit has to say. Start the car."

Vinny turned the key. "Where we going?"

"It doesn't matter," I said. "Just drive."

"Take the highway," Fat Paulie said.

Then he leaned back in the seat, smiling comfortably, as if he were the pope on tour. He outweighed the pope, though, by at least a hundred pounds. His cheeks were so chubby they pushed his eyes closed from below. Fifty years ago he'd probably been a cute kid. Adorable. Now he was a bookie and a loan shark and a few other things that he'd been charged with but never convicted of. And, like the pope, he'd never been in prison.

Vinny turned right on Thirty-eighth Avenue and headed toward the freeway. There was little traffic. A cop car went by in the other direction. But we were invisible to him behind our darkly tinted windows.

"So," Fat Paulie said, "here we are driving in the car. Smooth, huh? My wife loves it. She's waiting for me at home. So what do you want to talk about, Dumb Shit?"

"About whether I should shoot you or not."

"What?" he said, surprised and angry but certainly not scared. "I don't even *know* you. Who're you working for?"

"Right now I'm working for myself," I said.

"So what's your problem?"

Vinny steered the Caddy under the railroad bridge, then around the ramp onto southbound I-25. He kept our speed at fifty-four miles an hour. Cars zipped past as if we were crawling.

"My problem, Paulie, is that you sent a pair of goons to terrorize my friends and I'm not very happy about it."

"You hear that, Vinny? He's not happy."

"I heard him, Mr. DaNucci. You want me to do it now?"

"Not yet, Vinny."

"Not ever, Vinny," I said. "Either one of your hands comes off the wheel and I blow your boss's head all over the windows."

"Just say the word, Mr. DaNucci." Vinny acted as if he hadn't heard me.

"So, who are these friends of yours?" Fat Paulie asked me conversationally.

"Eunice Zenkowski and her boyfriend, Milton."

Fat Paulie shrugged under his overcoat. "Never heard of them."

"Maybe you don't know their names, but you know who they are. You sent Johnny Toes Burke and—"

"Johnny Toes? Hah! That little prick don't work for me no more. I got rid of him when I found out he was selling drugs to kids. He'd do anything for a dollar. I fired him what, Vinny, a year ago?"

"At least a year, Mr. DaNucci."

"There, you see?" Fat Paulie said. "So what *else* is on your mind, you dumb shit?"

"You've got a nasty mouth for a guy who could get blown away at any moment."

Fat Paulie snorted. "Number one, you're not gonna shoot me or you woulda done it back there in the parking lot. And number two, I called you a dumb shit because number one, you gotta be a dumb shit to pull something like this, and number two, I don't know your name."

"Jacob Lomax."

"Lomax. What the hell kind of name is that?"

"A last name."

"You hear that, Vinny? A comedian."

"I heard."

"Okay, so, Mr. Jacob Lomax, now you know that I never heard of your friends, and you know that Johnny Toes don't work for me anymore, so now can we all go home and go to sleep? It's late."

"Nice try, Paulie, but I happen to *know* you sent those two clowns to my friend's apartment." I didn't know it at all. "And after that they paid me a visit."

"You don't listen so good, do you, Mr. Jacob Lomax? What've I just been telling you? Okay, wait, let me ask you something— Why would I send a guy who don't work for me anymore to push around—is that what he did, push?—to push around some people I never heard of? Tell me why."

"To get Joseph Bellano's books."

"Books? What books?"

"His bookmaking records. Mainly his accounts receivable."

"What, are you kidding me? I don't have enough trouble right now with *my* records and an upcoming trial that I gotta be collecting *another* guy's records?"

"They're worth a lot of money," I said, but I was beginning to lose my conviction.

"Maybe to a cheapie like Johnny Toes they're worth money, but not to me. To me they'd be more trouble than they're worth. I've got all the accounts I can handle."

I was beginning to believe him.

"You're telling me Johnny Toes did that on his own?"

"I'm not telling you anything," Fat Paulie said. "You're the one doing the telling. But it looks that way, doesn't it? One thing that surprises me, though, is that I didn't think Johnny Toes had the guts to push *anybody* around, much less a guy your size. Which reminds me, why don't you put away the gun? Your hand must be getting tired."

It was, but I kept it pointed at DaNucci's grand belly.

"Johnny Toes had help," I said. "A bruiser named Bruno."

"Bruno Tartalia?"

"I didn't catch his last name."

"A big ugly guy with dead eyes?"

"That's him."

"You're maybe lucky you're alive there, Mr. Jacob Lomax. This Bruno is a very nasty character, especially if he doesn't get what he wants."

"So you do know him."

"Sure I know him. He used to work for me. For a very short time. Then I fired him. Actually, I asked him to resign, because with a guy like Bruno, you don't want to get him too upset."

"I coulda handled him, Mr. DaNucci."

"Sure you could," Fat Paulie said to the back of Vinny's head. Then he glanced at me, rolled his eyes, and shook his head, like one parent to another. "The trouble with Bruno," he said to me, "was that he'd forget himself. Like he'd forget that all I wanted him to do was talk to a guy and ask him why he was late with an interest payment. Just talk to him. Scare him with his looks. Not break both the guy's arms so the guy couldn't even go to work to pick up his paycheck, much less *endorse* the damn thing."

Fat Paulie shook his head and chuckled to himself, his round body moving under his coat.

"The government wants to do something about Iran," he said, "they should fly Bruno over there and tell him all of them owe us money, then drop him out of the plane. Couple of weeks that whole country'd be a hospital ward."

When nobody laughed, Fat Paulie sighed.

"Yeah, well," he said. Then, "So Bruno and Johnny Toes are after poor Joe's books, huh?"

" 'Poor Joe.' Like he was a friend of yours."

"As a matter of fact, he was. It was a terrible thing that happened to him. I'd like to get my hands on whoever did it."

"Some people think you did it."

Fat Paulie jerked around in his seat, and for a moment I thought he was going to attack me. I raised the Magnum so he could see it better.

"That's bullshit!" he yelled at me. "Do you hear me? Joe

Bellano, God rest his soul, was my friend since we were practically kids."

"He told me you were afraid he'd testify against you."

"Afraid? More bullshit. I knew he'd never testify against me. He was an honorable man. Besides, he couldn't hurt me no matter what he said, not at the trial, not anywhere. My lawyers already told me not to worry about the trial. Now you tell *me* something. What's your connection with Joe Bellano?"

"He hired me to find his daughter the day before he was murdered."

Fat Paulie blinked at me a couple of times.

"I knew there was a private dick trying to track down Joe's kid. So that's you, huh?"

"How did you know that?"

"You hear things," Fat Paulie said. "You wanna put away the piece now? I think maybe we're on the same side."

"Maybe," I said. I didn't see how. "But now that I've threatened you, maybe I need the gun for protection."

"That gun would do him a lot of good, wouldn't it, Vinny?"

Vinny laughed. Fat Paulie joined him.

"What's so funny?"

"Nothing," Fat Paulie said. "Vinny, turn us around."

Vinny took the next exit, then swung us under the freeway and back up the on-ramp heading north. I knew now that Johnny Toes Burke and Bruno Tartalia were working on their own. I also realized I'd been sidetracked from my main objective—locating Stephanie Bellano—by my own desire for revenge. I'd harassed Fat Paulie for nothing. The problem was that I *had* harassed him. I'd have to start checking the Olds for bombs.

"So," Fat Paulie said to me as if I'd been wrong about that and we really were pals, "have you had any luck looking for Joe's kid, what's her name, Stephanie?"

"Not much," I said.

"God, poor Angela. She must be going crazy. I know, I've

got three daughters. Of course, they're all grown now, with families of their own."

I figured next he'd show me pictures. Maybe we *were* pals.

So I told him about the four customers and Big Pine and the church near Wray. I told him there was probably a connection between Stephanie's running and Bellano's death. I also told him about the only connection I'd found: Both Stephanie's father and her ex-employer in Big Pine had been murdered with military weapons.

"The cops traced the bomb—it was a land mine—to a theft at the armory last year."

"No shit?" Fat Paulie tugged at his fat bottom lip. "This armory thing—" he said. "Let's say I know a guy who knows a guy who.can tell me where that stuff went. Would that help?"

"It might."

Fat Paulie nodded. "If I hear something, I'll call you."

I put away my gun, tentatively, then dug out a card. Fat Paulie held it up as if it were a rare stamp.

"Hey, Vinny, he's got business cards and everything."

"I'm impressed," Vinny said.

We drove back to Giancio's. I opened my door but didn't get out.

"I apologize for threatening you, Paulie."

"Believe me, Mr. Jacob Lomax, you were never a threat. The main thing is, you find Angela Bellano's kid."

"Right. And what do you mean I was never a threat?"

"He's curious, Vinny."

"I noticed."

"Should I tell him?"

"I wouldn't, Mr. DaNucci."

Fat Paulie grinned at me like a chubby little juvenile delinquent. "Promise not to tell?"

I promised.

"You see," he said, unable to keep his wonderful secret to

himself, "I had some novelties installed under the seats—one up front next to Vinny, two back here. In fact, you're sitting right over one. It's a short steel tube with a 10-gauge shotgun shell, and it's pointed right up your ass. Vinny pushes the correct button with his foot, and my upholstery gets ripped all to hell. Of course, so do you. Nice, huh?"

I tried to grin and swallow at the same time.

"Yeah, nice."

I turned to get out, and Fat Paulie grabbed my shoulder. When I looked back, I was looking at two guns—one in Fat Paulie's hand, one in Vinny's.

"These things go off real easy," Fat Paulie said in all sincerity. He wasn't smiling. "You gotta be careful where you point them."

"Yes, sir."

"Sir. I like that. Something else you should know. I won eight hundred bucks tonight playing poker. It put me in a very good mood. Consider yourself lucky I didn't *lose* eight hundred. You hear what I'm saying, Mr. Private Detective?"

"I hear."

"He hears, Vinny."

"He'd better," Vinny said.

I got out.

They drove away.

CHAPTER

22

IT WAS NEARLY FOUR in the morning when I got home.

The confrontation with Fat Paulie had left me drained. It had also left me worried. Fat Paulie was not one to ignore an embarrassment. And I had definitely embarrassed him. In front of his bodyguard, too. Sure, he'd acted as if all were forgiven since I was trying to help the widow of his old, dead pal Joe.

The key word, though, was "acted."

If Fat Paulie wanted to get even, how long would he wait? I wondered when I could stop looking over my shoulder. If ever.

I slept until eight and woke up feeling as if I'd been too long in bed. I showered, shaved, got dressed, and ate some breakfast. Then I began to refocus. I'd been distracted by Johnny Toes Burke, Bruno Tartalia, and Fat Paulie DaNucci. My best chance at finding Stephanie still seemed to lay with the four customers.

Since Johnny Toes was being so blatant about Bellano's records, I doubted he was involved with Bellano's daughter. And Mitch Overholser hadn't struck me as the type to mess with young girls *or* with land mines. That left Gary Rivers and Stan Fowler. I needed more information on each of them.

I phoned station KNWZ. Gary Rivers was not working

today. But Carol was. She remembered me. I worked for a newspaper.

"Carol, you told me before that Gary's wife went to live with her parents in Colorado Springs."

"That's right," she said.

"Is she still there?"

"Yes."

"Would you have the address?"

"Just a moment."

I heard her flipping through a Rolodex. "Here it is."

I wrote it down.

"You said that Mrs. Rivers has been down there since sometime this summer, correct?"

"Yes. She went to live with her parents in early August."

"And this was because of a death in the family?"

"It was their son," she said.

"Their son? How old was he?"

"He was just a few months old. It was sudden infant death syndrome."

I found myself squeezing the receiver.

"Did this happen in Denver or Colorado Springs?"

"Neither. They were in the mountains."

"Where, exactly?"

"Big Pine Lake."

I was silent for a moment.

"But you're not going to print that, are you?"

"What? Oh, no, of course not. Just one more question, Carol. Was Gary Rivers ever in the military?"

"No."

I thanked her and hung up.

Gary Rivers and Stephanie had both been in Big Pine this summer. Betty Phipps had shown me the record of a dead infant that had been brought to the clinic. The baby's last name wasn't Rivers, but that didn't mean it wasn't his kid. Stephanie had seen the baby. She must have seen Rivers, too. But why would that make her afraid of Rivers?

I'd ask him.

Carol had said he'd never been in the military. However, he could still be familiar with military weapons. Land mines, for example.

I'd ask him about that, too.

I phoned his house. Not that I wanted to chat with him over the phone; I just wanted to see if he was home. He wasn't. I tried his car phone. He didn't answer that, either.

I considered my options. I could look for him. I could break into his house and wait for him. I could drive down to Colorado Springs and talk to his wife.

Or I could talk to Stan Fowler's wife.

Just because Rivers looked very suspicious right now was no reason for me to forget about Fowler. After all, he'd hustled young women in the Lion's Lair. And he'd owed Stephanie's father nearly a hundred thousand dollars.

Rivers's wife or Fowler's wife?

Fowler's was closer.

Everyone knew where Stan Fowler lived. He'd frequently used his house for TV commercials. We'd all seen what a regular guy he was, standing on his front porch, asking us in to look at his new TV sets and appliances.

I took Speer Boulevard across town, then drove west on Thirty-second Avenue all the way into Applewood.

The Fowler residence, a sprawling split-level ranch-style monstrosity was on Crabapple Road, less than a mile from Rolling Hills Country Club. Coincidentally—or maybe not—the house was also less than a mile from the armory at Camp George West. I left the Olds in the wide circular drive and went up to the front door. Actually, they were double doors, which made it convenient to usher in camera crews.

Mrs. Fowler answered the door.

Stan's salesman, Mr. Roberson, had told me she was an alcoholic. He'd been right.

Her hair was messy, and I could smell the gin from out on the porch. She wore brown pants and a yellow sweater with a fresh stain on the right cuff. She was well into middle age, and she'd probably once been attractive. Now she just didn't care. She'd done a halfhearted job of putting on her makeup this morning. Her lipstick was smeared at the corner of her mouth, giving her a lopsided grin, like a clown.

"What do you want?" Her voice was husky from years of pouring booze down her throat.

I introduced myself and held up a card. She leaned forward, squinting, then caught herself from falling into the screen door.

"I can't read a damn thing without my glasses," she said. "What's this all about, anyway? You're a detective?"

"A private detective. I'd like—"

"A private eye? Like on TV or something?"

"I wish. I'd like to talk to you about your husband."

"What's the bastard done now?" she said without hesitation.

"Could we talk inside?"

She gave me a coy look. "You wouldn't try to take advantage of me just because I'm home all alone, would you?"

I started to say I wouldn't, but she'd already unlatched the screen and pushed it open.

The front room was enormous. The furniture was arranged in clusters, reminding me of a showroom. Everything was neat and tidy, so it was a cinch Mrs. Fowler had a cleaning woman.

"What're you drinking?" she wanted to know.

"Nothing, thanks."

"Come on, now."

"Okay, beer, if you've got it."

"I've got whatever you want." She believed it, too. "Have a seat."

She walked a crooked line to the kitchen. Not even noon and already bombed. I wondered if living with Stan had done that to her. I sat in the nearest furniture cluster—an off-white sofa and matching chairs arranged around a black lacquered coffee table. A big ugly green porcelain frog squatted on an end table. There was a lamp stuck in his back.

Mrs. Fowler returned with a bottle of Heineken and a tumbler of gin and ice. She plopped down next to me on the couch, spilling a little gin. She set the beer bottle on my knee, and I took it from her.

"So. A real-life private eye."

"Mrs. Fowler, your hus—"

"Call me Madge."

"Right. Madge. Now about your—"

"And you are? Where the hell'd I put that card?"

"Jacob Lomax."

"Jake. I like that. Drink up." She showed me how. "So what's on your mind, Jake?"

"I'm working for the parents of Stephanie Bellano. She ran away two weeks ago, and no one's seen her. It's possible your husband may have known her and—"

"How old is she?" she asked me matter-of-factly.

"Eighteen."

"Then Stan probably knew her." She took a big bite out of her drink, leaving blood-red lipstick on the rim.

"Why do you say that?"

She waved her hand and stared across the room as if she were addressing a crowd. "Because he likes them young, Jake."

"Have you ever heard him mention her name?"

"Nope." Then, "What was it again?"

"Stephanie Bellano."

She shrugged. "Nope. How's your beer?"

"Fine. Was Stan ever at Big Pine Lake?"

Madge Fowler smiled at me and cocked her head as if she'd just remembered something. "Wait a minute, now. Is Stan in some kind of trouble? I mean, cop trouble?"

"It's possible."

"Good!" she said, grinning, then slapped my knee. "I

always knew that son of a bitch would end up in prison. Serve him right. At least it'll keep him out of the kiddy bars, where he tries to dip his noodle into everyone under twenty-five who wears panties. He hasn't even *tried* to get it up for *me* in two years." She swallowed some more of her drink. Her eyes lost what little focus they'd had. "He wants a divorce, but there's no way I'll give it to him. I'm having too much fun making his home life hell. Hell, I *want* him to go to prison. The convicts will do to him what he's been doing to those young girls."

She rattled the ice in her glass. There wasn't much gin left. Then she shook her head and smiled politely at me.

"Now, where were we?"

"Has Stan ever been to Big Pine Lake?"

"Sure. We used to go all the time." She smiled at the memory. "He'd take me fishing out on the lake."

"Did you go there this summer?"

"*I* didn't go. He hasn't taken me anywhere in years."

"Did Stan go there?"

"Sure he went. We've got a cabin. He goes a couple times a year. Says it's to entertain business clients. I let him think I believe him, the stupid son of a bitch."

"It's not business, then?"

"Hell, no," she said. "He takes fresh meat."

"Do you mean girls he picks up in bars?"

"That's exactly what I mean." She pulled herself unsteadily to her feet and downed the rest of her drink, keeping the ice in the tumbler with her teeth. "Ready for another?"

"Why not?"

I set down my full bottle of beer and followed her to the kitchen. I wondered if Stan Fowler had managed to lure Stephanie into his cabin. I wondered if she was there now, perhaps against her will.

"Where exactly is your cabin?" I asked Madge Fowler.

"God, it's so beautiful up there in the summer." She pulled open the left-hand door of the stainless-steel refrigerator and began filling her glass with ice. "The pine trees and the blue sky and all of it reflected in the lake. And the smell! God, it was nice." She closed the door with a whumpf.

"Where's your cabin?"

"Around the back of the lake," she said, reaching for the bottle of Beefeater. "Do you know Big Pine?"

"Somewhat."

She poured gin and told me how to get to the cabin. Then she said, "Why don't we put on some music and get comfortable?"

"I really can't stay."

She looked disappointed.

"Are you sure? Stan doesn't lock up the store until six tonight. And God only knows what time he'll make it home."

"Maybe next time. One more thing, Mrs. Fow—"

"Madge." She wagged her finger at me. "Madge."

"Madge. Was Stan in the service?"

"The service? You mean the army? Sure." She smiled broadly. Another fond memory. "God, you should have seen him in a uniform. Jesus Christ, he was handsome."

"What did he do in the army?"

"Do? I don't know. The usual things, I guess."

"Was he mostly in the office?"

"Who, Stan? No. He was in demolitions."

"Are you sure?"

"Sure I'm sure. He was in the Korean War. Except they called it a 'conflict.' He even won a medal. I think he got it for blowing things up."

After I'd left Madge Fowler's house, I'd driven east on Thirty-second to catch I-70, then headed into the mountains. The roads had been pretty good all the way, and it had taken me only a little over two hours to get to Big Pine.

I figured if I found Stephanie in Fowler's cabin, I'd bring her home and *then* go talk to Stan. If "talk" was the proper word. If she wasn't there, I'd talk to him, anyway. However, I didn't see any reason to listen to his lies *before* I went up there. Either way, we'd talk. I now had two connections between him and Stephanie: the Lion's Lair and Big Pine Lake. More, he was handy with military explosives.

I steered around the lake. The sky and the water were the same weak shade of gray. I drove past numerous cabins, including the one belonging to Betty Phipps. It didn't look as if she was home.

I found Fowler's cabin and parked before it.

I waded through shin-high snow to the front door. Fowler's last name was burned into a wooden plaque and nailed to the door. There were no visible footprints but mine. I knocked anyway. The snow in my shoes was beginning to melt into my socks. I knocked again.

No answer.

I waded through crusty snow to the side of the cabin and peered through the window. There was a small front room with a fireplace and rustic furniture.

I broke out a pane of glass. Then I unlocked the window, raised it, and pulled myself over the sill.

It was at least as cold inside the cabin as it was outside. I followed my cloudy breath from room to room—one small bedroom, one small kitchen, one tiny bathroom. All empty. All cold. The place was obviously closed for the winter.

I unlocked the back door and looked out over smooth, even snow. It hadn't been disturbed for weeks, maybe longer.

I found some duct tape in a drawer in the kitchen and some cardboard under the sink. I put a temporary patch over the broken windowpane. Then I drove back to Denver, letting the air from the heater dry my pants cuffs.

I didn't expect much cooperation from Stan, so I went home before going to his store. I wanted a gun. The phone was ringing before I got the door open. It was Gary Rivers.

"I've been trying to reach you for hours," he said. He sounded agitated.

"*You're* looking for *me?* There's a switch."

"I'm at Mrs. Bellano's house, and she—"

"You're where? What're you doing there?"

"I'll explain later. She told me to call you. You'd better get over here right away. She's received a ransom demand."

"What?"

"Stephanie's been kidnapped."

CHAPTER

23

ANGELA'S BROTHER, Tony, answered the door and let me in.

"We're in the kitchen," he said, leading the way.

I expected the "we" to include plainclothes cops. But there were only Angela Bellano and Gary Rivers. He fidgeted with his tie as if it were out of place. In my opinion, *he* was out of place.

"What happened?" I asked Angela.

She was sitting at the kitchen table, fingering a rosary. Not praying, just worrying the beads. There was a plain white envelope on the table. It had been ripped open at one end. On top of it lay a gold ring.

"They've got Stephanie."

"Angela got a call this morning," Tony explained, putting his hand on her shoulder. "The man said he had Stephanie and that if we wanted to see her again we'd have to pay him a hundred thousand dollars."

"Did you call the police?"

"No!" Angela came half out of the chair, then settled back down. "No police."

Tony kept his hand on her shoulder. "The guy on the phone said if we called the cops he'd kill Stephanie."

"I think we should call the police right now," I said, "no matter what this guy told you."

"No." Angela was firm.

"Listen, I know you're concerned for Stephanie's safety. But believe me, the safest way to handle this is with the police. They—"

"No, please."

"They can put a tap on the phone. They can do a hundred different things that we can't do to—"

"We can pay the ransom," Tony said flatly. "And that's what we're going to do. Now, you can help us with that, or you can get the hell out."

"Tony . . ."

"Yeah, yeah."

He let go of her shoulder, then moved toward the refrigerator, bumping into me on the way. Rivers jumped out of his path like a startled squirrel.

"Mr. Lomax," Angela said, "we can't call in the police. Not until Stephanie is safely home. We can't take the chance. These men, they might be watching the house. And if they found out— You understand my concern, don't you?"

I understood it, but I didn't agree with it.

"Sure," I said.

"Then you'll help?"

"If I can."

"And no police?"

"No." At least not this minute.

"Just be sure about that part," Tony said. He was standing by the refrigerator with a carton of milk in one hand and a half-full glass in the other. Ulcers.

I sat at the table with Angela.

"When exactly did the man call?" It was nearly five.

"Just after noon," Gary Rivers said. "I remember checking my watch."

I looked at him. "You were here?"

He nodded yes.

"Doing what?"

"Don't you know?" Tony said, a wiseass grin on his face. "He *works* for you."

"He said that?"

"I said I was working 'with,' not 'for.' " Rivers looked at me. "I told you I was going to help you find Stephanie, remember?"

"We'll talk about that later." I turned to Angela. "Tell me what the man on the phone said. Exactly."

"Well, first he asked me if I was Angela Bellano. Then he told me to look in the mailbox. He said there was a present for me. Then he hung up. I thought it was some kind of a joke. I went out and found this."

She nudged the envelope toward me. I picked up the ring. It was a simple yellow gold band with tiny flowers etched in the surface. There was a single word inscribed inside: Bellano.

"It belonged to Joe's mother," Angela said. "Joe gave it to Stephanie on her sixteenth birthday."

I set the ring down. Angela stared at it wistfully.

"A few minutes later the man called back," she said. "He said, 'We have your daughter and—' "

"He said 'we'?"

She nodded. " 'We have your daughter, and if you want her back alive, you'd better come up with one hundred thousand dollars in cash. Fifties and hundreds.' I asked him if Stephanie was all right. He said she was fine now but she wouldn't be if I didn't get the money. I said I wanted to talk to her. He said not until I got the money. I begged him, but he wouldn't listen. He said if I called the police or told anyone I'd never see her again. I told him I didn't know how long it would take me to get that much money, you know, all in cash. He said, 'Have it by Monday.' Then he hung up."

No one spoke for a few moments. Angela shifted her rosary to her left hand and picked up Stephanie's ring. She rubbed it slowly between her thumb and forefinger as if it, too, were a talisman against evil.

"Do you remember anything else he said?"

"Isn't that enough?" Tony asked sarcastically.

"Nothing else." Angela touched the ring to her bottom lip.

"How did he sound? Young? Old? Ethnic?"

"He sounded . . . funny. As if he was trying to disguise his voice."

Disguise? I wondered if he was afraid Angela would recognize him.

"There's something here that bothers me," I said.

"You mean *besides* my sister's kid being kidnapped?" Tony sounded mean. He looked it, too, milk glass or no. Maybe Angela wanted me here, but he sure as hell didn't. I wondered what he thought about the presence of Rivers. I glanced over at the smaller man, who was standing quietly in the corner, trying hard not to be noticed.

"They didn't let Angela talk to Stephanie," I told Tony.

"So what?"

"How do we know they really have her?"

"The ring, for chrissake."

"Right, the ring."

That bothered me, too, and I wasn't sure why. Maybe because it seemed like an unusual item to send as proof. More to the point would have been Stephanie's driver's license. Or articles of clothing. But a ring? How did they know Angela Bellano could identify it unless they knew it was something special? Or unless they'd removed it from her finger and read the inscription? Maybe that's what had happened. The next question was, had her finger been warm or stone-cold?

"How do we know she's all right?" I said.

"She *is* all right." Angela was staunch. Her eyes, though, were moist. "I know she is."

"We can't know for sure unless they let us talk to her."

"Hey." Tony crossed the kitchen in three long strides. "We *know* she's all right." He shoved me so hard I almost fell out of my chair.

I stood. Tony squared off, ready to punch me out.

"Tony, no!"

Rivers came forward, like a small referee in a heavyweight bout. He got between us and raised his hands to our chests.

"Take it easy, both of—"

Tony shoved him aside, not hard, but hard enough to knock Rivers back against the counter.

"Stop it!" Angela cried. "My God, what are you all doing? It's my little girl." Her hands were fists. Stephanie's ring was clenched in one, the rosary in the other. The black beads stood out on her skin like drops of blood.

Tony pushed past me to get to his sister.

"There, Angela." He pulled my chair next to hers, sat down, and put his arm around her shoulders. "There, it's gonna be all right. Everything's gonna be fine." He looked at me and glared, as if this whole thing were my fault. "Why don't you leave us alone for a while," he said.

"We'll be in the next room," I said. I looked at Rivers, then walked out. He followed me. I led him through the dining area to the living room, then turned to face him.

"I know you're wondering why I was here when—"

"You lied to me, Rivers."

He blinked. "What?"

"Last Monday you told me you'd never met Stephanie Bellano. You said the first time you saw her was in her father's barbershop the day she ran away."

"That's true."

"No, it isn't. She was working at the Big Pine Medical Clinic last July when you brought in your dead baby son."

He turned pale. "How did you . . . ?"

"I asked around. Why did you change his name on the medical report? What were you trying to hide?"

"Change his name?"

"Thomas Rhynsburger."

Rivers cleared his throat, regaining his composure.

"Rhynsburger is his name. It's *my* name. Everyone knows me by 'Rivers,' but that's my professional name."

"Why didn't you tell me you'd seen Stephanie at the clinic?"

"I *didn't* see her. I didn't know she was there until just now."

"You're lying."

"No, I . . . Look, if you say Stephanie was there, fine, I believe you. I mean, I knew *somebody* was there besides the doctor, but I honestly didn't look at her face. I was . . ."

He looked away.

"It's painful to talk about," he said, avoiding my eyes. "My wife and I and Tommy were up there on vacation. In fact, now that I think about it, I might have heard about Big Pine from Joe Bellano. Anyway, we rented a cabin on the lake. On the second morning there my wife went to take Tommy out of his crib. He wasn't breathing. She started screaming, and I ran in there and tried mouth-to-mouth. Nothing. We rushed him to the clinic. Dr. Early tried to revive him, but it was too late. He was already . . . gone."

He looked up at me and shook his head.

"I guess I remember someone else being there," he said. "But before today I couldn't have told you if it was a man or a woman. I was, well, in shock."

"I see." I think I was beginning to. "I'm wondering if it was you that Stephanie ran from that day in the shop."

"Me? But why?"

"In a minute. First, I want to know what you're doing here."

He shrugged his shoulders. "Trying to help."

"Help who?"

Some color rose to his cheeks.

"You think I'm pretty selfish, don't you, Lomax?"

"As a matter of fact, yes."

"Well, I don't give a damn what you think. The truth is, I feel *sorry* for this woman. I want to help her if I can. If nothing else, I can give her moral support. Is there something wrong with that?"

"These people are hardly your best friends. I think you're hanging around waiting for a news story to happen. And wasn't it a coincidence that you were here when the phone call came?"

Now his whole face turned red.

"Yes, it *was* a coincidence. This is the third time I've been here since Monday. And, okay, maybe it is for selfish reasons. I think this is a great human-interest story, and I want to be around when Stephanie comes home. I think other people would like to hear about this."

"In other words, Angela's suffering has market potential."

He gave me a grim smile. "If you want to put it in those terms, fine. But before you start condemning me, remember, if it weren't for her suffering, you wouldn't be working here, either."

"Not the same thing, Rivers."

"According to you. Now tell me what you meant about Stephanie running from *me*."

I glanced toward the kitchen. I could hear Angela and Tony talking.

"Your Dr. Early performed an abortion on Stephanie," I said, keeping my voice down.

"What?"

I nodded. "It was a few weeks before you brought in your dead child. Apparently she was still deeply depressed."

Now it was Rivers's turn to glance toward the kitchen.

"Do they know?"

"No. And before I got involved, the only people who knew were Stephanie, her doctor, her nurse, and her priest. She felt certain that none of them would tell. But she wouldn't have been so certain about you."

"Me?"

"You might not have recognized her, Rivers, but I think she recognized you. When she saw you in the barbershop, she probably connected you with the clinic and Dr. Early.

And there you were, pals with her father. She ran because she thought you'd tell him about her abortion."

Rivers was shaking his head.

"But I didn't even *know* about it. And what if her parents did find out? It was only an abortion. What's the big deal?"

"Are you really that stupid? We're talking about a strict Catholic family. An abortion is about as big as you get."

Rivers looked angry. He didn't like being called stupid.

"If you're right about all this," he said, "then why didn't she come home after her father was killed? Are you saying she's been held by kidnappers all this time?"

"I don't think she's been kidnapped at all."

"What do you mean? Her ring. The ransom demand."

"Listen, four days ago Stephanie was on a farm in Wray. She phoned a man in Denver, and he picked her up. This kidnapping business sounds like something she and this man might have cooked up between them."

I thought now I knew who the man was. Mostly by process of elimination. I'd even considered the Reverend Lacey, but only briefly. He didn't seem the type. Besides, I figured he was too smart a man to try something like this, especially after having admitted that Stephanie had lived in his house.

"You think Stephanie is party to her own kidnapping?"

"It's possible. I know one thing, if she'd truly been kidnapped four days ago, Angela would have received a ransom demand before now. Kidnappers are generally in a big hurry."

"Jesus, I can't believe Stephanie would put her own mother through this."

"She might have gotten encouragement. From her 'man.' "

"What kind of a sleazeball would—"

"The kind that likes money and young girls." I looked at my watch. "And it's just about time for me to go talk to him. Say good-bye to Angela for me."

I left Rivers staring at my back.

CHAPTER

24

FOWLER'S TV & APPLIANCE CENTER stayed open until six on Saturdays. I got there at five fifty-five.

"We're closing," Mr. Roberson told me. He acted as if he didn't recognize me. Maybe he'd had a long day.

"Stan's expecting me," I said.

"He's in the back. You want me to call him?"

"Don't bother."

There were several other salesmen in the vast store. I was the only customer. I walked between two rows of cold, colorful stoves to the back doors. The warehouse area was silent and empty save for a horde of crated appliances.

Fowler's office was to my left. As I started toward it, I heard a forklift.

I ducked behind a crate. The forklift stopped nearby. The gorilla who climbed off was one of the pair who'd ushered me out the last time I'd been here. He went into Fowler's office. A few minutes later he came out laughing and saying good-night over his shoulder. He pushed through the doors and was gone.

Madge Fowler had told me that Stan locked up the store. I hoped he did it after everyone else left. It would be easier to squeeze the truth out of him if we were alone.

I had nothing solid on Fowler. In fact, everything I had might be merely coincidence. Somehow, though, I doubted it. There was just too much.

Fowler frequented the Lion's Lair, and so had Stephanie. He'd entertained young women at his cabin in Big Pine, and Stephanie had worked there the past two summers. According to his wife, he was a demolitions expert. And someone familiar with military explosives had put a bomb in Stephanie's car, which had ultimately killed her father. Fowler lived within a mile of the armory from where those explosives had been stolen. And he'd owed Joseph Bellano almost one hundred thousand dollars—the exact amount now being demanded for Stephanie's return.

If Stan were holding Stephanie—or harboring her—he'd done so since last Tuesday, when she'd left Wray. But why had he waited until now to try to "sell" her?

I'd already decided that neither of us would leave this building until I had the answer.

Now the swinging doors opened, and Roberson came through. I watched him walk to Fowler's office. He stood in the doorway.

"We're ready to lock up, Mr. Fowler." Pause. "Okay, then, see you in the morning."

Roberson returned to the front of the store. I waited a few moments, then stepped out of my hiding place and peeked through the crack between the double doors. I saw Roberson follow the other salespeople out the glass front doors. He waved good-bye to them, twisted his key in the lock, then walked out of sight.

I unholstered the Magnum and walked into Fowler's office. He was alone at his desk, intently studying some papers.

"Hi, Stan."

"I thought you'd—"

He stopped short when he saw it wasn't Roberson who'd returned. He gave the gun a passing glance. The fine network of broken capillaries stood out fiercely on his face. He looked angry, not scared. Maybe I needed a bigger gun.

"What the fuck are *you* doing here?"

"Where's Stephanie?"

"Get out of here before I call the police," he said.

"You're not calling anybody. Tell me where she is."

"Did you hear what I said?"

He stood up and puffed out his chest to scare me away. He was almost big enough to do it.

"Get out."

"I'm not here to play games with you, Stan."

"That's it. I'm calling the police."

He lifted the receiver.

I shot the phone off his desk. It exploded into white shards, like an old, fragile skull.

I'd seen Lee Marvin do that once in a movie. It had worked for him. *His* guy had turned to jelly. *My* guy looked surprised, sure. Maybe even shocked. But he wasn't scared. Unless he was a good actor.

I waited for the Magnum's ringing to leave our ears.

"Where is she, Stan?"

"You're going to pay for this." He laid the receiver on the empty place on his desk where his phone used to be. His hand didn't even shake. "And I don't know anything about Stephanie, much less where she is."

His voice was smooth and steady, sincere enough to sell a freezer to an Eskimo. I didn't believe him for a minute.

"I'll shoot you, Stan. I mean it."

He didn't seem convinced. Maybe I wasn't, either. It wasn't that I didn't have the stomach for it. In fact, at that moment I think I would have enjoyed it. Not kill, just wound. But it's tough to merely wound someone with a .357 Magnum, especially at point-blank range. Even if I shot Fowler in the foot, the hydrostatic shock from the high-velocity, 158-grain slug would probably knock him unconscious. Or cause his heart to seize up. At the very least, it would blow off his appendage. He might bleed to death. He'd certainly be spiteful. He might not tell me where to find Stephanie.

"Where is she, Stan?"

"I'm telling you I don't know." And then he must have seen something in my face, because he set his jaw and gave me a tight grin. "And you know what else, Lomax? I don't think you're going to shoot anybody. You're not the type."

"Let's go," I said, motioning toward the door with the Magnum, which now felt as heavy as a cinder block.

"I'm not going anywhere with you."

"Right now." I raised my aim to his face and thumbed back the hammer until it clicked.

Fowler hesitated. He didn't *think* I'd shoot him, but he wasn't totally certain. Neither was I.

He came around the desk.

I shoved him out the door.

I kept the gun pressed to the middle of his beefy back and steered him through the warehouse area toward the huge roll-up doors at the rear of the building. This was where crates were opened, and sometimes resealed for shipment back to the factory. Running along the wall next to the doors was a counter with crowbars, heavy-duty staplers, box cutters, and the like. I picked up a thick roll of fiber tape.

"Put your hands behind your back."

"What are you going to do?"

"First, tie you up."

"You're *crazy* if you think I'm going to just stand here and let you—"

"Fine," I said. I put down the tape and picked up a crowbar. "Then I'll knock you out first."

He let me tape his wrists together behind his back. I shoved him toward a refrigerator-sized crate, then turned him around so his back was against it. Then I knelt and taped his ankles together. I stood before him and holstered the Magnum.

"Look here, now, Lomax. This has gone far enough."

He was starting to sweat. Finally.

"I'll be the judge of that."

His movements were now limited to hopping, bending over, and falling down. I'd fix that. I left him for a moment to get a stapler. When I returned with it, he looked genuinely worried.

"I don't know what you want," he said. "Just tell me what you want."

"Where's Stephanie?"

"I don't *know* where she is."

"I think you do."

"I'm telling you I *don't*."

"We're going to find out for sure, Stan."

I pulled out a three-foot-long strip of tape and flattened it horizontally on the crate, with Stan's fat neck in the middle.

"Wha—"

"Shut up."

I pounded a few staples through the tape to make sure it held. Then I ran four or five more strips across his neck—not tight enough to choke him but tight enough to hold him.

"What . . . what are you going to do?"

I looked him over. I didn't like it. If he started squirming and twisting his head, he could probably move sideways. I ran a half-dozen long strips across his chest and another half dozen across his knees. Then I stapled them as close to his body as his bulk would allow.

It all looked pretty sloppy. But effective.

"Lomax, seriously, you don't think you're going to get away with this, do you?" His voice had gone up half an octave.

"Get away with what, Stan?"

"With . . . whatever you think you're doing."

"I'll tell you what I'm thinking, Stan. I'm thinking that you're lying to me, and—"

"No, I—"

"—and I'm sick of being lied to. I'm also frustrated, Stan. I've done about all I can do to find Stephanie. And still no Stephanie. I'm beginning to wonder if she isn't in a shallow grave somewhere."

"Look, I don't—"

"I'm wondering if maybe you conned her and seduced her. Used her up and threw her away."

"I don't—"

"Oh, you're scared, now. Maybe too scared to talk. But I think you're scared that I've found you out and you're on your way to prison. Am I right?"

He shook his head as much as his sticky, stringy bonds would allow.

"Well, Stan, there are things worse than prison. Much worse."

I went to get the forklift.

I'd never operated one before, so it took me a while to figure out which levers did what. I raised and lowered the twin forks. They were a few feet apart and parallel to the floor. Each steel prong was about four feet long and six inches wide. Each was several inches thick at the base, tapering to a rounded quarter-inch-thick point. I raised the points to about belly height. Then I steered the bulky steel contraption between rows of crates toward Fowler.

His eyes got as big as hard-boiled eggs.

He yelled something incoherent.

There was a crate next to Stan's. Like his, it held a refrigerator. I drove the forklift into it, spearing it with one prong. The crate slid back a few feet, and the prong went in about halfway. When I backed it out, there was a scream of metal. I think Stan Fowler screamed, too.

I know he screamed when I steered the forklift toward him.

"NO!"

When I stopped, the tip of the right-hand prong was two feet from his belly. I stayed in the driver's seat.

"Where's Stephanie, Stan?" My voice wasn't as steady as I'd hoped. But I don't think he noticed.

"Jesus, Lomax, I don't know! Don't you think I'd tell you if I did? For God's sake!"

I slowly rolled the forklift toward him, and he started screaming again. He stopped when the tip of the fork pressed against his stomach, midway between his belly button and his sternum. He sucked in his gut and tried to push himself backward through the crated refrigerator.

I climbed off the forklift and stood next to him.

His face had gone dead white. He kept shifting his stare from my eyes to his stomach. The tip of the fork had disappeared between two rolls of fat.

"Jesus God, Lomax." His voice was strained from holding in his belly.

"Where is she, Stan?"

"I'm telling you I don't know! For God's sake!"

I started to climb back on the forklift.

"No, wait. Wait! I was with her, that's all!"

I stopped.

"At the Lion's Lair," he said. "I tried to hit on her in there a couple of times. Okay? Is that what you want to hear?"

I went back to him. He shifted around, trying to ease the pressure of the steel prong nudging his gut.

"Keep talking," I said.

"Look, I've been going in there for years, okay. I mean, I like it, I can't help it, I just do, I mean, making it with young chicks, it's the only thing that excites me anymore." He was beginning to babble. I let him go on. "I mean, all the rest of it, the business, who cares anymore? Cars, booze, none of it means a damn thing, there's just these little pleasures now and then, maybe it's the fear of growing old, I don't know, or the conquest, that, too, I buy them drinks, maybe give them little presents, and they're grateful, so what's a little harmless sex? I take them to motels, sometimes I take them up to my cabin for the weekend, maybe they get scared, maybe I have to force them a little, but it's just harmless sex, I never really *hurt* them."

"It sounds like rape to me, Stan. What about Stephanie?"

"Stephanie, right. Like I said, I saw her in the Lion's Lair a few times, a good-looking chick, nice body and everything, so I talked to her, tried to move on her, but she was shy or something, I never got to first base, all I knew was her first name, I mean, I didn't even know she was Joe Bellano's kid or I never would've messed with her. When she came in his shop that day and started screaming and then looked around and got scared, I thought it was because she recognized me. Christ, *I* was scared she'd tell her old man and he'd cut my throat right there in the chair, but she ran out. That's all, I swear, that's all there was to it."

He was out of breath, and his shirt was soaked with sweat. He stank. I almost believed him.

"There was something else going on," I said. "That's why you wired a land mine to her car."

"What? No."

"No problem for you, an old army demolitions man. But poor old Joseph used her car first and got blown up in her place. Meanwhile, she was hiding out on a religious commune near Wray."

"She was?"

"You went there and took her away."

"No."

"Then you hid her someplace, maybe killed her, and now you're—"

"No."

"—you're trying to bleed some money from her mother, the same amount of money you owed Bellano when he was killed."

"No, Lomax, I don't know anything about *any* of that."

"I'm out of patience, Stan."

"I'm telling you the *truth!*"

"One touch on that lever is all it would take, Stan. I'd probably get off easy, too. Temporary insanity. I mean, what *sane* man could run another man through with a forklift? Oh,

I might spend a few years behind bars. But it would be worth it just to watch you squirm like a bug under a needle."

I put one foot on the forklift.

"No, *please!*" he screamed.

And then he started to weep.

". . . I swear . . . I swear . . ."

I went to the counter for a box cutter. I freed Stan from the tape. Then I helped him squeeze around the tip of the prong. He sat down on the cold concrete floor and hugged his knees. Tears ran down his pale, bloated cheeks.

"I'm sorry, Stan," I said, and I was.

CHAPTER

25

I DROVE away from Fowler's store. I felt sick and disgusted. Sick at the image of him groveling and disgusted at myself for making him do it.

I'd taken it farther than necessary. I'd known Fowler had been telling the truth when he'd admitted his minor involvement with Stéphanie. He'd been scared spitless. Right on the edge. But I'd wanted to push him just a little more. Watch him fall. Watch him lose his manhood and his dignity. Take out my frustrations on poor Mr. Stanley Fowler. Stan the Man. Except he wasn't feeling like much of a man right now.

Neither was I.

I found a bar on the way home and started killing brain cells. At some point during the night, I think I bought the house a round. At some later point, I think I challenged the house to a fight. Lucky for me, they left me alone.

When I awoke Sunday morning, I was still in my clothes. At least I'd made it to bed. I couldn't remember driving home.

However, I could remember Fowler and what had occurred last night in his store. I still felt sick about it. But it was difficult now to separate that from the more immediate nausea of alcohol consumption. I was hoping that when the one went away the other would follow.

I was pretty sure it would. After all, Fowler might inspire pity, but he couldn't sustain it, not with his cabin conquests and his sneaky, sly form of rape.

However, he did have one thing in his favor: He wasn't a kidnapper. Or a murderer.

I bumped around the kitchen, knowing I should eat but not feeling like it. I made some coffee, took one sip, and poured it in the sink. Then I fixed a Bloody Mary. It fortified me while I heated some olive oil in a pan, dropped in some sliced onion, pepper, and ham, then poured in four scrambled eggs and a quarter cup of salsa. I pushed it all around with a spatula until the eggs set. Then I fixed another Bloody Mary.

I was rinsing out my dish in the sink when the phone rang. It was Fat Paulie DaNucci.

"You been hiding behind any garbage cans lately?"

"Not lately," I said.

"There's hope for you yet. Have you found Stephanie?"

"No."

"Okay, then, listen up. You remember that guy I told you about? That guy who knows a guy who might know a guy?"

"This last guy knowing something about the armory burglary?"

"Knowing. Right. Try Ramón Quinteras."

"Who's he?"

"A two-time loser living in Northglenn."

"How is he tied to the robbery?"

"Let's just say if the armory people wanted to find their toys a good place to look might be Ramón's basement."

"Okay, thanks."

"Is that going to help you find Stephanie?"

"I don't know. But it's bound to help the police find her father's killer."

"Almost as good. And Lomax."

"What?"

"If you ever want a real job, give me a call."

"A real job? You mean like scaring people into paying you what they owe?"

"Hey, banks do it."

"Right."

I hung up and called the cops. MacArthur sometimes worked on Sundays. Not this one, though, I was told. Since he was the only cop I felt like talking to, I called him at home. He wasn't pleased to be disturbed on his day off.

"How'd you get this number?"

"You gave it to me, remember?"

"I thought I'd had it changed since then."

"And I thought we were friends."

"Yeah, yeah. What do you want? And it better be important. My kids are waiting for me to read them the Sunday funnies."

"I've got a name for you on the armory burglary. Ramón Quinteras." I repeated what Fat Paulie had told me.

"Where'd you get this information?"

"From a reliable source who wishes to remain anonymous."

"I'm not about to ask a judge for a search warrant on the basis of a 'reliable source.' I need a name."

"His initials are F.P.D."

"F.P.D. Who the hell is that?"

"F as in Fat."

He paused. "*He* told you about Quinteras?"

"Yes."

"And you believe him?"

"I do. He wants Bellano's murderer as much as you do."

"Then tell your fat friend to pick up a paper. We made an arrest yesterday morning."

"You did? Who?"

"Mitch Overholser."

"What?"

"That's right," MacArthur said. "Our property clerk Isenglass finally talked. Apparently he's had previous dealings with Overholser; namely, he's placed bets through him. He said Overholser approached him the day after Bellano was killed and tried to bribe him to steal or destroy Bellano's records. When Isenglass balked, Overholser threatened him. He said, and I quote, 'What I did to Bellano, I could do to you.' So Isenglass brought a magnet into the property room and messed up Bellano's computer disks."

"What does Overholser say?"

"He's confessed to everything except placing the bomb. He said he just made up that story to scare Isenglass."

"What do you think?"

"What I *know* is that Overholser owed Bellano forty-six thousand dollars. He said so himself. People have killed for a lot less than that."

"Do you have any other evidence?"

"What are you, the grand jury? Of course we do. We finally got a warrant late last night and searched Overholser's apartment and car. You know what we found hidden under a blanket in the trunk of his car? A land mine. Just like the one that got Bellano. Of course, Overholser says he can't imagine how it got there. And something else. In his younger days Overholser served in the Colorado National Guard and spent time at—guess where?—Camp George West."

After I hung up, I phoned the Bellano house. Tony answered. He'd already heard about the arrest of Mitch Overholser.

"I'm glad they got the bastard," he said. He didn't sound glad. He sounded depressed. "We haven't heard from them again."

"Them" being the kidnappers.

"How's Angela?"

"She's . . . holding up. Um, listen, Lomax, maybe I gave you a hard time before, but—"

"No problem."

"But tomorrow morning I could use your help."

"Anything."

"While the three of us are out getting the money, we need someone to stay here by the phone, you know, in case they call."

He obviously knew that as a seasoned investigator I'd had experience answering the telephone.

I said, "The three of you?"

"Rivers is going with us."

"Why?"

"Angela seems to think he can help—at least with the banks."

"What do you think?"

"I think he's a pain in the ass," Tony said. "But he's involved now, and there's not much I can do about it."

"You know he's hoping to get a TV special out of all this, don't you?"

"Look, Lomax, I don't like him any more than you do, all right? I tried to change Angela's mind about the guy, but I couldn't." He sighed. "See, when the kidnappers first called, Rivers was here and I wasn't. Angela went to pieces, and she leaned on him. He let her. So now she trusts him. Plus he was a friend of Joe's."

"So he says. But why let him hang around?"

"Hey, I didn't call to argue. Rivers wants to help and Angela says we let him and that's the way it is. Now are you with us or not?"

"Sure."

"Then be here at eight-thirty tomorrow for breakfast."

He hung up.

Now what? I had an entire Sunday with nothing to do. I phoned Rachel. No answer. Maybe she skied on Sundays. Maybe I should take it up again.

I'd skied in my college days. Sure, I'd never gotten very good. In fact, I'd never gotten past lousy. But I bet I could do it again. Strap on those ol' slats and aim them down a powdery slope, then watch the solid encroaching trees whiz by at sixty miles an hour with nothing between me and their immovable trunks but sharp branches and thin mountain air.

Or not.

I started to call Vaz. Then I remembered he and Sophia were still in Phoenix. I missed brainstorming with him while he beat my brains out at chess. Maybe I could do it by myself. I got out the board and set up the pieces.

I moved pawn to king four.

Hey, it worked. I thought of something useful to do.

I spent the rest of the day getting a cellular car phone installed in the Olds.

On Monday morning I arrived at the Bellano residence at a quarter after eight.

I parked behind Gary Rivers's car, a white BMW with darkly tinted windows. It looked like a polar bear with sunglasses. I knew it was his car, because he was climbing out of it. He was carrying a briefcase. He looked relieved to see me. We went up the walk together.

"I'm glad you're here," he said. "I don't think Tony likes me very much."

"Well, we can't hold that against him."

He shook his head at me.

"I'm trying to help them, too, you know," he said.

"How, exactly?"

"For one thing, if Angela and Tony have any trouble getting their money out of the bank—I mean, in cash—I might be able to use my notoriety to expedite matters."

"Where's your camera crew?"

"Listen, goddammit!" His face was red. He worked his jaw and forced himself to calm down. Okay, so maybe I *was* needling him. "Listen, Lomax," he said, burying his anger, "I'm putting up five thousand of my own money to help them with the ransom. And I got the radio and TV stations I work for to each kick in ten. That's twenty-five thousand dollars."

I grabbed him by the lapels of his overcoat and nearly yanked him off his feet. He dropped his briefcase.

"Hey, wha—"

"You've already told the *media* about this?"

"What? No, goddammit. Let go of me."

I did and gave him a little shove while I was at it. He smoothed his coat and tried to look more offended than scared.

"All I told them was that there was a big story in the making and I was right in the middle of it and—"

"With exclusive rights."

"That, too. So what? Anyway, they okayed the money. All I have to do is pick it up at the bank." He picked up his briefcase and wiped off traces of snow. "Satisfied?"

I didn't bother to answer.

Tony let us in and led us to the kitchen. This was command central in the Bellano house. The table was already set. We sat down with Tony while Angela Bellano dished up Italian sausage and eggs. After she sat down, I asked how they planned on getting the money.

Angela said, "Joseph had set up a money market account for us. Also, he bought some long-term CDs. I'll cash them in."

"Banks are often reluctant to hand over that much cash. At least right away."

"It's her money," Tony told me.

"Right." I didn't see any point in arguing. "Whose car were you planning to take?"

Tony shrugged at Rivers, and Rivers shrugged back.

"Take yours," I said to Rivers.

"Any special reason?"

"You've got a car phone, right? So do I. That might come in handy later if we need to keep in touch on the road."

"What've you got in mind?" Tony asked me.

"Maybe nothing. Let's see what the kidnappers have to say.

And one other thing—you'd better be careful driving around today. You're going to be carrying a lot of cash."

"Don't worry about it," Tony said. "I'm bringing a gun."

"Why doesn't that make me feel better?"

After breakfast, they all left in a group—Angela with her rosary, Tony with his pistol, and Rivers with his briefcase for the money. I felt like a kid the grown-ups had left behind. I went back to the kitchen and washed the dishes.

I watched daytime TV for a while. Finally, out of boredom, I snooped around the house.

Joseph's den looked the same as it had the last time I'd seen it—unused. I walked into the master bedroom. It had dark mahogany furnishings, with a large wooden crucifix over the bed and a painting of the Virgin Mary and Child beside the dresser mirror. The next bedroom had no personality and looked to be for guests. Tony had probably spent a few nights there lately. My guess was it had once belonged to Diane Bellano.

The last room was obviously Stephanie's. The dressing table held carefully arranged bottles of cologne and lotions. The bedspread was white, with pink and yellow ruffles. There was a small pewter crucifix on the wall at the head of the bed. Maybe she should have had one of those big wooden ones, like her parents'. Although it hadn't done Joseph much good.

The phone rang.

It was ringing in the living room and kitchen. I hustled into the kitchen, because it would be easier to copy down demands and instructions while standing at the counter. I got out a pen and pad and picked up the receiver. It was Rivers.

"Has anyone called yet?" he asked.

"No. Any problems?"

"Nothing serious," he said, "but it's taking longer than we thought. So far we've only collected my money and the stations'—twenty-five thousand. Talk to you later."

"Later" turned out to be four o'clock, when they all trooped in. I could see by their faces that all was not well.

"What's wrong?"

"Did he call?" Tony asked.

"No."

He brushed past me toward the kitchen.

"We only got fifty-eight thousand," Angela said, worry etched deeply in her face. "What are we going to do? What if the man wants it all tonight?"

Rivers and I dumbly shook our heads. She joined her brother in the kitchen.

"We spent all day at her bank," Rivers explained. "They let her cash in her money market account, but the hassle was getting it in cash. They finally came across, though—thirty-three thousand in fifties and hundreds. But the CDs are a different story. They said she'd have to wait twenty-four hours. Bank policy, and there's no way around it."

I nodded and started toward the kitchen. He stopped me.

"This business about the car phones," he said.

"Yes?"

"What do you have in mind?"

"For the ransom drop. When it comes time to pay off the kidnappers, they're probably going to tell Angela to take it someplace and leave it. I want to be able to follow her and stay out of sight."

"Wait a minute. Do you intend to *try* something during the payoff?"

"Absolutely."

"Jesus, Lomax, are you sure about this?"

"I'll make sure Angela is safely out of the way."

"I'm thinking about Stephanie."

"I'll be blunt, Rivers," I said, keeping my voice down. "There's a chance Stephanie may be dead."

He looked shocked. "Why do you say that?"

"The kidnappers didn't let Angela talk to Stephanie. In my

mind that means only one of two things: They don't have her, or she's dead. Either way, we risk nothing by trying to grab them. If we don't try, or if we miss, we may never find out what happened to Stephanie."

"But what if she really is alive and being held captive?"

"Let the kidnappers prove it."

"And if they do?"

"Then we proceed more cautiously," I said.

He nodded. "I take it you've dropped your earlier theory about Stephanie being a willing accomplice to all this."

"I'm keeping an open mind. Remember, when she left Wray, it was *willingly* with a man."

Rivers and I went in the kitchen. Tony was helping Angela fix dinner. I asked if they needed any help. They gave me withering looks. I sat down and shut up.

During dinner I explained a few things to Angela and Tony. Not as bluntly as I had to Rivers but just as assertively. Tony balked at first but eventually agreed with Rivers and me. Angela wasn't sure. But she did agree to tell the kidnappers that she didn't know how to drive a car. Then we all sat around and sipped coffee and waited for the call.

It came at nine o'clock.

CHAPTER

26

ANGELA BELLANO WAITED until I was ready by the phone in the living room. Then she picked up the extension in the kitchen.

"Hello?"

"Mrs. Bellano?" It was a man.

"Yes."

"Did you get the money?" His voice was fuzzy and distorted, as if he were holding a piece of cloth or paper between his mouth and the telephone.

"We got fifty-eight thousand, but we can't get the rest until tomorrow."

"I told you to get it all today." He sounded angry.

"I know. We tried. But our bank is making us wait twenty-four hours before they'll—"

"You're lying. You're trying to stall."

"No, I swear to God. We begged them. If you don't believe me, call the bank and—"

"Wait a minute. You said 'we.' Didn't I tell you to keep your mouth shut if you wanted your daughter back?"

"Yes, but—"

"Did you think I was kidding about that?"

"No, of course not." Angela's voice was surprisingly calm. "My brother Tony has been staying with me. He was here

when you called the first time. I had to tell him what was
going on because I needed his help with the bank. And for
another thing, I can't drive a car," she lied. "He had to take
me around. He and I are the only ones who know. I swear."

Hell, even *I* believed her. But the caller was silent. Angela
looked at me from the kitchen doorway, a pleading question
on her face.

We waited.

"You're sure he's the only one?" the man said finally.

"Yes, I swear."

"All right, I'll call tomorrow night, and you'd better have
the money. And I mean all of it."

"Wait. Please let me talk to Stephanie."

"Put the money in a gym bag and have your car gassed up
and ready to roll, you understand?"

"Yes, of course, but I want to talk to Stephanie. How do I
know she's—"

"When you get the money, you can talk to her. And you'd
better not screw up, lady." The line went dead.

I hung up the phone.

"What did he say?" Rivers asked me. "Did he put Stephanie on the phone?"

I waved him off as Angela came toward us from the kitchen.

"Did I do all right?"

"You did fine," I told her.

Then Tony and I discussed how we should proceed. First,
we assumed that he and Angela might be watched all day.
Therefore, Rivers agreed to let them use his car, starting now.
Tomorrow I'd stay close by in the Olds, but out of sight. Tony
would drive Angela and stay in constant communication with
me. He wouldn't be seen with the phone to his ear because of
the BMW's dark windows.

It *sounded* easy enough. I could think of only a hundred
and twelve things that could go wrong.

Then Rivers wanted to know where he'd be during all this.

"As far away as possible," I said.

"Absolutely," Tony agreed.

"Now, wait just a minute," Rivers said.

He tried to argue that he was just as much a part of this as any of us. Tony and I quickly voted him down. But Angela said yea, and that was that. Hers was the only vote that counted. After all, it was her daughter who'd been kidnapped.

Tony and I agreed that Rivers could do the least damage if he rode with me. I didn't like it, but there it was.

Rivers and I left the house by the back door. It was snowing again. Which I'm sure delighted all the children in town, since Christmas Eve was only ten nights away and Santa needed a slick surface for his sleigh. The Olds, however, did not have runners, and this weather could only make things more difficult.

We walked through the snowy yard, past the ruined garage, down the alley, and around the block to my car. I asked Rivers where he lived. He gave me an address in an upper-middle-class neighborhood just off South University Boulevard. I drove east on Thirty-eighth and winced only slightly when we passed Giancio's Italian Restaurant. Then I got on I-25 heading south.

"I'm pretty nervous about this," Rivers said. "I mean, it could be dangerous tomorrow, couldn't it?"

"It could be."

"Then maybe we should call in the police, no matter what Angela and Tony say."

"Maybe we should."

We rode for a few minutes in silence.

"I have a gun at home," Rivers said. "A hunting rifle."

"Lucky you."

"Maybe I should bring it tomorrow. I admit I haven't fired it in years, but—"

"Forget about it."

"But maybe—"

"Forget it, Rivers. The last thing I want tomorrow is an amateur in my car with a loaded gun."

The next morning, on my way to pick up Rivers, I decided to try out my car phone. Sure, I'd used it right after the guy had installed it. I'd called my office answering machine. But I'd been *parked,* for chrissake. Now I was on the move. A happening guy. Just like all the other people who had car phones—big shots or people who wanted to be big shots or people who thought they were big shots. Or traveling sales-men.

I tried hard not to look like a salesman. I picked up the phone. I nearly ran into the guy in front of me.

Okay, so when this was over, I'd rip out the damn phone.

I called Rivers and told him I was on my way.

When I pulled into his driveway, he came out the front door. He was cradling a long, narrow bundle wrapped in a blanket. It was obvious what he had, but at least he wouldn't scare the neighbors. He laid the bundle in the backseat.

"I thought I told you to forget about the rifle."

"I know," he said. "But maybe we can use it."

"Well, we *can't* use it."

I drove to the Bellano residence. When we were a few blocks away, I pulled over and used the phone. Tony answered. I gave him my number and told him we'd follow them to the bank.

"Call me along the way," I said. "I want to see how these phones work in traffic."

"They work fine," Rivers told me.

"What's that?" Tony asked.

"Nothing. Just call me as soon as you and Angela get started." I hung up.

"They work fine in traffic," Rivers said.

"Okay, okay." Big shot.

Tony and Angela got the cash from the bank without a

hitch. Then we all went back to the house to wait for the call. We waited through lunch and through dinner.

The call came at six-thirty. Rivers and I listened in on the extension.

"Mrs. Bellano?" It was the same voice that I'd heard last night—muffled and distorted.

"Yes?"

"Did you get the money?"

"Yes. It's in fifties and hundreds, just like you wanted. I have it in an athletic bag."

"Good. Now I'm going to bounce you around the city to make sure you're not being followed. You won't know when I'll be watching, but believe me, I will be, and if I see anything that looks even a little bit suspicious, you'll never see your daughter again. Understand?"

"Yes, of course. Let me talk to her now, please."

"When I have the money in my hands, you can talk to her all you want."

"But you said when—"

"Shut up and listen. There's a pay phone in front of the 7 Eleven on Thirty-eighth and Irving. It'll start ringing in five minutes. You'd better be there to answer it."

"Wait. Don't hang up. I want to talk to Stephanie before I leave the house."

"Bring the money," he said. "You're down to four and a half minutes." He hung up.

"I don't like it," Rivers said to me.

"Neither do I. Let's go."

Tony and Angela went out the front door. Rivers and I slipped out the back and hustled down the alley to my car. The convenience store was only six blocks away. I drove slowly, giving Tony and Angela time to get there. When I crossed Thirty-eighth, I saw Angela huddled against one of the pay phones in front of the store. She was spotlighted by the headlights of Rivers's car. The windows were so dark I could barely see Tony inside. But I could see customers inside the store—a man standing by the news rack and two kids playing a video game. And they could see Angela.

I kept driving slowly south on Irving. The phone chirped a few blocks later. Rivers picked it up.

He listened for a moment, then told me, "Tony says they're being sent to another convenience store."

This one wasn't too far, on Thirty-ninth and Tennyson. But then we got sent to another one across town on East Colfax. And the fourth one, also on Colfax, was nearly all the way to Aurora. There was a lot of traffic on Colfax. It was possible Tony and Angela were being followed. I paralleled their course but stayed one block over on Fourteenth.

The phone chirped, and Rivers answered it.

He listened, nodding. "Okay," he said to me, "we're driving back across town to the Southwest Plaza Mall. The guy wants Angela to walk alone through the southwest entrance and bring the bag. There's a phone near the elevator. She's to wait there for another call."

"Tell Tony to take his time so we can get there first."

I took Thirteenth back into town, then swung over to Eighth Avenue, and finally Sixth Avenue heading west. I'd been trying to visualize the mall.

"Call Tony."

Rivers did.

"Tell him to walk with Angela to the entrance, then wait there. He should keep his eyes open for anyone carrying the bag out. Not that it'll do much good—there's a dozen ways to get out of that mall. But I'll come in from the other side and be watching the phones before Angela gets there."

Rivers relayed the instructions, then hung up.

"Do you think they'll try to take the bag in the mall?"

"They might."

"With all those people around? The place will be jammed with Christmas shoppers."

"That's the idea. Assuming they try it. They could grab the bag and get lost in the crowd. The other way—the way I was hoping they'd try—would be in a deserted area. That would make it easier for them to watch for cops. Of course, it would also expose them. Which is probably why they want the crowd."

I got off Sixth onto Wadsworth and drove south for twenty minutes to Cross Drive. I entered the shopping complex from the north side.

The stores closed at nine, which was barely an hour from now. However, the parking area was as busy as if it were the middle of the day. I drove to the northeast entrance of the mall, between Joslins and Sears. There weren't any empty parking slots. Not even Handicapped Only. I left the Olds in a red zone.

"Should I bring that?" Rivers was indicating his lethal bundle in the back seat.

"What, are you kidding? Just wait by the entrance and keep your eyes open."

I went inside with the rest of the happy shoppers. "Jingle Bells" was coming over the PA system. Oh, what fun. I pushed through the throng until I neared the elevator. It was beside the huge opening in the floor, which allowed one to see the crowds on the lower level. I could see kiddies and their moms lined up to talk to Santa. I stayed on this side and window-shopped at Merle Norman Cosmetics.

Ten minutes later Angela Bellano walked hesitantly through the crowd.

She spotted the pay phone by the elevator and walked directly to it. Either she didn't see me, or she acted as if she didn't. She stood nervously beside the phone.

Finally, it rang. She answered and listened for a few moments. Then she nodded her head, hung up, and walked back the way she'd come, carrying the bag.

I followed her to the exit and saw Tony meet her. She said

something to him. He looked up and spotted me. Then he
scratched his ear, mouthed the word *phone*, and led Angela
out to the parking lot.

I ran back the other way, dodging shoppers as if this were
the big game and we were behind by six points.

Rivers was waiting at the mall's entrance. I sprinted past
him to the car. The phone was chirping when we got there.

"We're going to Mile High Stadium," Tony said in my ear.
"There's some pay phones near the south end of the east
stands."

I drove north on Wadsworth and passed Tony and Angela
before we got to Sixth Avenue.

"How long do you think this will go on?" Rivers asked me.

"Who knows? Until they feel safe."

"Do you think someone besides you was watching the
telephone in the mall?"

"It's possible."

I took Sixth east to Federal Boulevard, then drove north to
Seventeenth Avenue. I turned right and drove slowly down
the hill between the parking areas for Mile High Stadium and
McNichols Arena.

There was a stop sign at Bryant Street at the southeast
corner of the stadium parking lot. I stayed there for a few
moments and surveyed the area.

Back to my left the stadium rose up stark and silent and
empty, with the big white bronco rearing up over the south
stands. There was an eight-foot-high chain-link fence running
around the structure. At the south end of the east stands, and
on this side of the fence, was a cluster of pay telephones.
Between me and the phones were a few acres of parking lot.
The lot was surrounded by a waist-high chain-link fence
broken by gates in several places around the perimeter. On
Sunday morning the lot would be packed with buses filled
with orange-clad fans. Now it was an empty white expanse.

I pulled across Bryant Street toward the I-25 underpass.

The highway hummed and whistled with Tuesday night traffic.

The street curved right and then left under the freeway. Then it turned north between the freeway and the Platte River. I pulled into the long, narrow parking area above the riverfront bike path. Then I turned the Olds around so it was pointed back toward the highway bridge, a hundred yards away.

Rivers and I waited. Our view of the stadium parking lot was blocked by the busy elevated freeway. The stadium bleachers rose up beyond it like the remnants of a dead civilization.

Ten minutes went by.

Fifteen.

The phone chirped.

"We got the call," Tony told me. "He told Angela to set the bag outside the car, then for us to drive home. If the money is all there and there's no interference, he'll call and tell us where Stephanie is."

"Okay, Tony, take Angela home. I'll—"

"Bullshit," he said. "I'm pulling away from the phones right now, but there's no way I'm leaving the area."

"Goddammit, if they see you, they'll—"

"They won't see me. Where are you?"

"On the downtown side of the freeway."

"Okay," Tony said, "I'll cover the west side of the stadium. You do what you have to do, Lomax."

He broke the connection.

CHAPTER

27

I PULLED AHEAD, almost forgetting about Rivers. I stopped under the freeway.

"You'd better get out," I told him. "You can wait here."

"But I can—"

"Now."

He hesitated. Then he reached over the seat for his blanket-wrapped rifle and climbed out.

"What do you think you're going to do?"

"Maybe I can help," he said.

I didn't have time to take away his toy.

"Just stay here, Rivers. Stay the hell out of the way."

I steered around the curve to the stop sign. Then I turned right and drove slowly north on Bryant Street—the stadium and the parking lot on my left, the freeway high above me on my right.

The lot was empty. Rivers's car with Tony and Angela was nowhere in sight. Near the cluster of phones I could see a small dark shape in the snow—the bait, a gym bag filled with money. Except now the bag might as well have been stuffed with comic books.

I drove well past the stadium, then killed the lights, made a U-turn, and stopped.

To my left the freeway was alive with traffic. So was Federal

Boulevard, beyond the stadium and up the hill. Down here it was as still as a cemetery. I punched up the number of Rivers's car. Angela answered.

"Where's Tony?"

"I don't know," she said. "I can't see him, but he ran toward the stadium. I'm scared, Mr. Lomax, maybe—"

"Where are you?"

"I'm a few blocks away on Seventeenth."

"Stay there," I said. "Stay in the car."

At that moment a late-model Monte Carlo entered the parking lot from the southeast corner.

I put down the phone and picked up my gun.

The car sped directly toward the cluster of phones. I slammed the Olds into low, steered through the nearest gate, and started across the lot toward the phones. The Monte Carlo got there well ahead of me. It slid to a stop. The passenger door swung open, and a man reached out for the bag. I was fifty yards away. I hit the lights. Bruno Tartalia looked up, momentarily frozen against the open door, his hand poised above the bag.

Then he grabbed the bag and slammed the door. The Monte Carlo started spinning its tires in reverse.

I braced myself against the steering wheel, flattened the gas pedal, and drove the Olds straight into the car. I smashed into the car's trunk and stayed with it, driving it forward, crashing into the cluster of pay phones and shoving the whole mess into the chain-link fence, which wrapped up the front end of the Monte Carlo like a net over a wild animal.

The collision must have dazed me, because when I saw Bruno, he was moving in slow motion.

He climbed out of the passenger side of the Monte Carlo. He had the gym bag in one hand and a fat automatic pistol in the other. He raised his arm. I fought with the door handle. His gun boomed, the windshield shattered, and I rolled out of the Olds onto the snowy asphalt. I peeked over the hood of

the Olds, ready to return fire. Bruno saw me and fired first.
Then suddenly the front of his coat burst open in bloody
eruptions, and a microsecond later I heard the whap-whap of
Rivers's rifle. Bruno fell heavily against the Monte Carlo,
then dropped to the ground, dead.

Johnny Toes Burke was already out of the driver's side of
the car. He had a gun in his hand, but he was interested in
flight, not fight. He began run-limping for his life toward the
west side of the stadium. I went after him.

He'd covered less than twenty yards when Tony stepped out
of the shadows in front of him. Johnny Toes fired wildly, almost
by accident; then he dropped his gun and raised his hands.

"I give up," he said.

Tony shot him.

Johnny Toes let out a yell and grabbed his side and fell to
his knees. Tony and I rushed over to him. Tony pointed his
gun at Johnny Toes's head.

"Don't do it, Tony," I told him.

He wasn't listening. "You've got ten seconds to live," he
said. "Where's Stephanie?"

Johnny Toes rocked back and forth, holding his side and
wailing, "Oh, sweet Jesus, I'm shot, I'm bleeding, Jesus, get
me a doctor."

"Tell me where you've got her or I'll blow your fucking
brains out."

Tony meant what he said. I stepped between him and
Johnny Toes.

"Put down the gun."

"I'll kill that mother—"

"If you do, we won't find Stephanie."

His eyes lost some of their fever. He put away his gun. I
noticed for the first time that his pant leg was wet with blood.
I looked around for Rivers and saw him jogging toward us
from the distant corner of the lot. Then I saw his car speeding
down Seventeenth. Angela steered through the exit, stopped

to pick up Rivers, then headed toward us. She slid the car to a halt a dozen feet away, then jumped out and ran to Tony. Rivers climbed out the passenger side.

"Call nine-one-one," I told him. "We've got two men wounded."

"Wait," Tony said, disengaging himself from his sister. "I'm just scratched. Don't call anybody. Not until this shit tells us where he's got Stephanie."

Rivers stood beside the open car door.

"Well, Johnny," I said, "do you want to talk now or kneel there and bleed to death while we watch?"

"We never had her, I swear, Jesus, please call me a doctor."

"Where is she?" Angela begged.

Before Johnny Toes could answer, Tony stepped up and kicked him in the shoulder. Johnny Toes cried out and toppled over in the snow. His hands never left his side. Blood oozed between his fingers. I was afraid he might die before he talked. I motioned for Rivers to make the call. He nodded and climbed into his car.

"Talk to us, Johnny, and we'll have an ambulance here in minutes. Where's Stephanie?"

"She's on a farm near Wray. Oh, Jesus. Some kind of religious commune."

"You're lying," I said. "I was there a few days ago and she'd left."

"No, she's there."

"How do you know? How did you know she was there at all?"

"A guy I know, a junkie named Dexter, told me."

I remembered the name. Reverend Lacey had said someone named Dexter had quit the commune the very day I was there—Thursday.

"Tell us about it, Johnny," I said. "All of it."

He did, in between moans and groans.

Dexter was a junkie who'd bought drugs from Johnny Toes. He'd tried to kick the habit at the commune in Wray, found the going too tough, and left. But before he'd gone, he'd stolen Reverend Lacey's stash. This was the communal pot that Lacey created with the help of all new followers—everyone had to surrender their cash and jewelry to him.

When Dexter got back to Denver, the first person he looked up was Johnny Toes. He wanted coke, and he gave Johnny Toes everything he had, including Stephanie Bellano's ring. Johnny Toes saw the inscription and asked Dexter about Stephanie. When he learned that she was isolated out of town, he cooked up the fake kidnapping. With a little help from his new partner, Bruno.

"We figured Bellano's old lady would have plenty of cash after she collected on Joe's books, so—ah, God, oh, shit, I'm dying here, where's that doctor?—so nobody would even get hurt, you know?"

"Do you think he's telling the truth?" Rivers said from behind me.

"I don't know," I said. "Did you call?"

Rivers nodded. "The police and the paramedics are on their way. I think we'd better check out this slimeball's story as soon as possible."

I agreed. If Lacey had lied to me about Stephanie, perhaps he was holding her against her will.

"I searched that place from top to bottom," I told Johnny Toes. "Where was Stephanie?"

"How the hell should I know? Ah, God."

Maybe Rachel Wynn had been right. Maybe there *was* a hidden room in that house.

"I'll take your car and drive up there tonight," I told Rivers. "You'd better stay here and explain everything to the police."

"I'm going, too," Tony put in.

"No." Angela grabbed his arm. "You're waiting here for the ambulance."

Rivers turned to me. "Do you want me to go with you? You might have trouble with Lacey and his followers."

"I can handle it," I told him. "Besides, and don't take this the wrong way, you're the one who dropped Bruno. The cops might get very nervous if they have to come looking for you."

"You're right. I'll stay here."

"Please," Angela said to me, "you should go now."

I looked down at Johnny Toes lying on his side and moaning. He was still bleeding, but not profusely. Maybe he'd live, after all.

"Promise you won't kick him again?"

Tony grinned. "I promise."

I walked toward Rivers's car. He fell into step beside me.

"Before you drive up there, there's something you should know."

"What?"

He glanced back at Tony and Angela. Obviously he didn't want them to hear. He went around the car and got in the passenger's side, leaving the door open. I climbed in behind the wheel.

"What is it?" I started to ask him, but he already had his rifle pointed at my chest.

It was a hunting rifle, all right. The kind used to hunt men—an M-16. Rivers's finger was on the trigger.

"Ever seen one of these before?" he asked me casually.

"Not up close."

"But you saw what it did to Bruno."

"I saw."

"Close your door and put your hands on the wheel."

I did so. He jammed the muzzle of the combat rifle into my ribs. One squeeze from his finger and my heart and lungs would be all over the car.

"Don't panic," he said pleasantly. "We're just going for a little ride. If you try anything now, you die. So do Tony and Angela. Do you understand me?"

"More or less."

He leaned his head out the door but kept the weapon pressed against my side.

"Mr. Lomax decided he wants me to go along. We'll be back as soon as we can. You probably shouldn't tell the police where we're going. Not until we're certain Stephanie's all right."

I watched Angela and Tony through the dark windshield. They looked puzzled. Tony took a step toward us. Rivers waved good-bye and closed the door.

"Let's move it, Lomax," he told me.

I did so.

CHAPTER

28

I DROVE out of the parking lot.

Rivers kept his military machine of destruction nuzzled against my side. He had me drive under the freeway and pull into the long, narrow parking lot near the Platte River. Somehow I doubted he'd phoned for the police and the paramedics.

"Kill the lights and shut off the engine," he told me.

I did.

We sat alone in the dim city glow. Alone, that is, except for a hundred people per minute zipping past on nearby I-25. They were on their way to family or friends, or maybe a late dinner or movie, as many destinations as there were people, and you could bet that not one of them was wondering if they were about to get their guts blown out.

Across the river the downtown towers of speckled light stood still and watched.

Rivers reached over his weapon with his left hand and opened the glove compartment. His right hand never strayed from the stock and the trigger. He rummaged around and came out with several plastic restraints, the kind cops use when they arrest a crowd of people—cheaper than handcuffs but just as effective. He shook one loose.

"Did you buy those from Ramón Quinteras, along with the rest of your arsenal?"

He gave me a smile of admiration.

"You got that far, did you?"

"Not soon enough, though."

"That's right, Lomax, not soon enough. Turn around and put your face against the window and your hands behind your back."

I didn't have an effective argument. I did what he said. He bound my wrists together with the thin plastic strip.

"To answer your original question," Rivers said, "no. I appropriated the restraints from the Denver police department when I was filming my special on drug busts."

"And what 'special' included Ramón Quinteras?"

" 'Illegal Arms Sales,' what else?"

Rivers pulled me around, opened my coat, and took the Magnum from my shoulder holster. Then he laid the M-16 on the backseat. He climbed out the passenger's side, then pointed my gun at me.

"Slide over here."

When I did, Rivers put the seat belt on me, tight across my lap and chest. I could move my head and my legs, and that was about it. Now I knew how Stan Fowler must have felt. Rivers tossed my gun in the glove box. Then he went around to the driver's side and got in.

We drove out of the parking lot toward the on-ramp for northbound I-25. Rivers slid the BMW smoothly into the flow of traffic. He kept the speedometer under sixty. It wouldn't do to be stopped by a cop.

"I need to take I-76, don't I?" he asked pleasantly.

"You don't think I'm going to *help*, do you?"

He grinned. "I believe you will. Later."

I didn't know what he had in mind, but apparently he needed me. At least he thought he did.

"Why did you put the bomb in Stephanie's car? Is she that much of a threat to you?"

"Yes."

"She could hurt you?"

"She could ruin me."

"How? I know it has something to do with you and your wife and baby in Big Pine."

"It has everything to do with that."

"Let me guess. Little Thomas Rhynsburger didn't die of sudden infant death syndrome. It was something more sinister than that, and Stephanie found out."

"Right you are."

"What happened?"

He shrugged. Then he saw the sign for I-76 and moved over into the right-hand lane. We began heading northeast, away from the city.

"I . . . killed my son," he said. "Of course, it was an accident," he added quickly. "He was screaming, crying about God knows what, he wouldn't stop, as usual, and my nerves were on edge, I mean, I'd been under more strain than you can even imagine, and—"

Rivers eased back on the gas. We'd been well over the speed limit.

"I was at a turning point in my career," he said calmly, "and I needed to get myself together. I took my family to Big Pine to relax. And it seemed like that goddamn kid was crying from the moment we left the house. It went on for almost two days. So . . ." He shrugged again. "I hit him. Not hard at all, just enough to shut him up. But he didn't shut up, he just got louder. I guess I lost my temper. I hit him again, and again, and well . . ."

"Then you took him to the clinic."

Rivers sighed. "He was bruised and bloodied, and he'd stopped breathing. I was in a panic. My wife was practically hysterical and—"

"Why didn't your wife come forward with this?"

"First, because she loves me. And second, because she's an accessory after the fact and she knows now that if she talks she'll go to prison, too. 'Felony child abuse resulting in death,' they call it. A parent can do a lot of time for that. *Both* parents. I made sure she understood."

"I see."

"Also, she's been a basket case since it happened. She's with her parents now. She rarely leaves the house."

"Lovely."

"Yes, well. Anyway, we rushed Thomas to the clinic, but it was too late."

"Stephanie was there, and she saw the baby."

"Yes. It was obvious what had happened to the child. But at that point I was too upset to care. I mean, about hiding the fact. Then Dr. Early and my wife and I had a long talk. He agreed that calling in the police would not bring back Thomas. He understood our predicament, our grief, and he was very sympathetic. So he faked the death certificate."

"One for all and all for one. You avoid arrest, and he picks up ten thousand dollars."

"How did . . . ?"

"I went through Early's books."

Rivers laughed. "Jesus, he wrote it down?"

"Anonymous donor," I said. "Why did you kill Early?"

His smile faded. "Because a month or so after Thomas's death, he called me, demanding more money. Blackmail, pure and simple. He said if I didn't pay he'd have my son's body exhumed and prove that he'd died of a broken neck. So I did what I had to do."

"Then you went looking for Stephanie."

"Actually, no. To tell you the truth, I'd pretty much forgotten about her until the day she stormed into her father's shop. She was yelling about people going to prison before she even saw me. And when she *did* see me, well, she got scared, and so did I."

"So you put a bomb in her car."

He nodded.

"Why did you choose that method? If you don't mind my asking."

"For one thing, I already had what I needed. You see, when Quinteras sold me the stuff last year, it was a package deal. An M-16 with clips, a couple of mines, some grenades . . . You know, the usual stuff your average high school gang member might carry in his car. And it seemed like the surest way to get her. And the safest, for me. With Bellano's alleged ties to the mob, the cops would assume the bomb was meant for him. No one would look toward me."

"Don't be too sure about that."

"Oh, I'm sure. It would've worked, too, if Stephanie hadn't run away. Everyone, including Joe, assumed she'd be back home in a day or so. It was just his bad luck that she stayed away and he tried to use her car."

We rode in silence for a few miles. The last of the suburb's buildings were falling behind us. Ahead lay blackness.

"I assume you planted the mine in Mitch Overholser's trunk."

"That was too good an opportunity to pass up. When one of my newsroom buddies told me he'd been arrested, I got to his house as fast as I could. My guess is he'll do time for Bellano's murder. That is, if things work out tonight."

"What things?"

"Can't you guess?"

"Look, Rivers, you might as well just give it up. You're finished, anyway."

"No, I'm not." He believed it.

It was nearly midnight when we got to Wray.

A gibbous moon rose before us. Its sickly light fell on the snowfields and the scattering of dark structures. For the past few hours I'd been trying to work my hands free from the plastic restraint. All I'd managed to do was rub my wrists raw.

So now I just sat strapped to the seat and watched the desolate scenery slide by.

Rivers stopped at a gas station—the same one I'd used to find Christine Smith's house. He got the tank filled. He also got directions to the Church of the Penitent.

Forty minutes later we were on the dirt road that led to the commune and Stephanie Bellano.

Rivers drove past the gate before he saw it. He backed up, then turned into the drive and stopped before the gate. It was padlocked shut. Far beyond it stood buildings, dark and isolated in the midst of fields of snow. I could see a few warm yellow lights in the main house. Late-night prayer meeting.

"How many people are in there?" Rivers asked me.

"Maybe ten."

"Okay, then, here it is. Either you help me get Stephanie out of there with no hassles, or I'll go in alone and kill all ten of them. Eleven, counting you. And don't think for a minute that I can't take them all. You should see the goodies I've got in the trunk."

I said nothing.

"I'd rather not do it that way, though," he said. "Too messy. And too difficult to explain. That's why I want your help. Think of it as saving nine lives."

"What happens to me and Stephanie? Assuming I can get her out of there."

"Well, what I had in mind was a fiery car crash in which you two perish and I am miraculously thrown free. Don't worry. I'll make sure you're both unconscious first. I'm not a sadist, you know. In any case, all you have to decide between is two people dead or eleven people dead."

As sick as it was, his point was valid.

"How do you know Stephanie's going to walk out with me?"

"That's your problem," he said. "Tell them her mother is dying or her father was resurrected from the dead or whatever you have to. But you decide right now."

Some decision. "Okay."

Rivers shut off the engine and pulled out the keys. Then he climbed out of the car. He opened the trunk, got out a tire iron, and used it on the padlock. It took him a while to break the lock. When he'd done it, he swung open the gate, put away the tire iron, and slammed the trunk closed. Then he opened my door and undid the seat belt.

"Get behind the wheel."

I scooted over. He got my Magnum from the glove box, then climbed in the backseat and closed the door.

"What can we expect when we drive up there?" he asked.

"Anger and resentment."

"Do they have firearms?"

"I doubt it." Here we were, chatting like old army buddies. "When I was here before, they threatened me with hand tools."

"Lucky for them. Okay, now when we get to the main house, you start honking the horn until people come out. If one of them is Stephanie, fine. You get out and grab her and we leave. Otherwise, you send one of them back inside for Stephanie. Make sure there's someone outside with you at all times. One false move and you and whoever's with you die immediately. Then I go inside and finish off the rest. Is that clear enough?"

"Absolutely."

"Once Stephanie's in the car, the three of us will drive quietly away."

"Sounds easy enough."

"It had better be easy, Lomax, or I'll be the only one leaving here alive. Lean forward."

When I did, he cut the plastic restraint with a pocket knife. I rubbed my wrists. Then he poked the gun muzzle in my back and handed me the keys.

"Let's go."

I drove through the ruts in the snow toward the buildings. Before we even reached the house, more lights came on.

Reverend Lacey came out the side door wearing a bathrobe over his pajama pants. He squinted against the glare of our headlights. Two more men came out behind him—the same two who'd confronted me before. The tall bearded one was carrying his trusty ax.

I shut off the engine.

"Do it," Rivers said, nudging me with the M-16. "And remember, this can take out the four of you in about three seconds."

"I'll keep it in mind."

I climbed out of the car, quietly slipping the keys from the ignition. When I slammed the door, I glanced back and saw that Rivers had opened his window half an inch. The better to hear. And no one could quite see in.

"Get right back in that car and get out of here!" Lacey shouted at me from ten feet away. "You're trespassing, and I won't stand for it!" Lacey's face was red, even in the cold glare of the headlights.

"Just shut up and listen," I said loudly enough for everyone, including Rivers, to hear. "We've come for Stephanie Bellano, and we won't leave here without her. My associate in the car is ready to call the sheriff if you don't cooperate."

"We've been through this before!" Lacey shouted.

"Not like this we haven't," I said, and moved right up until we stood toe to toe. When I spoke again, it was for his ears only. "The man in the car murdered Stephanie's father. Right now he's pointing an automatic weapon at us."

"What?"

"Look at me, Reverend, not at the car. Listen, you've got to believe this or we're all dead. Look at me, Lacey. Reverend. He's the man Stephanie is hiding from. He's a murderer, and he wants to take Stephanie. He's prepared to kill us all."

Lacey searched my face. Then he glanced at the car.

"If this is a trick of some kind . . ."

"Goddammit, Lacey."

His eyes held mine for a heartbeat.

"What . . . happens now?" he asked.

"The place where you hid Stephanie, is it in the house?"

He paused. "Yes."

"Is there room for all of you?"

"Yes."

"Okay, have these two get everyone there fast."

Lacey turned to the two young men and told them to take everyone to the room in the canning cellar. They left us and went into the house. I looked at the blacked-out windows of the BMW and gave Rivers a thumbs-up sign. I hoped it relaxed him, if only slightly.

"What about us?" Lacey asked me.

"How long will it take everybody to hide?"

"A few minutes."

"We'll give them one," I said, then told him what to do.

When our minute was up, we both faced the open door.

"It's all right, Stephanie, you can come out." Lacey spoke loudly to the empty doorway, as if someone were standing just inside, out of sight of Rivers. "Come out here now."

And we both dove for the door, Lacey hitting the floor first, with me right behind, scrambling like boot-camp recruits under live automatic-weapons fire, which splintered the door frame, smashed apart cupboard doors, and exploded crockery on the kitchen counter. Lacey made it to the basement door on all fours, went through, and shut it behind him. I ran through the kitchen and risked a look out the window.

Rivers was out of the BMW. Its windshield was shattered. He was slamming another clip in the M-16. I ran through several rooms to the far side of the house, opened a window, and dropped down into the snow.

I didn't know what Rivers would do. He might set fire to the house and wait for people to come out. Or he might go in shooting.

I stayed below window level and moved around the house.

I peeked around the corner. The BMW was about twenty
yards away. The trunk was closed, so Rivers didn't have
another key. And he'd probably decided he couldn't shoot it
open, since the gas tank was back there. On the other hand,
he may have already taken out what he needed.

I held my breath and listened.

Except for the cows lowing in the barn, there was no sound.

I ran in a crouch to the car, yanked open the passenger
door, and looked inside for my Magnum. No surprise, it
wasn't there.

I glanced toward the house and pictured Rivers moving
through it room by room. Soon he'd tire of his sport and torch
the place. I used the keys to unlock the trunk.

It looked empty.

I pulled away the panel that hid the spare tire. Jammed in
with the tire was a small army-green canvas sack. Inside were
two fragmentation grenades. I pulled the sack from the trunk
and looked toward the house just as Rivers appeared in a
window. He saw me and swung around his weapon. I dove
toward the side of the car. The side windows exploded,
showering me with pebbles of glass.

It was death to stay in the open. But where to run? I
scanned the buildings. Barn. Chapel. Greenhouse. Chicken
coop. Garage. I had in my sack exactly two chances to get
Rivers. If I missed . . .

Think positive, Lomax. Pray, if necessary.

I got in a three-point stance, then sprinted for the chapel.

Rivers didn't fire. Was he out of ammunition? Doubtful. I'd
probably caught him climbing through the window or heading
for the door.

I made it to the chapel and slammed the door behind me.
It was the only way in. Or out. The only other opening was
the window, high above the pulpit. It let in feeble moonlight.
I hurried up the aisle between the rows of high-backed
wooden benches, stepped up on the small stage, then

crouched behind the heavy wooden pulpit. I took the grenades out of the sack. They were smooth and cold and heavy.

I waited.

The door creaked open.

Silence.

Then a wild blast of steel ripped through the air. One slug slammed into the heavy pulpit and knocked a fist-sized chunk of wood off the corner.

The sound of the muzzle blast hung in the darkness for a long moment.

The lights clicked on. I blinked against their brightness. Then I squeezed the handle of one grenade. I pulled the pin.

When I peeked over the pulpit, I saw Rivers coming forward, carefully looking down the rows of pews. Then he saw me and brought his weapon to bear. I lobbed the grenade toward him as high as I could, high up near the peaked roof of the church, high enough to go beyond him to the bottom of the open door. Rivers saw it, fired a wild burst at me, then backpedaled frantically—directly in line with the falling grenade. He saw his mistake and dove toward the corner of the room. Which was where I hurled the second grenade as hard as I could, then dropped behind the pulpit just as the first one exploded. It threw shrapnel into the wooden pulpit. There was a scream. But it was cut short by the second blast.

I peeked around the pulpit.

Rivers was not in sight.

I stood and went down the aisle. The air smelled of cordite. I saw an ugly red smear in the rear corner of the church. I walked over to it.

Rivers lay on the floor beneath the smear. His shoulders and head were propped against the wall. His clothes were shredded and covered with blood. The M-16 lay at his feet. So did his right arm. His eyes were open, but he wasn't looking at anything.

Not in this world, anyway.

CHAPTER

29

I BRUSHED BROKEN GLASS from the front seat of Rivers's car. Then I used the phone to call the county sheriff's office. They said they were on their way.

I walked into the house and down the basement steps. The basement was empty except for shelves of preserves. They lined the walls. I hollered for Reverend Lacey and his flock to come out of hiding.

A section of shelving slowly swung out from one wall. Behind it was a small room with more shelves. It was packed with parishioners.

"It's safe now," I said. "But don't go in the chapel."

They filed out and tentatively climbed the stairs. Lacey came last. He ushered out a young girl. She wore a drab cotton dress and a faded sweater. Her eyes were wide and dark, and her hair was long and black.

"Stephanie Bellano?"

"Yes," she said in a clear, quiet voice.

"I'm afraid I've come with bad news. Your father is dead."

Lacey and I walked her up the stairs to the kitchen. One of the women already had a kettle going for tea. I sat beside Stephanie at the long wooden table.

"My father," she said. "How did . . . ?"

"A few days after you ran away, he was murdered by Gary

Rivers." I briefly filled her in on the events of the past two weeks. She took it much better than I thought she would. Perhaps the time she'd spent in the commune had strengthened her. Or maybe she'd been pretty strong to begin with.

"How is my mother?"

"She's worried about you," I said.

"If I'd have known, I would have left sooner." She glanced at Lacey, then at me. "When you were here before . . . ?"

"Yes?"

"Did you tell Reverend Lacey about my father?"

"Yes."

She looked at Lacey.

Lacey looked doleful.

"I'm sorry," he said. "I probably should have told you, but I was thinking of your welfare. I knew you'd want to leave right away. But I also knew there was danger present. And at that point I didn't trust anyone. Not even Mr. Lomax. I thought it would be best for you to stay here a while longer. If I was wrong, I apologize."

She smiled and touched his sleeve.

"Thank you," she said. She turned to me. "I want to go home now."

So did I. But we had to wait for the cops.

In the following days, Ramón Quinteras, under advisement from counsel, confessed to the burglary of the armory. He also admitted selling part of the take to Gary Rivers.

Mrs. Gary Rivers had a severe nervous breakdown. It wasn't clear whether this was precipitated by the death of her husband or the questioning by the police. In any event, she confessed to knowledge of her son's wrongful death. Due to the circumstances and to her present mental condition, the district attorney decided not to file charges against her.

The murder charge against Mitch Overholser was dropped. However, he still had to stand up for his part in the

destruction of Bellano's records. He was expected to get off
easy.

Fat Paulie got off easy, too. A few days before Christmas he
plea-bargained down from "operating a gambling business" to
"operating a wagering business without paying a special occu-
pational tax." He paid a nominal fine, and they let him go.

The same would not be said for Johnny Toes Burke. As soon
as he recovered from his gunshot wound, the Denver DA
planned to drag him over broken glass for attempting to extort
money from the widow Bellano.

As for Angela, she rejoiced in Stephanie's return. And just
before Christmas, too. Of course, Stephanie had a few
depressing things to confess, but I figured they were both
strong enough to handle it.

I even thought about making their Christmas a little
brighter by returning the unused portion of the five thousand
dollars Joseph had given me. It was the season, you know.
Besides, I didn't need the money. Oh, I could *use* the money.
But I didn't need it. Then again, I thought, neither did
Angela Bellano; Joseph had left her quite comfortable.

I wrote out the check, anyway.

I mailed it to Reverend Lacey, care of the Church of the
Penitent. Merry Christmas. Besides, he'd need to buy paint
for the chapel walls.

Then I began making plans for *my* Christmas.

They were limited, if not nil. For the past few years I'd
spent Christmas day with Sophia and Vaz. We would ex-
change small gifts and then go caroling with Sophia's church
group. Well, they'd carol. Vaz and I would stand in the back
and sort of hum. Then, in the afternoon, the three of us would
go back to their apartment. Some of the other tenants in the
grand old house would join us, and we'd all feast on stuffed
goose, cranberries, homemade bread, and so on.

But this year the Botvinnovs were Christmasing in sunny
Phoenix. I considered flying down there.

Then I got a call from Angela Bellano.

"I'm having Christmas dinner at my house," she said. "Lots of people, lots of food. I'd like you to come."

"It sounds great, but . . . I might be leaving town."

"Visiting loved ones?"

"Yes."

"That's nice. But if you don't leave, please come."

We hung up.

I called her right back.

"Can I bring a friend?"

"Of course."

I phoned Rachel.

"I've just been invited to a Christmas feast at the Bellano residence," I said. "Would you like to go? Or are you doing something with Pat?"

"No, she always spends Christmas back East with her parents and her brother."

"Well, then?"

"But I do have other plans."

"Oh."

"I was going to stay home alone and eat a frozen dinner and watch *It's a Wonderful Life*. It's sort of a tradition."

"And a fine one, at that."

"What time will you pick me up?"